THE NIGHT ROAD

The Author

John Charles Woodman had a conventional childhood and education, gaining a degree in philosophy.

He was recruited into his work by a tutor and has since been employed by several government agencies, working for a short while with the UK based arm of an American company. He still holds his blue badge.

His early career was in the field where he developed a specialization in the security of civil and military nuclear sites. During this period, he had close contact with Special Branch.

For a while in the mid-80s, he was invalided out of active service, concentrating instead on research and development in his specialist areas. When he was passed fit, he trained with the SAS and returned to fieldwork at a senior level, heading east and working both sides of the Wall.

After a further period working in hostile locations, he was promoted to a senior desk with responsibility for an entire region of activity.

Although he has now retired, he still does research and acts as a consultant in areas of expertise. He cannot and will not make personal appearances.

John Charles Woodman is not his real name.

THE NIGHT ROAD

John Charles Woodman

Monkey Business

Paperback – ISBN 978-1-909295-17-9
E-Book – ISBN 978-1-909295-18-6

2 3 4 5 6 7 8 9 10 11

Cover design by Graeme K Talboys

Acknowledgements

I am deeply indebted to LD, DC, EA, & AP who recruited me and taught me how it was done. Their work and support has been invaluable.

This is a novel. Whilst I have given it real settings and used documented events, there are places where my imagination has taken precedence. I have no idea, for example, if you can get macaroni cheese and chips in a public canteen in the James Paget Memorial Hospital.

Fiction or not, a number of people helped with the background to the story. Of those I can name, my thanks go to: Dame Sue Black DBE, FRSE, FRCP, FRAI who told me about skeletons and other aspects of forensic anthropology; various members of Suffolk Constabulary past and present (especially Simon Manthorpe) who patiently answered my questions even whilst they were involved with very real and horrific crimes; staff at the Forestry Commission who explained forestry in general and Rendlesham in particular; Suffolk Archaeology for the latest on the efficacy of geophysical surveys and for allowing the use of their name (although all personnel depicted in the novel are fictional); Dr Newman for some chemistry.

In memory of the real John Charles

01

(Sunday morning, early hours)

If you were to ask me what my idea was of a good Saturday night out, standing in the rain watching the police look for a body in a river would not feature high on the list. In fact, it wouldn't feature on the list at all. I'd had to do it once before and there was nothing about the process that made me any more excited about it this time round. Still, I suppose I should be grateful for small mercies. At least this time it wasn't Christmas Day.

When the call came through, I had been watching a re-run of *The Big Sleep* with my feet up and a take-away on a tray on my lap. Which does feature on my list, by the way. Make of that what you will. I had been tempted to pull rank and tell whoever was calling to shove off. It wasn't something I liked to do. It still surprised me I had been trusted with any level of seniority. But then they said a car was already on its way. A driver would take me out as far as the M25 while I was briefed and then they would hand over the keys. It didn't make me like it any more, I treasured my nights off, but it had to be serious if they were throwing those sorts of resources at me in these days of austerity.

My doorbell rang before I had finished packing an overnight bag. I used to keep one ready. In the old days. The dark days. These days were better. Most of the time I knew where I would be on the following day. And the only weapons my opponents wielded were committee papers and memoranda, written in that bizarre version of English that bureaucrats use to communicate.

The driver wasn't anyone I knew. Which wasn't that much of a surprise. It had been a few years now. I tried to keep my hand in at the old place, but it wasn't the same when you were based elsewhere and looked on as an outsider. After scrutinising each other's IDs, he sat in the kitchen while I went round and checked everything was switched off and secure.

With the alarm set, we clumped along the worn lino of the corridor and headed down the narrow back stairs. At the bottom, we passed the kitchens of the Chinese restaurant, where I left a note for the owner in his office. He would keep an eye on things for me, keep my post safe.

At the car, I got the full treatment. Door opened for me and closed with a solid clunk as I settled in the rear seat, bag stowed in the boot. It just made me more suspicious. As we pulled away into the scrum of Saturday night traffic, the driver reported in. The tiny blue light of his earpiece was bright in the dark interior. Not long afterwards, my mobile purred in my pocket and I listened to the bad news. As much as they cared to share. Which wasn't much. As briefings go, it really lived up to its name.

I was already settled back into my seat and comfortable to the point of dozing off when we pulled into the car park of the Holiday Inn at Brentwood. It's a soulless, three-storey brick building that smells of loneliness, all the more bleak at night. The driver found a spot as far from the building as he could, handed me the keys, and climbed out. As he walked away, I also climbed out and stood a moment, watching. The black Ford that had been tailing us whisked my driver back off into the City and I was left alone to climb in the front.

Out of habit, I checked the controls over, and then watched the car park for a while whilst trying to look like a driver taking a break. Satisfied, I pulled a road atlas out of the glove compartment and studied it by the shielded light of a torch to plot my route into the wilds of Suffolk. SatNav is all very well, but it's no substitute for knowing the landscape you are entering. Even if it was meant to be routine. Only fools believe it's ever just that.

That had been hours ago. In some other world where the last few comfortable years had been swept away. Now I was standing in the shadows on the edge of nowhere with my hands in my pockets and my collar turned up, the old wounds aching in the damp. I had long since worked out places of cover and several covert routes back to the nearest road. It was frightening how quickly the old instincts came flooding back, even after years of desk work. I settled down to wait, clearing away the thoughts and speculations.

The nearby halogen lamps on their extendable stands cut a complex chunk of nothing out of the night. Half-hearted rain flickered through it to the tangle of bleached wiry grass on which I stood. At one end of the floodlit area was the rear offside of a four by four police patrol car, parked on the flat top of the embankment. Its rear door was open, displaying a cornucopia of equipment. At the other, parked beside a World War Two pillbox, was a van. The flat, white surfaces of the rear doors were closed against the weather. It had already been there when we arrived. The four by four was designed for this terrain, but I admired anyone who could manoeuvre a van like that along the narrow tracks and up that steep bank.

I stood huddled in the dark where I belonged and watched the intermittent rain for want of anything better to do. Somewhere on the far side of the empty patch of light, down a slope, beyond a wire fence that had seen far better days, was the River Ore.

Beyond that in the impenetrable darkness was the tail end of Orford Ness. After that it was the North Sea, as cold and dark a place as you could not want to be in or near early on a Sunday, even in the summer. If you have never been there, I can tell you it is a bleak and unforgiving place, haunted by its own species of ghost. And I've known a few of those in my time.

From the dark to my left, somewhere up river, the sound of an outboard motor drifted in and out of hearing as an inflatable quartered the waterway. It was an insipid noise, lost in the darkness and sounding ineffectual in all that space. I listened but could make nothing more of it.

PC Crane, the copper who had driven me there in the four-by-four re-appeared from wherever he'd been keeping himself warm and dry. His head was tilted to one side as he listened to the radio nestled beneath his reflective jacket. I could see his eyes flicking in my direction. He tried to hide it, but I could tell he wasn't very impressed with what he saw.

Fed on a diet of movie and television superheroes laden with gadgets dispensed by a prescient quarter-master, saving the day with lots of running about, shouting, and sharp-shooting, a super-model hanging off one arm, he probably didn't see much of anything to get his teeth into and fire his imagination. Just a pale Crown servant in his early fifties, bleary-eyed, unshaven, dressed in clothes that any self-respecting charity shop would probably put straight in the bin. A weary man who had grown used to his desk and who was making lists in his head of where he would rather be and what he would rather be doing on a Saturday night and Sunday morning.

"Do we know anything about the boat that called it in?" I asked for want of anything else to do. You can only stare into the dark for so long before it gets Nietzschean on you and starts staring back.

"Not yet, sir. We will. But if he was on his way out he wouldn't want to miss the tide. And if he were coming in and stayed anonymous he was probably up to no good."

He looked at me and I looked back.

"Smuggling, sir. Ciggies and booze mostly."

"Drugs?"

"Not so's you'd notice. Unless it's a bit of coffee shop cake from Amsterdam. We know the locals too well for them to chance anything else and any strangers'd stick out, like. If they didn't get their selves caught in the mud."

A sweep of light in the darkness picked out dull ripples on the water and then raked along the bank in front of us. The pitch of the inshore boat's engine changed as it swept round. As the sound faded, I could hear another engine further off. A car picking its way along the grass track from the Young Offenders Institution at Hollesley Bay. We turned to watch.

The headlights lurched across the marshy fields, disappearing and then coming back into view before swinging round toward us. They picked out the track and the dull grey concrete of the old defensive wall that led up to the pillbox. The shadows of the bushes that grew in its lee lurched in black and white B movie style. At that point the cimbalom should have started and the opening credits should have rolled. In other circumstances I might have cracked a private smile. But not this particular morning.

The spectral set of extra shadows that had swung into the pool of light disappeared as the car's headlights were doused. PC Crane took his hands from his pockets and straightened himself at the sound of a very expensive car door closing. I began going through my pockets in anticipation of the little pantomime that I knew would follow.

Out of the shadows appeared a senior policeman, overcoat unbuttoned just enough to let me see he was in full uniform. He looked at the Constable who took the hint and scuttled off to find himself something to do out of earshot. I finally found what I was looking for and handed it to the DCC.

"Home Office?" he asked, fumbling the little folder open with gloved hands.

"Something like that," I replied.

"Box 500?"

Box 500 was the official wartime address of the Security Service. Some people liked to use it to prove they were in the know. Especially those who didn't really know. And it's easier to say than Box 3255. I wasn't in the mood for sparring, though. "Leave the fishing to your people in the boat. If you need confirmation, phone Simon Gass's office." He didn't reply. I looked at him as he flicked through an interior card index. "Joint Intelligence Committee," I added. "Cabinet Office. One of your regional CTU people will know the number." I thought about that. "I hope."

He didn't look happy. He was probably used to deference and the local press getting his best angle, but I didn't like brass nosing around. There was no need for him to be there. It would just put everyone on edge. Like me. And my edge is apt to be jagged.

PC Crane reappeared on the far edge of the pool of halogen light, close to the top of the river bank. He had wellington boots on. "Sorry to interrupt, sirs. They've found something."

The DCC handed back my little folder and crossed through the light to stand by the wire fence. I stayed where I was. I'd only be in the way. And they'd have to bring whatever it was they had found up to the level ground here. So I shrugged deeper into my jacket and tried not to think of other times and other places. Of rivers. Of sudden death.

Watery sounds filled the silence that followed the cutting of the inflatable's engine. Its light dimmed as it drifted to shore. Into the quiet, two men emerged from the white van, yawning in the cold, damp air. They walked down each side and opened the rears doors. From the dark interior, they took out a large sheet of plastic that they spread on the grass, anchoring the corners with weights. One of them went back and got a body bag and the pair of them climbed over the fence and joined the melee down at the waters edge.

A dead body is heavy. Add to that the weight of soaking wet clothes, the intractable nature of something with so many moving parts, and a stranger watching intently from the distance, it is no wonder it took a full ten minutes of muffled exhortation and cursing to transfer it from boat to bag and then carry it up the bank, over the fence, and onto the top of the dyke where I was standing.

It was the two men from the van who manoeuvred the bag onto the plastic sheet and laid it down. Before they moved out of the way, one of them unzipped the bag and they lifted the body out. Given what they had just had to cope with, they were surprisingly gentle. Given what I now saw laid out before me, I was extremely grateful. They moved back into the shadow of their van. A flame lit their faces and cigarettes glowed.

At this point, SOCO would normally be all over the scene like ghosts in their white suits. I had ruled that out. They were sitting in a van at the head of the track by the western end of the prison. If this had turned out to be nothing to do with me, they would have been summoned. There are police procedures when a body is found, designed to preserve forensic evidence. As it was, this was unlikely ever to become a police case.

The plastic sheeting crackled beneath my well-worn boots as I stepped forward and looked down. On the fringes of my vision, I could see the shiny toe caps of the DCC's shoes and the dull matte green of PC Crane's wellington boots. For the moment, however, my attention was fixed on the face below me.

"Could I have some gloves please?" I asked, clearing my throat.

Crane looked at his superior. I looked at the DCC as well. He could get sniffy and play it by the rules. He could try. In the end I would get my way and we would all have wasted a lot of time in the cold and dark. He was smart enough to know that and nodded. PC Crane stepped across to his car, rummaging in the rear before coming back to me with a pair of blue latex gloves.

I pulled them on, realising that my hands had become very cold. After a moment massaging my fingers under the guise of getting the gloves to a decent fit, I looked back down at the body. Water was draining away from the clothing, forming runnels and puddles in the creases of the plastic. He hadn't been in the river for too long. Not long enough to distort his features or hide the ugly mark on his forehead. Probably long enough to wash away useful traces of evidence.

Choosing a dry spot, I knelt. After another glance at the face, I turned to the feet, unlacing the shoes with difficulty and pulling them off. Happy they were empty and that the socks concealed nothing, I laid the shoes and sodden Argyles neatly by the feet and began to search through the trouser pockets. Someone laid a large evidence bag beside me, I didn't see who. Into it went a neatly folded soggy handkerchief and some loose change. From the jacket pockets I extracted a mobile phone and small diary which I put to one side along with a set of car keys. The wallet, in an inner pocket, contained nothing but money, a driver's licence, and a company credit card. There was nothing else a quick search could find. Others would look closer.

I nodded with approval, tidying wet hair from his cold, white brow. "Good lad," I said quietly. "But what the hell were you doing out here in the first place?"

As I stood, I could hear another car approaching, saw the lights leap up and down as it found the potholes on the track. I hoped it was the Police Surgeon. I didn't want it turning into any more of a circus than it already was.

Pocketing the phone, diary, and car keys I turned to the DCC who was now on my side of the plastic sheet. "I can formally identify him," I said. "His name is Charles Smith. And that's all you'll get from me. I will notify next-of-kin. And someone will be down from his employer's legal office tomorrow to do the rest of the formal stuff." I looked down at the body. "Where will he go from here?"

"The James Paget in Gorleston. They've found his car."

I nodded. "The press does not get to hear of this. From anyone. Everyone who sees the body will be required to sign the Act, so try to keep it to a minimum. What about the boat; the ones who called it in?"

"We'll find them. They won't talk."

"Thank you. Look after him," I said nodding to Charlie, sparing him a last, fond look. At least I now knew why it had been me who took that call yesterday evening.

He must have heard something in my voice. I had tried to keep it steady, but when you look down at the corpse of a good friend, it isn't easy.

"We will, sir," he said.

I turned to the constable who had brought me out here. "I take it you're local, Crane?"

"Sir?"

My hands still felt cold as I peeled off the latex gloves and dropped them by the evidence bag. I fished out a pair of fingerless mittens and slipped them on. "Take me to his car, please."

I climbed into the front of his vehicle and closed the door, fishing round for the seat belt. At least it had stopped raining and I could peer out into the dark. Something I did altogether too often. Crane packed his equipment back into the rear of his vehicle and changed out of his wellingtons. There was a pause while he said a shy hello to the young police surgeon.

I bent forward slightly and caught a glimpse of her in the wing mirror. She looked fey enough to have come from nearby Woolpit, and certainly seemed to have enchanted PC Crane who was still smiling to himself as he climbed into the driver's seat.

The first half of the journey was across a night dark countryside, saturated with rain, shadow, and secrets. We bumped slowly along the dike, down at an alarming angle onto a faint set of tracks across a marshy field and then made our way along a stretch of road by HMP and YOI Hollesley Bay before driving round the edge of another field and slowly through a farmyard. I'd have been lost in ten seconds.

Even on the roads we seemed to be going in several different directions, turning first one way and then another. I was aware of trees, the occasional house and cottage, a sharp right at a crossroads, a barn. After that I gave up. There wasn't much point in trying to make sense of the landscape, especially in the dark. That would be someone else's job. I hoped. At least Crane kept his own counsel.

The vehicle's lights picked up a hedge on our right and a field on our left with nothing between itself and the road but a low grassy bank. At the far end, where the road swept round the right, was a dark grey Focus ST. What Charlie had made of that is anyone's guess. He had a second-hand Yeti.

As we drew closer I could see he had parked it just off the road at the ungated entrance to two fields. Close behind it, half on the road, was a police patrol car. Crane flashed his lights and the patrol car backed onto the road and turned to face us. As it passed, a ghostly hand waved.

Crane parked where his colleague had been and I climbed out into the fresh night air. For all the rain on the coast, it was reasonably dry here and there were one or two stars visible in the rips in the cloud. Although the memory of Charlie's dead, white face was still vivid, my hands were warmer. Which was good. I would be angry. But sometime later. Right now, Charlie needed me focussed.

The Ford was tucked in against a hedge, its back to the road. Charlie had either not had the time to turn it round and back in, or he had forgotten a basic of field craft. Probably the latter. Charlie was a researcher, an analyst, a man who could track down the most obscure pieces of information and make sense of them with the same ease I could strip down and re-assemble my Beretta or a dozen other small arms in the dark. He should not have been out here in the first place.

Leaving PC Crane to his own devices I searched the car. It was specially adapted and I was pleased to see that Charlie had at least switched off the brake and reverse lights. It's all very well dousing your headlights if you're tailing someone, but the red glare of your tail lights is just as much a give-away.

There was nothing else to be seen. Not that I had expected anything. But then I hadn't expected to be dragged away from my flat on a Saturday evening and sent to Suffolk to identify Charlie's body. I shook my head. What the hell had been going on?

I locked the Ford and looked around. Although it was not much past two in the morning, it was light enough now to see shapes. The cloud was clearing away fast. A quarter moon and bright stars filled an ever-widening sky.

Crane was flashing a small torch around. "Can't see any other tyre tracks here, sir."

"What?"

"Doesn't seem to have been another car here."

He was being a good policeman, puzzling out how Charlie had got from here, where his car was parked, to the river. Or how someone else had taken Charlie to the river.

"How far is it?" I asked. "To the river."

"Bout three and a half mile as we drove it. Same if you head for the most convenient upstream point."

"Easy to find?"

He shook his head slowly. "You'd need to know the way."

Someone with local knowledge. I looked around again, across the fields. "Turn your torch off for a moment, will you?"

He switched off the torch and it went dark. My eyes adjusted. Stepping carefully, I took a few paces into the open field. It wasn't too rough. The grass had been cut recently for silage and there was only a gentle slope upward away from the road. About three hundred yards away, on the far side, a dark mass filled the horizon.

Crane was sitting in his patrol vehicle when I got back and climbed in. "What's that up there?" I asked pointing across the field.

"What? The trees? That's Rendlesham Forest."

02

(Sunday morning)

The early part of my working life was spent on the wrong side of the wire. Based in Pardubice, I worked as a joiner's assistant, playing the role of an idiot country cousin. It helped explain my accent and my absences. Because my real job was first serving and later running several networks of workmen. They used to gather information from and about people and places that would have got us all shot if we'd been found out. I must have done a good enough job. We all survived.

When the Eastern Bloc fell apart and the Czechs began to share information on Semtex and the places it was sent, I was rewarded with new employers. After a brief interview and handshake at Century House, I was shunted off to 140 Gower Street. There was no time to become acquainted with it as I was promptly sent to one of the other ends of the supply line. Northern Ireland. Some reward. But I did a good enough job there as well, working in a team. Most of us survived.

I mention all this for a reason. It's not some dewy-eyed reminiscence of the good old days. It's so you'll understand that it's not something I claim lightly when I say walking up the short suburban path in front of me was the most difficult thing I have ever done.

There had been a nightmare quality to the drive back from Woodbridge. Twenty years worth of bad memories seethed like a choppy ocean, fighting for attention. And all they did was bring up all the old resentments and angers that hard work and time had failed to sink deeply enough. Which is why I drove straight to the house.

I should have driven into the City and reported. Actually, I should have phoned in a preliminary report and then driven into the City and given the full version to whoever was expecting me at Thames

House. Instead, I kept going. Across the river and down to Herne Hill. When I parked the car, I gave myself time to cool down. It also gave me time to pluck up courage.

The house was a Victorian end of terrace and still had its little patch of front garden. A shaggy hedge leaned over the recently repaired fence. The gate opened onto a tiled path that led to the front door, white with black diamonds. Recycling boxes were lined up neatly to one side.

I closed the gate and looked at my watch as I stepped up to the door. It was just after five thirty. There was no way to soften this. Any visitor at that time of the morning is going to be bringing bad news. My hand hesitated on the bell push. They would be asleep. I was about to tear their world apart. But there was no way in hell I was going to let anyone else do this.

Charlie had talked of getting one of the sound people to rig up a bell that played Leslie Philips saying 'Ding-Dong'. The plain old double chime was a relief. I pressed again, just to be certain and leaned against the brickwork, staring at the tiny car parked neatly on top of the meter box.

"Who is it?" The electronic voice sounded a long way away.

I looked up and turned to face the camera. A lock clicked and a chain slid before the door opened.

Rose has been described as wan, slight, pale, even delicate. Someone I know once called her anaemic, although it wasn't to her face, as he is still walking on his own legs. She certainly looked almost child-like standing there in the doorway wearing a dressing gown two sizes too big with her feet in the cute fluffy cow slippers I'd bought for her last Christmas.

"Alex?" She stood a moment, still emerging from sleep. "What are you doing here? Come in. You look awful." She herded me into the hall. "Charlie's away just now." She put it all together very quickly. "Oh shit. Oh no." Tears began to roll.

I closed the front door and slipped the chain back on before putting my arms round her, holding her shaking body tightly against me, shedding a tear of my own. Charlie and Rose were a truly odd couple. She had been an enforcer at Thames House and at one time had been assigned to track me down – a polite way of saying 'make it look like an accident'. Charlie knew I hadn't gone bad and was on hand in time to stop Rose, using a length of timber to knock her unconscious. Typically of Charlie he visited Rose in hospital when she was recovering and it was there that the shy desk officer and the hard as nails field agent fell for each other.

"Mummy?"

The voice drifted down from the top of the stairs, uncertain. Rose straightened and looked up at me, a vast emptiness in her eyes. She scrubbed at her face with a tissue fished from the pocket of her dressing gown and reassembled herself as best she could. "It's OK, Georgie. It's Uncle Alex. He's got some..." she swallowed.

"Come on, George," I said and watched as the four-year-old came down step by step in his pyjamas, a frown on his face. Lifting him up, I put my other arm round Rose and guided her into the kitchen.

We told George his father was dead and we cried together sitting on the bench at the table. George cried himself to sleep although I'm not sure he truly understood. Rose found no such escape. Once I was certain George was properly tucked in under his blanket, I made tea and toast. Mostly for myself.

We talked quietly for a while, skirting the issue until Rose was ready.

"What happened?" she asked as I poured myself a second mug of tea. She gripped her own without drinking, her knuckles white.

I shrugged. "I wish I knew. I got a call yesterday evening. From a night duty officer at Thames House. Would I go down to Suffolk? Woodbridge Police Office. The locals there had found... They needed someone to go down and look at someone."

Rose looked at me, bewildered.

"They left it to a local copper to fill in the details," I said, feeling the anger return. Some gutless wonder at Thames House hadn't had the courage or the nous to let me know what was going on. "What the fuck was Charlie doing in Suffolk, Rose?"

Yawning, I plodded up the broad, shallow steps of the Millbank entrance of Thames House and went through the central doors between the two ornate black lamp posts. There were no talking animals on the other side; it was a world far more bizarre.

I had stayed with Rose until her mother arrived, put Georgie on the sofa beneath his blanket and waited until he went back to sleep. I then went through the whole gut knotting experience again, phoning Charlie's parents to break the news. Now I was in search of explanations.

Within the lobby there was no telling it was early on a Sunday morning except perhaps for the absence of politicians on a jolly. It was the same imposing place, marble and glass arranged in a way that said 'Get Lost' but said it expensively and politely in a hushed voice.

I went across to the right hand side where the public reception window was and rang the bell. A face appeared, looked at me for a moment and then smiled.

"Hello, Mr Grant. Long time, no see."

"Hello, Stan. You still here?" He was a fixture from the old days when I worked in the building.

"Only place you can get a decent cup of tea these days," he said with a commendably straight face.

"I would imagine I'm expected."

"Just like the old days, sir." And I'll swear he winked before he glanced at a screen I couldn't see. "Someone's on their way down for you now. Number two."

Opposite the doors to the street is a curved wall of security doors, revolving tubes of armoured glass that admit you one person at a time and can lock you in if there's anything suspicious about you. I went to number two and waited. Eventually a smartly dressed young woman appeared on the other side and opened the tube to let me in.

As the glass turned I watched her. She returned my impassive expression, hugging her blue clipboard folder. When the door let me in, she led me to a table and I went through the rigmarole of signing in and clipping the visitor's badge to the less than reputable collar of my coat.

I followed her to the lifts and then through familiar corridors. It was a good few years since I was shown the door, but little seemed to have changed. They were still getting their personnel from the same cloning facility. The carpets were the same horrible blue that contrived always to look slightly grubby. And there was still that hushed and over-heated atmosphere you find in seedy chain hotels.

The room we went to was little different. Very like my own office had been except this one had two doors and enough room for two of those low backed chairs you find in waiting rooms and staff rooms all over the world. I declined her offer of a seat while I waited. I had no intention of waiting and, besides, it would be a long way back up to my feet after being up all night.

She knocked on the inner door and after opening it a fraction, slipped through and closed it. I leaned to peer over the stack of trays on her desk, but she had been diligent. The monitor was switched off and all her folders were closed. When she re-emerged I was staring at the mud flaking off my boots onto the carpet.

"Mr Whickramasan will see you straight away."

I should bloody hope so, I thought as I smiled and went through into the office beyond. This one had a window. Senior staff now, then. A product of Harrow and Oxford, he exuded the arrogant confidence of one of God's gifts. He stood as I entered the office, waiting patiently until I had closed the door before leaning across his desk to offer me a hand. I ignored it.

"What was Charlie Smith doing in the field, Chandra?"

Unphased, he sat down. He'd met me before. "I take it you have identified the body, then."

"Of course I have. I've just come from telling Rose."

He stopped in the process of opening a folder. "Oh. I wish you had left that to the personnel department."

"Not bloody likely. Rose and Charlie are friends. Good friends."

"Be that as it may, you were asked to look at the body, nothing else."

"No. I was asked to identify someone. I wasn't even told it was a corpse until I got to Suffolk and a young copper told me. A corpse. Of a friend. And in case I hadn't already mentioned it, a good friend. What was Charlie Smith doing in the field?"

The folder closed. "I hope, Mr Grant, that you are not going to make a fuss."

Wrong fucking answer. I smiled. "Fuss? No." For a second he looked relieved. "Fuss does not even begin to cover what I am going to make if someone here doesn't give me an answer."

We looked at each other across his desk. His long fingers skittered nervously along the edge of the folder. He could do that as long as he liked. Had I still worked for the Security Service he could simply have asked me to leave his office. But I hadn't worked there for a while now. I had been kicked out. And up. I had the clearance, clout, and sheer bloody-mindedness to turn him and his department inside out and upside down if I wanted. And I had a boss who would back me up.

He caved in and picked up the handset of his phone.

(Sunday midday)

I doubt that I was a pretty sight, I rarely am, but at least by kicking the conference room door open and coming in backwards, Sally Barrett gave me time to wake up. A bit. I stretched as she manoeuvred round the door carrying a large stack of files and then watched as she dropped them on the conference table. It was a dull sound, ominous.

Pushing the tray with the remains of my meal to one side, I yawned. Then I smiled. "Sally," I said.

"Alex," she replied.

To say that Sally Barrett and myself had history would be something of an understatement. We had prehistory and archaeology as well. And most of it was best left undisturbed.

She sat directly opposite me with the width of the mahogany table between us. "I was sorry to hear about Charlie. How's Rose? And little Georgie?"

"Remember me when Lesley was murdered?" It was an unfair question and I felt like a heel as soon as I asked it. "Sorry. That wasn't fair. " Sally had watched my back in the building more than I had appreciated at the time. Lesley had been my fiancée, one of the Security Service's watchers. Someone had put a bomb in my flat and she was the one that opened the door. "You're the first person who has bothered to ask about Rose and George."

She sighed. "Things have changed."

"So people keep telling me. They've been telling me that since November of '91, and they started all over again ten years later. All I see are the same cock-ups followed by the same excuses and blandishments. But Rose is family. Does that count for nothing in these changed days? And more to the point, what in the name of hell was Charlie Smith doing in the field?" My anger was beginning to make me incoherent.

"All in good time. First, I need to know if you're happy..." she grimaced "...it wasn't an accident. Sorry. Poor choice of words."

I waved it away. "Charlie's car was a mile and a half as that poor bloody crow flies, possibly more, from the river where his body was found."

Sally nodded. "OK. In which case, I've been asked to brief you. First..." she pushed a slim blue folder and a pen across the table, "...read and sign. You know the drill."

I knew the drill, but I read the papers anyway. Someone might have slipped in an extra clause. My soul had long been traded away, but they might be after my first born, or collection of Chandler and

Hammett. "Has this been cleared with—" my brain clicked into gear and I held up my hands. "Stupid question." My present employers would already have given the go ahead otherwise I wouldn't be sitting there.

"Temporary re-assignment. Limited access to the building." She emphasised the 'limited'. "Access to Registry through me."

"What, no invisible ink, wrist radio, and code disc?"

Sally gave me a frosty look over the top of her glasses. I signed in the appropriate places, closed the folder, and pushed it back across the table.

"Who do I report to?" I asked as she checked the contents of the folder, presumably to make sure it was my name I had signed.

"Me."

"You?"

"Why the surprise?"

"I thought you were Director of Strategic Planning these days."

"I am. But I know you."

"And they don't want me upsetting anyone else."

Again, the look over the glasses, but this time it was more difficult to read. I had the feeling, though, that I had put one of my muddy size nines a bit too close to where it wasn't wanted.

There was still a sandwich left on the tray, along with some cold coffee. While Sally sorted through the other files, which looked like they had arrived en masse via the internal monorail, I helped myself and wandered over to the window. The traffic on Lambeth Bridge was still light, a sunny haze sitting on the Thames. Sunday morning tourists were getting a thrill from taking pictures of the building. For once I didn't get the urge to wave.

"Last week… Are you listening?"

I turned from my contemplation of Lambeth Palace and went back to my seat, brushing crumbs from the front of my jumper.

"Last week," said Sally again, "there was a sudden influx of CIA field agents."

"Sudden influx? Are we talking invasion? Coach party?"

"Three."

"Three? Seriously. How many currently stationed here?"

Sally ignored the question. I knew the answer and she knew I knew the answer. The legals, anyway. And three extra did not constitute an influx, sudden or otherwise.

"Two," she said, "were on active service here in the latter half of the '70s. The third disappeared off the radar about 12 years ago."

"And we picked up on them because?"

"There were three of them."

"So what?" Although I thought I knew what the answer to that would be.

"They all ended up in Suffolk."

"And you sent Charlie out there to find out why."

"No, Alex. I didn't."

"No. But someone did. He's not… wasn't a field agent. You know that. It was on his bloody personnel file. I put it there. 'Not to be deployed in the field'. Underlined in red. You endorsed it. Because he was useless in the big outdoors. He's an Analyst. Probably one of… shit." It still hadn't sunk in, despite seeing him there in that body bag on the river bank. "And, for good measure: fuck."

"He wasn't meant to do anything. Simply go down, locate these people, and confirm their identity."

"A job for a probationer on a second-class day return. Not a top class analyst."

"Things have changed."

"I wish people would stop saying that like it was a reason for anything."

"There wasn't anyone else."

I looked across the table. This was not the Sally I knew. She was career minded, it's true, but she had never been an apologist for incompetence.

"You could have used a retread for Christ's sake."

"There's no need to shout, Alex."

"Yes, Sally, there is. This is Charlie Smith we're talking about. Charlie and Rose Smith. And little Georgie. Charlie Smith who is now dead. It should have been a day trip for someone who knew what they were doing.

"Budgets are tight."

"Don't give me that crap. Budgets have always been tight. Half of C section or whatever it's called these days would have paid out of their own savings to get out of this bloody building for a couple of days if you'd asked. Now you're going to have find a widow's pension and retrain someone to fill Charlie's shoes. And you know that's not going to come cheap. Especially someone of his class. Bloody hell, I'd have gone out there for the price of a ticket and a pack of sandwiches. Happy to get away from all the political, inter-departmental bickering. Face it, Sally. Someone screwed up. Big time. I sincerely hope there's going to be an internal enquiry."

Sally is someone I would never feel happy about sitting opposite at a poker table. It's why she was good at her job. It's why I had always liked her as my boss. She let me have my say knowing I was less likely to take my concerns back to my bosses at JIC and the Cabinet Office.

"OK," I continued, feeling calmer, thinking things through. "So assuming my name did come up, why wasn't I sent?"

"Because there are Americans involved. You have a..."

"Reputation?"

Sally shrugged by way of reply.

"So why am I being used now?"

"Because there are Americans involved."

"And I have..."

"Because you won't be deferential."

"That's got to be an understatement," I said sourly.

But I was pleased. At least I now knew why they wanted to retain me. And it was Sally's way of letting me know that the great and good were not happy about what had happened to Charlie. She pushed one of the thick folders across to me.

"That has a copy of everything that Charlie was given. Abstracts of the CIA operatives' biographies, basic information about the area, and background on US activity there. Plus transcripts of Charlie's phone-ins." I didn't open the folder. "There may be stuff in his hotel room."

"Give him some credit, Sally. He may have been an Analyst, but he wasn't daft. Where are the Americans now?"

Sally didn't answer.

"Seriously. Are you telling me that we have lost a good man and the Americans have slipped sideways out of the picture? What kind of set-up are you people running here these days?"

Sally didn't answer that, either.

So I read the file. There wasn't much once you'd sifted out all the dross they like to put in these days. There was certainly very little to go on. But at least I knew what the 'influx' looked like. Two tired looking men who were well past field duty retirement and a severe looking woman in her early forties. When I'd finished, I slid it back across the table, paid Sally some genuine compliments, then went and spoiled it by asking for time in the Thames House firing range.

03

(Sunday afternoon)

Rested, showered, and properly fed, I packed for a longer stay away from home and then drove back into town. They'd let me keep the official car and I found half a parking space in Mason's Yard. The offices on Duke Street St James's, where I worked were quiet, which suited me. Just security on the door and someone singing quietly to themselves in the stock cupboard. Our kind of work can have that effect on some people.

Officially we were the Joint Intelligence Committee Internal Affairs Investigation Department, but that was a mouthful so everyone called us Juvenal. It was our remit to provide oversight for the many Intelligence units and organisations, investigate problems, sort out the constant interdepartmental wrangling – guard the guards.

Unlike my work with SIS and the Security Service, you tended to get the weekends off and very few people had the wherewithal to shoot at you. They had recruited me a number of years ago, although I hadn't known it at the time. There had been a problem within the Security Service and my particular talent as an obstinate bastard had been used to wrong foot people. It had been successful. Eventually. People lost their lives and others, like myself, came close. I had been a bit too zealous for the liking of some, but I had never lost any sleep over that. Plenty of other things, yes. But never that.

In my bright little office high in the narrow building, one of the perks of being Deputy Director, I sifted through my overloaded in-tray and sorted the work into non-urgent piles of casework that could be offloaded to junior staff. Another of the perks of being Deputy Director. Sunshine broke in through the south facing window in the corridor outside my door. After a couple of hours without the normal round of phone calls and other interruptions, I had all my urgent stuff up to date with recommendations for further action pencilled in.

I loaded all the files onto one of the small trolleys we used in-house and wheeled it along to my boss's office next door, each pile neatly labelled. Letting myself in with my key, I put the urgent material and the three year review of the Joint State Threats Assessments Team on her desk and left the rest for her to distribute as she saw fit. My own desk was now empty for the first time in years. It was a momentous occasion. I took a photograph of the bare surface and e-mailed it to myself. I was going to print it up, have it framed, and hang it on the wall. No one would believe it otherwise.

After I had signed out, I let the SatNav guide me to Ilford where I picked up the A12 and drove to Suffolk. Resources at Thames House, or whatever they called themselves these days, had booked me into the same hotel in Woodbridge that Charlie had been staying. Sally had e-mailed all the information to my office.

Just off the market square and not too far from St Mary's Church was a rambling red-brick structure that had settled comfortably over the centuries. I took the car through a high, covered passage round to the back and parked, taking a moment to check my surroundings.

It was a peaceful spot. The early evening was warm and bright with the sounds of evensong on the air. Trees and shrubs grew around the edge of the car park and, in the garden at the rear of the hotel, bird song added to the general atmosphere of well-being. And there I was, leaning against the car, sick at myself for being glad to get away from the office for a few days and do what I always did best.

After checking in to my room, three doors down from what had been Charlie's, I wandered around the town for a bit and down towards the river. It made a change from my home turf of narrow congested streets, endless takeaways and charity shops. I had a meal in a pub, then went back to my room and fell asleep over a Margery Allingham. It's all part of the hectic life we lead.

(Monday morning)

Detective Sergeant Hopper wove his way along the length of the crowded CID room carrying two mugs of coffee. You could tell he'd done it before. I went back to reading the report he had left on his desk for me on top of a pile of other paperwork. After stopping to talk to one of his colleagues, he squeezed between his desk and the window and sat in the other chair.

"It doesn't matter how big they make a building, there's still never enough space," he said.

He didn't need to tell me. I had shared a room in Thames House before promotion gave me an office of my own, a space that had originally been intended as a cleaner's cupboard. I hadn't seen much of it before all the business that still meant I was given a wide birth. I suppose if you clean their stables for them, some of the stink lingers. My current office at JICIAID wasn't much larger, though it did have a window.

I closed the report. We were currently sitting on an upper floor of the main block of Suffolk Constabulary Headquarters at Martlesham Heath. I'd been in a lot worse places. At least there was a view of trees. And a sports field.

"Not a lot there, I'm afraid," he added, nodding at the file. "We still have no idea how Mr Smith got down to the river from where his car was left."

"Is it far?" I asked, knowing the answer.

"Not if you know the area."

"But?"

"Well, I'm assuming your Mr Smith didn't know the area." He looked at me for an answer. I didn't have any.

He was an unassuming man who looked young for a DS, but then they all looked young to me these days. Like the jolly brigade that still inhabited Thames House with the brittle accents that betrayed their backgrounds. And I would go on believing they were recruiting them younger rather than giving into the idea I was getting older.

"And anyway," he resumed, realising I was going to be an awkward bastard, "why park where he did? If he had been headed for the river, he only needed to go up that road a bit to Capel. Turn right there and that takes you down to the Butley at Boyton Dock."

I still wasn't familiar with the landscape, though I had brought some maps with me, so I took his word for it.

"If he was headed for the river." I said. "A big 'if', though. He certainly wasn't dressed for it, was he?" But then, he hadn't been dressed for wandering about the Suffolk countryside, either. I shook my head. "Is there anything special about that stretch of water?"

"The Butley? No. Unless you like wildlife."

Not Charlie. "So what do we know about where he went into the water?"

"I've got a couple of uniforms down there now talking to locals. But we think it was the dock."

"Well signposted is it?"

"Sorry?"

"Would you need to be a local to think about that and find your way there?"

"Someone who knew the area," he said. "Someone who knew the area well," he added.

"OK," I said after a bit of thought that didn't really get me anywhere. "And the post mortem?"

"This afternoon. Sorry it wasn't sooner, but the pathologist has been busy with the skeletons."

"Skeletons?"

"Yes. A couple of them turned up in Rendlesham Forest."

And this is why you put experienced people in the field, people with an instinct for things. I had no idea if the skeletons were relevant, but they were better than nothing. "Tell me about your skeletons," I said. "Tell me about Rendlesham Forest."

We drove down to Woodbridge, along the bypass and crossed the bridge over the River Deben. From there on I was lost. There was the inevitable golf course. Trees lined the road, offering glimpses of houses and water, farms and light industry. Bare fields and more trees. Fields, and then the forest; endless lines of conifer planted in neat rows, behind scrubby hedge and fence.

After a mile or more, we turned right. More blocks of dense plantation lined the road on both sides. Hopper announced a long gap to our right as the old airfield. A small holding was tucked in between the road and the perimeter fence. Not the best situation I would have thought, directly under the flight line. You had to wonder at the tenacity of someone who had hung on to that piece of land for all those years.

After that, there were more trees. It gave me the creeps. It was far too much like swathes of East

Germany and Czechoslovakia. The wire fence of the airfield hadn't helped. Too many old memories. Days spent in the forest avoiding patrols and trying to get photographs. I could almost hear the dogs barking. Perhaps I should have stayed in my office with its view of fire escapes, rooftops, and the unlovely blunt end of The Cavendish. Like I had a choice.

And then it changed. Broad leafed trees, parking areas, picnic and camping sites, houses, people dawdling in the road, and then a narrow track where we pulled up on the grass verge behind an empty patrol car.

"It's on foot from here. All very civilized, though. These days."

A warm breeze drifted between the trees carrying the sound of laughter as we climbed out and he locked the car.

"Busy."

"Since the Forestry Commission put in facilities. Before that it was a grim sort of place, even after the airbase closed. This way."

We cut across a grassy open space. At the far end, two large pine beams formed a triangular frame to which was attached a large notice. The Rendlesham Forest UFO Trail, it proclaimed. I looked at Hopper. "Don't ask," he said, shaking his head.

I asked.

"We've got a file on it somewhere. Bit slim. I'll dig it out for you if you like. We keep it cos we're always getting letters from..." he looked round to make sure no one was close, "nutcakes, and it's useful to have something we can print off without wasting time."

"Not a believer?"

He gave me a quick look and decided I was winding him up.

"No. I mean, people do see all sorts in dark, quiet, country places, like this. Usually after closing time."

I nodded, all too sober. Like Charlie would have been. And what was it he saw out here after dark on his own?

"Pardon?" asked Hopper.

"Sorry. Just talking to myself. It happens to the best of us in my game."

We passed under the oaks and onto a wide, well-used path. Making its way towards us from the darker sections of the forest was a long, sinuous, noisy, and brightly coloured caterpillar of very young children. Herding them was an equally vivid coterie of adults laden with bags, clipboards, coats, plastic collecting jars, and packed lunches. I couldn't help but think of young George.

It became very quiet once they had passed, quieter still when we turned off the main path and onto a vague track leading into one of the plantation blocks. The air here was still and it felt uncomfortably close. Hopper loosened his tie and undid his collar button. I was glad I hadn't bothered.

We eventually came across a brighter area, ducking under the blue and white tape strung across the path. The clearing was thick with brown pine needles, soft and silent beneath the feet. On the far side was the start of a row of fallen trees, their large, shallow root plates levered upright. A uniformed policeman was leaning against the second one along looking down at the ground beyond it.

"SOCO have finished with the surrounding area," said Hopper. "There's a couple of archaeologists from Suffolk Archaeology checking the site in case there's anything else of interest in the exposed area."

"Archaeologists?"

The uniformed man must have heard us as he furtively straightened. Hopper grinned. "That's what he's looking at," he said quietly.

Keeping to a path everyone else had used, worn down into the soft surface, we approached the toppled tree. As we got closer it was possible to see the wide, shallow crater left in the sandy topsoil. Two young women with multi-coloured hair, wearing shorts and t-shirts were scraping at the soil. One of them swept the loose onto a coal shovel and tipped it into a bucket.

It was like a lid had been lifted onto a curious underworld, most of it stuck to the underside. A vast network of roots was woven together and the gaps were filled with hard, sandy soil. The exposed ground was a dry, whitish clay. It would be murderous if it got wet. The rain I'd stood in the day before clearly hadn't reached this far.

One of the archaeologists looked up and grinned.

"Anything else?" asked Hopper.

She shook her head. "Jilly found the bones of a rabbit, but that's about it."

Hopper turned to me. "The trees along this ridge came down last week in a storm. The forestry workers who came to clear them off the path over there," he pointed toward the crown of the tree, "found human bones. Some were tangled in the roots, others still in the ground."

"Shallow grave, then. Not long after the tree was planted."

"That's what we're assuming."

"Which was when?"

"This whole block was planted up during 1980."

It didn't mean anything to me. We watched the uniformed man take the bucket from Jane and wander off to the spoil heap at the edge of the clearing. She winked at me and got back down to scraping the soil. I bet the uniform bunch were lining up for this duty. We stood looking down for a few moments, alone with our thoughts.

"Anything on the skeletons?" I asked.

"We're still waiting for forensics. It might have arrived at the office by the time we get back."

Neither of us moved. "We could get arrested for this," I said. Hopper grinned. "Do you have any missing persons on your books?"

He sighed. "There's always missing persons on our books. It never ceases to amaze me, especially in this day and age. People walk out the door and are never seen or heard from again. But nothing for that time frame. And no one's come forward since it was in the papers, asking if we've found their long lost loved ones."

It was a dead end. This kind of work is full of them. I was reluctant to go looking for the Americans, though.

"Mind if I look around here for a bit?"

"Help yourself. My DI said 'all assistance'."

"I bet he wasn't smiling when he said it." Hopper laughed. "Which direction was Charlie Smith's car from here?"

That got him thinking. And me. I don't really know why I asked other than the fact Charlie had parked it facing toward the Forest. Hopper looked non-plussed, turning on the spot. He pointed to the trees on the far side of the clearing.

"That sort of direction. I think."

I made my way round the hole. "I won't be long."

Ducking under more police tape that hung between two trees, I ventured into the plantation. There wasn't a path, just that endless, brown carpet of needles. And suddenly I was alone. You're not supposed to get fanciful in my business, but pine forests are eerie places, plantations more so. They feel lifeless yet aware. And this one had clearly witnessed things meant to be kept secret.

The further from the clearing, the rougher it became. The original planting furrows were still visible beneath the drifts of needles. Recently fallen branches littered the spaces between trees. Little light penetrated, even on this sunny morning. Quite suddenly I came to a forest road, long and straight in both directions, with scrub on the far side before the trees started again.

I crossed, trying to keep to a straight line through what was clearly an older block of planting. And then there was another, narrower road beyond which was open space. Just to my right a hedge stretched away in a straight line to a distant road. To the left of it was a field, recently cut for silage. On the other side, a long garden and then buildings.

Looking diagonally across the field, I could see the road sweep away. There was an entrance from the road, and a hedge with a gap to the field beyond. It took a moment. But then I'd only seen it in the dark before. From down there. Because that is where Charlie had parked his car.

It didn't take much working out. He must have followed a car, having had the sense to douse all his lights. They would have pulled off the road directly in front of where I stood and walked up to the forest, following the hedge. Charlie would have pulled in over on the far side and followed them on a parallel path. He must have let his quarry get to the hedge or even the trees before following otherwise he might have been seen and they would have just faded into the background and waited until he was lost in the trees before driving off. And by now, he'd be home. With Rose and George.

I crossed along the top of the field, keeping to the tree line. Picking up the path Charlie must have taken was easy. After a last look down across the field, I walked back through the trees toward the clearing where the skeletons had been found, taking slow steps and watching the ground as I went. I had no idea what I was looking for or if there was anything to find. I found it all the same.

When I made my way back into the clearing, Hopper was leaning against the root plate talking to the archaeologists. The uniformed man was lugging another bucket of soil. Hopper looked up when he heard me, a slight frown replacing his smile. Perhaps because I had come back in from a different direction, perhaps there was something in my expression.

"I think I've got something for you." He straightened and started to walk across the clearing toward me. "And watch where you walk."

04

(Tuesday morning)

I smiled and said 'Thanks' as Sally's secretary held the door open for me, carrying the coffees through using my folder as a tray. She was a treasure, not least because she had somehow reduced Sally's infamously untidy desk to something resembling order. If they gave medals for secretarial forbearance, she deserved one.

Sally looked up for an instant, waved me to the empty chair, and went back to reading. I put the folder down and passed Sally's coffee across. She closed the file, signed the distribution sheet on the cover, and put it in her out tray.

Sitting back in her chair and stretching she looked at me over the piles of folders she had yet to read. I waited.

"You haven't made yourself popular," she said eventually.

"It's a talent," I said and sipped my coffee. Then pulled a face. Some things never changed. It still tasted like they'd filtered the contents of an ash tray.

"Chief Constable of Suffolk, no less. Via the Home Secretary. Doesn't appreciate 'amateurs' interfering in an investigation." She smiled.

"Bloody cheek. They were sloppy. Charlie's car had been found within easy walking distance of where the skeletons were found and they hadn't made a connection."

Sally pulled a face at her coffee as well. "Why would they?"

"I'm not a trained detective and I did. And I found tracks like a herd of elephants had gone through. Not fifty feet beyond their blue and white tape."

"Presumably they don't know anything about the American contingent, so they've no reason to make any connections."

"It's still sloppy work. It wouldn't have taken a uniform more than an hour to walk the woods round-about."

"I hope you didn't upset anyone else."

I thought about it. "The DS was OK with it. Hopper. But it wasn't his case. He's bright, by the way. Worth watching."

"Never mind the recruitment drive. What about our Cousins?"

I lifted my half empty cup from the folder I'd brought in. The heat had raised a ring on the blue plastic. I was treated to one of those over the top of the glasses looks as I handed the folder over. Others found them intimidating. To me they were just cute. Not that I'd ever dare say so. I'd sustained enough injuries in the line of duty as it was.

Sally sighed and snatched it from me. She lifted the cover and glanced at the contents. "Your hand-writing hasn't improved."

"I don't have access to one of them thur fancy writin' machines."

"Spare me the cod Suffolk accent. It was meant to be Suffolk was it? I'll read this later. Just tell me."

I was annoyed. That was my trick. Cuts out a lot of boring reading. "Nothing much *to* tell. After I'd upset the Chief Constable by pointing out the bits the local plod had missed, I went back to Woodbridge and had a nose round the hotel. Charlie's room is still sealed, but if the CIA *were* involved they will have been in and cleaned it."

"I hope you didn't try."

I gave her my full on walk-the-mean-streets-alone narrowed eyes. She grinned and held her hands up in a placatory gesture. "Just don't leave it too long before you send a team in," I said.

"They're already down there."

The phone warbled politely and she picked up the handset. Whilst she listened she stared at me, leaving me with the feeling I was the subject of the conversation. I hoped I wasn't. The file she pulled out from the bottom of the pile was thick and well thumbed. Cradling the handset between ear and shoulder, she flicked through the pages, scribbled something on a post-it note and slapped it onto the page. I tried to read it, but she closed it with a faint smile, said 'Thanks', retrieved the handset, and dropped it into the cradle.

"Sorry about that. Er... The Americans."

"This is where it begins to get... interesting."

"How so?"

"The two men, Stefan Cichy and Oliver Navarro, we know are still working for the Cousins. They have desks in Langley these days, different departments, although both could have retired years ago. They were originally posted to Vietnam and later transferred together to the CIA office on the US Air Force Base at Woodbridge. And I use the term 'office' loosely. From what I've been able to dig out so far, it was as big as London Station. The woman, Laurie Fiquenet, well, the nearest she ever got to working in this country was a six week secondment to Grosvenor Square. The file says it was part of an internal security review, but there's a question mark."

"OK, so why is that interesting?"

"As far as I can tell, they haven't met. Ever."

"And you know this how?"

"By doing my job, Sally. I sat and watched and I talked with people who work and watch. From what

I can gather, the two men don't know who she is. I'm not even sure she knows who they are."

Sally frowned. "Aren't the accents a bit of a give-away?"

"With Cichy and Navarro, perhaps. Everyone I spoke with knew they are American. The common assumption is they served on the base and are there for 'old time's sake'. The woman is different. Soft spoken, little trace of an accent that I could hear. And she keeps very much to herself."

I finished the coffee and wished I hadn't. Sally thought it through. "It's far too much of a coincidence."

"Assuming she is still CIA."

"Even if she isn't – and I've got someone looking into that – it is still too much of a coincidence." Sally thought some more. "And what brought them all here? And why are they still hanging around?"

"The skeletons." I continued through her sceptical expression. "The chronology fits. And Navarro and Cichy were stationed less than half a mile away at the time the bodies were buried."

"OK. I'll buy it for now. And if that is the case and Ms Fiquenet has been involved in internal security reviews before..."

"She might just be keeping a covert eye on the other two." I said. "In which case..."

We looked at each other across the piles of paperwork.

"It's possible she knows what happened to Charlie."

(Tuesday evening)
The washing machine was nearing the end of its spin cycle and I was hoovering the hall when the doorbell rang. I tapped the switch with the toe of my

slipper and the motor died. Two steps took me to the panel on the wall by the door at the head of the stairs. The little screen revealed Sally Barrett standing outside my front door in the long, featureless corridor. She was holding an overstuffed briefcase in each hand. At a discreet distance, her driver was doing the sore thumb act perfected by babysitters the world over.

I padded down the stairs and unlocked the door, letting Sally in along with a waft of cooking smells from downstairs. The driver nodded to me and waited until Sally was safely inside. I slipped the chain back on and went back up the stairs. Sally was in the kitchen by the time I closed the top door, rummaging in a cupboard, her briefcases on the table. The machine was winding down to silence.

"There's a fresh pack above," I said. She put the lid back on the empty jar and opened the cupboard.

"You've changed blend."

I fetched the basket from the hall cupboard and began to unload the washing machine. "This is creamier, less bitter."

She worked alchemy with the coffee while I took my clothes to the bathroom and hung them on the horse over the bath. By the time I'd finished, the scent of coffee filled the air and Sally was drying dishes and putting them away.

"I did the searches you requested."

"I'm honoured. The Director of Strategic Planning doing my legwork. And the drying up." I thought about the last time someone higher up the tree did me a favour and all the grief that had followed.

"You know they're never going to let you near Registry on your own again. You wouldn't be happy down there with someone looking over your shoulder all the time. And I know better than anyone what you want, which isn't saying much."

"I still have access through JIC." Via computer so I only had access to what had been digitised and there was a permanent record of everything I looked at. Which might give you some idea of how much I had disgraced myself, despite the fact I was saving their ungrateful necks.

"And how is that these days?"

"What? Oh, it wavers between desperate tedium and the desire to find the nearest political appointee and punch their lights out."

"You'll be spoilt for choice these days, then."

"What happened?" We looked at each other across the kitchen table. Sally with a tea towel in her hand. Me with an odd sock. "No. Never mind."

"Have you eaten?"

"No."

She produced a mobile phone from her jacket pocket. "Do they still do those superb spring rolls downstairs?"

It never ceases to confound me. My flat has a large, well appointed kitchen. All mod cons as the estate agent said. And a big table with comfortable chairs. Yet whenever I have guests, and you can count that on the fingers of one hand these days, we always end up eating in the living room. From take-away cartons. Off the ridiculously low coffee table.

Sally was prowling, looking to see what new books I had bought, touching the backgammon set she had bought me, ending as I knew she would at the framed photomontage on the wall. She looked at the smiling young woman.

"You still miss her." It wasn't a question. I began to collect the foil trays, stacking them and dropping them into the brown paper carrier bag. "It's been five years since she died, Alex."

"What's in the briefcases?"

She turned and looked at me. It wasn't an argument she would win so she didn't try. It wasn't because I had answers. Quite the opposite. But she knew the ice was thin. And how stubborn I could be. Instead she went out to her jacket and returned with a set of keys. Sitting on the settee, she pulled the heavy cases toward her and unlocked it. When I got back from the kitchen with more coffee, she had a pile of folders stacked up on the seat beside her.

"All that?" I asked, horrified. I had assumed most of it was homework for her.

She replied with a cruel grin.

First up was a slim file in a new, buff cover. "That's a copy of the outline of the history of the USAF base at RAF Woodbridge and Bentwaters. It's not classified, but try not to lose it. If you want the detailed file, let me know, but you'll have to come in for that as it contains personnel sub-files."

I opened it but Sally wasn't going to give me time to look at it, lifting the next, slightly thicker file.

"This," she continued, "is an abstract of police activity out of Woodbridge for the period..." She opened the cover. "May 1975 to the end of 1981."

"Why those dates?"

"Navarro and Cichy arrived in May 1975. We don't know when they left, but they were both in Langley by mid '81."

"That's a longish stint."

"We assume they were running something. There was, as you said, a big CIA presence at Woodbridge. I hadn't realised the extent of it until I read this. They serviced a lot of European stations and we presume it was the co-ordinating centre for stay behind and roll over agents and groups in the event of a Soviet incursion."

"What is it with them? Woodbridge stored nukes and was a primary Soviet target. Why do they always put their fall back and emergency co-ordination centres in the middle of the biggest, juiciest targets?"

It was one of the many bees in my bonnet. They still did it, even after the New York attacks. Sally ignored me. She'd heard it all before. Instead she handed me the file and then lifted up the other five. They were massive. Several thousand pages in each.

"Just to make you really happy, this is a copy of the five-volume file for an event that occurred at Woodbridge Air Force base just after Christmas 1980. The file is still open."

I perked up a bit at that and took the massive folders. Turning them, I opened the top one and read the title page. I read it again. Give Sally her due; she wasn't smiling when I looked up. There wasn't even the hint of a smirk.

"Is this for real?" I asked. I'd seen the slim file that the Suffolk Police kept. It hadn't even hinted at this can of worms.

"Oh yes," said Sally. "Field reports. Maps. Photographs. Intercepts. Queries. Endless queries. Mostly from the public. Debate in the House of Lords. The whole, sorry lot."

"Shit. This had my name all over it, didn't it? Grant, spelled S. U. C. K. E. R."

05

(Wednesday)

Coming through Prestwick was a bit like playing the probationers' first day version of Spot the Spook. The CIA resident was easy to pick out. They always are. And they wonder why they become easy targets. Here, of course, his cover was pretty much blown anyway so he didn't really try. But there were quite a few others hanging around in that unconvincing way you get from people whose job it is to hang around. Even in airports where everybody is just hanging around, the ones who have nowhere to go are easy to spot. They know the quiet moments when it's safe to go to the toilets; their newspapers are well creased having been read from cover to cover; the CTU plain clothes detachment manage to look like police officers; all of them have faces that are dull with terminal boredom. That used to be a funny joke. A long time ago.

None of them seemed to be interested in me, but you can never be certain. I crossed through baggage pick-up, skirting all the tired people waiting for their luggage, and hung about in the bookshop for a couple of minutes. I flicked through a few books and then bought a magazine. Even then I couldn't make my mind up. Sometimes you have to trust to an instinct honed by years in the field. So I didn't bother with the car that had been hired for me and made my own travel arrangements.

I could still see the plane's lurid orange seat backs as I stood outside the terminal building and waited for the bus. There should be a law against it. That and the safety card pasted up in front of you with its reassuring pictures of the plane nose-diving to land and to sea.

Sally picked up on the third ring. "Sally?"

"What's that noise?"

I looked up, shielding my eyes against the glare of the sun. "It's an old Westland Sea King."

"Oh." The chopper trailed exhaust as it lumbered off in the direction of Arran. More bloody memories. Literally. I was in hospital for months after that as they put me back together. "Are you there?"

"Sorry. Any more news on the break-in at the morgue?"

"Someone went through everything in a fairly dedicated fashion. Nothing was taken. And there wasn't much damage – unless you count the mess left by the sprinkler system. It could have been worse."

"That's something at least. Was the fire a serious attempt?"

"The Fire Brigade think so."

"Shit."

"You're assuming it's connected."

"I'm fresh out of belief in coincidences, just now."

"So what was the point?"

"Who the hell knows? Stealing a body? Destruction of evidence? It seems that someone is desperate. Or maybe trying to sell us a pup."

"Hmm. Are you staying up there overnight?"

"I don't intend to. I'll fly straight back to Stansted when I've finished if I can get a flight. Then I'll drive back out to Woodbridge from there. Let me know if you hear any more."

I climbed on the bus and settled down, wondering what the hell was going on. It wasn't the crudeness. I was used to that. It was a common solution: bullets, bombs, a can of petrol and a match. No one seemed to have the patience to gather and digest, to talk, to solve problems without leaving a trail of misery and a hundred more problems flowering poisonously in their wake. It was just bullying on an epic scale and I'd never liked that. But so far we had nothing that made sense, handfuls of puzzle picked at random from different boxes and mixed on the table. And a feeling that it was going to get a whole lot stranger.

A faint haze hung on the horizon and Arran was a damp watercolour of slatey blues and greens set in a flinty sea. The dark humped back of Holy Island squatted in front of it. A tiny white sail was bright against the muted colours.

The village, as I stood and enjoyed the scene, seemed deserted. No one was about and once the bus had gone there was no sound of traffic. So I walked back up the hill from the bus stop to the shop. It was packed from floor to ceiling with pro-visions and all those little extras that people didn't realise they would need when they came down to stay in the rows of caravans I'd seen earlier. I bought a local paper and a bar of chocolate for the goodwill and asked my way to Harbour Terrace.

It wouldn't have taken much working out. Half a dozen roads in the village and only one of them led to the harbour. So I went back down the hill, past the bus stop and followed the main road until Harbour Terrace appeared on my right. Number forty-four was a 1920s dormer bungalow at the far end on the highest point of land, screened by high hedges, but with a clear view of anyone approaching. Especially if you stood in the middle of the front room whilst you were using the phone.

The front door opened before I even reached for the gate. Clearly his contact had re-assured him about me.

I fished around in my pockets for my ID card while I was scrutinised by a pair of unfriendly looking eyes.

"Grant?" he asked looking up from the card. "That your real name?" I pulled a face. "Hmm. Stupid question."

"Are you expecting anyone else, then?"

"Have you eaten?"

"Not recently."

Richard McCullough. One time employee of the Security Service and sensible enough to retire to a place a long way away from London. He flicked an arthritic finger back towards the gate, produced a coat from inside the door and then slammed it shut.

"There's a place just up the hill," he said as he closed the gate, wrapping the coat round his gaunt frame. "Full of old fogies. The food's good."

I let him lead the way. Up the hill was obviously going to be approached via the beach. I cast a glance over my shoulder at Arran where shafts of light had broken through the cloud, picking out hazy detail.

"Don't say much, do you."

"I'm not here for the small talk."

He cracked a smile of sorts. "What are you here for, then?"

"1980. Winter."

He stopped for a moment and turned to me, clearly puzzled. "I'll need a bit more than that."

"You were based in Ipswich at the Post Office."

"I know where I was and I bet it still gets a smirk," he said sourly.

"No idea."

"Hmm. Still at school then, I expect."

"You were asked to go to Woodbridge..."

"Christ." He stopped again. "Not that bloody nonsense. I wrote a report, you know."

"Yes."

"Of course you do."

"There are some questions."

"Not about me," he said.

"No."

After a moment, he began walking again and headed towards a steep, gorse covered sand hill. I followed, hoping he'd warm up once we got to the food. Mind you, I can't say I blamed him. The last thing you want is someone appearing in your comfortable and peaceful retirement who starts asking questions about something you did nearly forty years ago. Especially in our game.

At the top of the hill, a set of buildings became visible. Low and hunkered down behind trees that had grown leaning away from the prevailing winds.

"Retirement home," he said, "for folk with more money than loving relatives."

There are worse places, I suppose, although it seemed bleak to me. Perhaps it was the golf that drew them here. Turnberry was just up the road. Or maybe it was the once genteel town of Ayr just up the other road. Or the views of Arran and the Mull of Kintyre on a clear day. It must have been one of those, because there was bugger all else.

The restaurant was clean and bright and half full. We were guided by a redheaded waitress to a table with a view of the harbour, slightly isolated from the rest of the tables. Clear view of the door. Perhaps it was his regular place. He may just have been in a desk job for most of his career, but he still had a fieldsman's eye. That, at least, made me feel happy, not least because it meant he was observant.

"So what about Woodbridge?" he asked once we had started on the soup.

"How much do you remember?"

He stared at the leek and potato for a bit. "I was based in Ipswich. Martlesham. Surveillance, mail, phones. All a bit primitive by today's standards." He thought for a moment more, spoon hovering. "I can't remember the exact dates, but it was just after Christmas. I'd been on duty all week. I got a phone call from Gower Street. There was something happening in my neck of the woods. Everyone else was still on leave." He blew gently on the soup and drank. "Could I tear myself away from my domestic intercepts and go and have a look? Well, why not. Anything to get out of the office for half a day. Besides, it wasn't exactly a request."

"That was it?"

"Pretty much. I was supposed to go to some RAF chap at Bentwaters. He would tell me what was going on."

"He would tell you what he wanted you to know was going on."

He stopped, and the soup spoon hovered again. "So there was something else."

"Sorry. Shouldn't have interrupted. Don't start second guessing. Just tell me what you remember."

"What is there to remember?" He broke off a chunk of bread and put it back down on his plate. "It was Suffolk in the winter. It was bloody cold. As usual. And I was chasing round checking up on rumours about a bloody..." he looked round quickly and lowered his voice even more, "...flying saucer."

"Is that where you first heard it?"

"Come again?"

"Were you sent to check rumours about a flying saucer, or did that emerge as you began asking questions?"

"Hmm. No. 'Incident involving security at a United States Air Force base' is how they phrased it. Something like that, anyway."

"Did that strike you as odd?"

"That something had happened or that the Service, muggins here, was asked to look into it?"

"Either. Both."

He crumbled more bread as a prelude. "Well, to be honest, I wasn't surprised that something had happened. It was a top secret nuclear weapons storage facility guarded by eighteen year olds a long way from home. At Christmas. That's a recipe for trouble in anyone's book. I'm surprised any of us got away with it."

I waited while he spread butter on one of the pieces of bread and popped it into his mouth. It was displacement activity, something to do while he was thinking. I let him get on with it and spooned in some of my own soup. It was very good.

"I think someone was probably worried about Reds in the forest or something," he continued, finally. "I'm not really sure. I didn't get that involved.

"Were there any Russians active in the area?"

He shrugged. "Probably. Not my department, though. Anyway, as soon as people started talking about flying saucers, a team from that Civil Defence outfit turned up and I was told to go back to Martlesham and write a report."

"CDI9?"

"Aye," he said brightly. "That's the bunch. You heard of them?"

"They weren't mentioned in your report."

He laughed. "A lot of stuff was left out. The whole thing was an utter shambles. Contradictory stories. People running round like blue-arsed flies. I was glad to be out of it. I tell you one thing, though. That place made me grateful to be back in Ipswich. In the 1980s. Can you imagine that?" He gave me a straight look. Perhaps he took my silence for some kind of judgement. "And you never had a report re-written by your superiors and handed over for your signature?"

I finished my soup, patted my lips with a heavy napkin. "When did you retire?"

He frowned, thrown by the change of direction. "What? Er… Three years ago."

"So you'll remember A Branch losing a whole team. The shooting on Arran." I flicked my eyes toward the window.

He looked out across the sea and then down at his plate for a moment before looking back at me. "Grant. All that trouble with Registry. And then *persona non grata*. Man hunt. So, that *is* your real name. And they've taken you back?" He sounded incredulous.

"Yes. After a fashion. Although I was never really out. But you could say my efforts on behalf of the Service were not appreciated. So, yes, I know all about signing reports that someone else has written for you."

He had nothing else to offer about Woodbridge, so we finished the meal trading small talk and walked back down through the village to his bungalow. The inside hadn't got much beyond the mid-1930s in terms of décor and amenities. Large, horse-hair armchairs either side of a fire place where he set a match to the newspaper crumpled beneath kindling and coal. An old wireless set on a large oak table, although the CD slot was a bit of a giveaway. Rugs. Polished floor boards. Somewhere a large clock gave deep measure to the civilized quiet.

Over a large pot of tea, he opened up a bit more and told me what he could remember about Suffolk that hadn't gone into the record. It wasn't much, but this what I was really after. He hadn't been happy about events and was glad to get back to his proper work in the warmth of an office.

"I drove over in the early afternoon," he said, "and reported to the RAF liaison at Bentwaters. He took me out to the Forest, but by that time it was getting dark and the place was heaving with CIA personnel. I got the distinct impression they were recovering a crashed reconnaissance plane. The base was an alternative landing site for U2s. It was probably the impression I was meant to get, the story they were putting about for those in the know. They flew in a lot of big planes and personnel over the next few days.

"The local police weren't happy, but there wasn't much they could do. The sergeant I talked to told me that a few locals had complained, but the areas that were put off bounds were MoD property in those days. And that was that. Normal rules didn't apply.

"The real problem came when a couple of gung-ho military types started waving rifles at a local who tried to drive down one of the approach roads to get to his smallholding. The whole thing was a fiasco as far as I could gather. Which wasn't much. The Air Force boys were kept away behind the wire of the base and the CIA wouldn't talk to me. The RAF chap didn't seem to know what was going on. The local police were helpless."

"Did you talk to any locals?"

"I was thinking about it. I'd started to make arrangements with the local police which is when they told me about the problems the locals had been having. Then the CDI9 team turned up and I was told to go back to Ipswich."

"Did you see any of the CDI9 people? Did they approach you?"

"No. I was just told they were turning up. And there weren't that many hotels in Woodbridge in those days."

"Bit of a convention, was it?"

"More like the bloody circus had come to town."

He stared into his mug for a moment.

"Look. I know it's stupid to ask, but what's this about?"

"I'm as much in the dark now as you were back then. But it might be worth taking a holiday. Somewhere random. Just a couple of weeks."

"What?!" He looked alarmed.

I know I shouldn't have said anything, but I also know how much I hate being kept in the dark. "In case anyone else starts sniffing around. It's not likely. But something turned up in Rendlesham Forest a couple of weeks ago that fits the 1980 timeframe and within days we had CIA agents flying into Heathrow anxious to be taking their annual leave in the UK. That level of activity made our former masters uneasy. They sent someone to have a look. I watched the police fish him out of the river a couple of days ago."

06

(Wednesday evening)

We dropped into Stansted through stormy weather and I sat and watched the upcurved wingtips flex while the air brakes rose and fell like increasingly impatient fingers. It was marginally better than staring at those orange seat backs. Then I changed my mind. A nasty crosswind had the plane looking at the runway from some alarming angles before the pilot picked his moment and the wheels thumped the concrete. The back of the seat in front of me had never seemed more inviting.

After the plane had landed, we rumbled along with a collective sigh of relief. Everyone then ignored the pilot's final announcements as they prepared to disembark. Like me they probably wanted to get out of that metal tube as quickly as possible.

Heavy clouds squatted over the airfield as we made our way out of the exit of the Airbus a319 and there was thunder rumbling in the evening air. The last of the sunshine glowed a sickly green through the tinted windows of the terminal buildings and the internal lighting struggled to compete with the elemental gloom. Even the fluorescent vests of the ground crew were muted.

Large drops of rain smacked the concrete and hit the windows as I followed the other passengers along the concourse. We made a scrum of it with other disembarking passengers and emerged into the main terminal. I went off to extricate my car from the Short Stay car park.

By the time I had negotiated all the roundabouts and slipped out onto the Colchester road, rain was bouncing back off the ground and even the most seasoned drivers were down to forty. The windscreen wipers worked double time all the way to

Ipswich and I began to feel the cloud was following me. Lightning flickered in the gloom as I crossed the Orwell. If I'd been superstitious I'd probably have turned round and headed for home.

It was still raining when I locked up and ran across the hotel car park and into the rear lobby. The dining room was still open and I gave it the quick once over before heading for the desk. The receptionist appeared in the doorway of the office and smiled, producing my room key from a hidden board.

"Your office called," she said handing me the key. "I explained we can only give you an extra ten days, not a whole fortnight."

"Ten days is fine by me," I said.

"Oh, that's good." She looked as tired as I felt. "Er, I have to ask you to pay now."

"Of course." I produced a credit card.

"Sorry about that. We had a couple of guests leave the other day without so much as a by your leave." I wasn't surprised.

"Shocking," I said, trying to look suitably shocked. "Bet they paid for everything with cash while they were here, though."

She put my card into a reader and began tapping keys. "If you could just enter your PIN." She watched the screen of her computer. "Do you know...? I think they did. Funny that. These days." A printer produced a receipt. "We can always refund if you have to leave early," she said, handing it to me along with the card.

"Thanks. Are they still serving?" I asked.

"Oh yes. Go right through."

With my key in my pocket, I slipped the receipt into my wallet and made my way toward the dining room. Before going in I pulled out my phone and selected a number from the contact list.

Strange acoustics formed a background to Sally's voice. "Where are you?" she asked.

I wondered the same about her, but thought it impolitic to ask. "Woodbridge. We need to talk."

When I rang off I looked in to the dining room again and decided to go in search of fish and chips instead.

(Thursday)

The clack of keyboards, the warble of phones, and subdued chatter formed a background to the crowded room. None of the fancy glass boards, stylish furniture, and acres of space you see on television. Just rows of bog standard desks piled high with the paperwork of petty and serious crime. A large side room housed a conference table and corkboards that had seen better days. Piles of stationery were stacked in one corner because the stationery cupboard was full.

I perched on an old plastic chair just outside the conference room, keeping out of everyone's way, listening to the sounds of the office, grateful for my comparatively spacious and quiet room in the JICIAID building. No doubt it was already doubling as a store cupboard and I would bet anything that my desk was piled high with all the casework everyone else was offloading on to me in my absence.

DS Hopper arrived with two mugs of coffee, placing them on the small table next to me.

"Thanks," I said.

"You've already tasted our coffee and you're still thanking me?" He disappeared with a grin and returned a few moments later with a pile of folders which he placed on the table when I moved my mug. "Rumour has spread through the building," he said with a glance first to make sure he couldn't be overheard.

"Oh. And what does rumour say?"

"It wavers between APACS and Box 500."

"And where has your money gone?"

He had the grace to look sheepish as he leaned against the wall and sipped his drink. "I'm barred 'cos of so-called inside knowledge, but I would've had an outside bet on something else. A little bird mentioned the Cabinet Office."

I had to think about it for a moment. Light glimmered but nowhere near as bright as the halogen lamps had been. "A Crane, I suspect. And what, precisely, is your outside bet?"

"JIC."

"Have you thought of joining Counter Terrorism?"

He looked at me, weighing things, clearly understanding the implications of my question. CT was a pathway to the Security Service. "No."

I nodded. I could understand why. Besides, most coppers just want to be coppers. "So. What's new?"

"Plenty," he sighed. "It hasn't got us much further forward, though."

"Let's start with what happened at the morgue."

"Break-in, suspected attempted arson." He pulled a folder off the pile and handed it to me. "A patrol car was called after someone tried to get into the mortuary. Alarms went off in the hospital's security office. The man was challenged and ran for it."

"I take it there's someone on duty there round the clock."

"Hospital security always is. And one of our cars will swing by at random every night."

"OK."

"We don't have the numbers to do anything more."

I held up my hands in a placatory gesture. He didn't need to tell me about shortages of personnel.

"What about Pathology?" He looked blank. "Charlie might be in the Mortuary, but your skeletons are in

Pathology, along with all the notes. While everyone was chasing the interloper..."

"Shit. Hang on."

He went over to his desk and used the phone. I read the report. It was mercifully straightforward. When he came back it was with a long face. "I've just been on to the Path Lab. They seem to think someone might have been messing with their computers."

"And the skeletons?"

"They were moved before this happened."

"Somewhere secure, I hope."

"They're in the building." I must have looked blank. "Here. Police Headquarters."

"OK. Sorry. Bit slow on the uptake, there. And what do we know about them?"

He lifted another folder and opened it.

"A man and a woman. Both old, probably in their eighties. Buried side by side in a shallow grave. Decomposition and the state of the bones is consistent with them having been there since 1980. We're still trying to identify them."

I let that sink in for a few moments. It didn't mean anything to me, but they still seemed to be the reason everyone was here. He placed the file on the table.

"What's next?" I asked.

Hopper picked another folder from the pile. "Your man. Mr Smith."

He hesitated a moment, looking at me. I nodded.

"Cause of death. Heavy blow to left temple with blunt object which caused severe haemorrhage. Blood found low on a tree at the scene – boy was there hell to pay for that – matches Smith's." He closed the folder and handed it to me. "That's it for now. Do you want copies?"

"Yes. Thanks. I'll see they get forwarded to the right people."

A young DC appeared, hovering by Hopper's shoulder. "Phone for you, Sarge."

"OK. I'll be there in a minute." He turned to me. "Sorry."

I smiled and took a look at the report on Charlie, wondering how Rose and young George were coping. Hopper wandered back from his phone call.

"There's someone downstairs wants to see me."

I stood and stretched, placing my mug on a nearby desk. "That's OK. I've got to go and find an American before CTU lose her as well."

Hopper raised an eyebrow. "Perhaps you'd better stick with me, then."

It was a 'chat with the public' interview room rather than one of the 'you're nicked' interview rooms. No tape recorders. Marginally better furniture. Mind you, it was still bolted to the floor so it couldn't be thrown around. There were posters on the wall. And a woman in her early forties that I recognised – tall, composed, severe. She looked at me and then Hopper as he closed the door.

"Now why do I get the feeling that my innocent little inquiry has turned into an interrogation?"

"Nothing like that, Ms..." Hopper looked at a piece of paper.

"It's pronounced like 'frequent', but without the 'r'. Laurie Fiquenet."

I made a mental note to tell Sally we'd been pronouncing it incorrectly.

"Please. Sit down. I'm Detective Sergeant Hopper. And this is my colleague, Mr Grant. How can we help?"

"Why," she asked as she sat, "doesn't he have a rank?"

"Because I'm not a policeman," I replied as Hopper settled himself opposite Ms Fiquenet.

She folded her hands on the table top in front of her. "And what if my inquiry is confidential?"

"Is it?" asked Hopper.

There was a moment's silence. She pursed her lips, flicked a glance at me where I stood in the corner.

"So," said Hopper. "What is this enquiry of yours?"

"I'm looking for a dead man."

It went quiet again for a moment. "Would you care to explain?" Hopper was doing a very good impression of a dull English copper.

Ms Fiquenet produced a folder from the pocket of her tailored jacket. She opened it and placed it on the table. Hopper looked at it without touching it. I stepped forward.

"May I?" I asked.

"Help yourself." If you listened closely there was an underlying hint of accent you could miss if you weren't paying attention.

I picked up the folder. You've seen them on television. Black leather with a badge nestled in a cut-out. The badge was gold with blue lettering stamped into it proclaiming the holder to be a Special Agent, Office of Special Investigations, Department of the Air Force. There was also an ID card. This had a passable photo of the woman sitting at the table. I took out my phone and selected a contact from the list.

"Don't mind me," I said. "Hope you left the Sig at home," I added as I waited for someone to pick up at the other end. "O. S. I. US Air Force – 002601/SI. Got that? Phone Andrews direct. I'll hold."

"Ms Fiquenet?"

"Let's wait for Captain Cody."

We waited. Eventually a voice asked me if I was there. I was. It told me the correct name and gave a passable description. "Do you want a photo confirmation?" it asked. I said I might as well and a picture appeared on my phone. I rang off and put my phone in my pocket, then closed the ID folder and placed it on the table.

"Thank you, Ms Fiquenet," I said. "It pays to be certain." She put the folder back into her jacket pocket. "And wasn't it *Commando* Cody?"

The look she gave me was sharp. She probably summed me up correctly. I don't think she much liked what she saw. I could live with that.

Hopper intervened, ever the gentleman. "And what can we do for the US Air Force, Ms Fiquenet?"

"The Office of Special Investigation normally deals with crime and certain aspects of security on US Air Force bases." Hopper nodded. "Occasionally, we get assigned to more... personal matters. So, yes, the Sig was left at home." I nodded. Perhaps it's catching. "A short while ago, the widow and mother of several USAF personnel wrote a letter to her Congressman. Mrs Pennyweather wanted to know why one of her sons was not brought home when he died. So did the Congressman.

"An initial check showed that her son had left the Air Force more than a year before he died. She has a terminal cancer and it was thought she was confused. Pain. Medication. But she produced a photograph of her son, for the local OSI agent. It shows her son in uniform, on the base. On the wall just behind him, there's a poster for a dance with a date just a few weeks before he died."

"Don't tell me," I said with a sigh. "A Christmas Dance. 1980."

That left a little dent in her calm façade. "Oh-kay."

"And how can we help?" chipped in Hopper with his favourite question.

"I get the impression you two are singing off different sheets."

"Same song," replied Hopper. "Different arrangement." He paused. I could feel it coming. "So how can we help?"

She looked at us both carefully. "In absence of a grave, which I will find eventually, I want to know how this boy died. The Air Force has no record. If he died in this country, there must be a paper trail."

"Very well. If you write down—"

A long envelope embossed with the USAF seal appeared on the table in front of her and she pushed it across to Hopper. "It's all in there."

"What prompted Mrs Pennyweather to ask about her son now?" I asked.

"As I said, she's dying."

"But why not in the nearly forty years she was living? Worth asking, don't you think?"

"If that's all? I have a grave to find."

That told me. She stood. Hopper followed suit and went to the outer door.

"There is one other thing," I said as he reached for the handle to let her out.

"There usually is," she said, her eyes narrowed.

"Your hotel."

"What?"

"Comfortable?"

"You're with the Tourist Board as well?"

"The two Americans who were there when you first arrived, Ms Fiquenet."

"I'm not with you."

"One time colleagues of yours."

Hopper kept a commendably straight face through this little exchange. Ms Fiquenet kept the puzzled expression to a minimum as she looked first at me, then at Hopper, then back at me.

"I've a feeling," she said, with a sigh, "that things just got a whole lot more complicated."

"Oh," I said, matching her sigh. "They usually do."

07

(Thursday)

It was a fine morning and I stopped just outside the main entrance of the police headquarters beneath the heavy looking portico to check my phone. Fish cruised in lazy fashion round the small fountain in the moat. As I flicked through the messages, Laurie Fiquenet left and walked past me without so much as a nod. She crossed the visitor's car park and climbed into what I presumed was a hire car. I'd know soon enough. I sent a short text and a photo then started to put my phone away.

It never made it to my pocket as a small Ford emerged from further back and set off after the US Air Force agent, an older looking couple in the front two seats. Moments later, another car swept past. Now, a police HQ car park is bound to be a busy place, but that was just a little too busy for my liking. And a bit bloody cheeky if you ask me. It wasn't our missing Americans as the driver was young and clean cut. A DC nipping home for an early lunch, perhaps. Or a civilian nipping down to W H Smith for some extra paper clips. Both of which I doubted very much. So I took a few more pictures and phoned it in and left it to others to sort out.

Traffic was light. I drove the three and a half miles back to Woodbridge, parked in the hotel car park and went for a walk. In the Market Square I admired the Market Hall; let a couple of cars, a shiny black van, and a bus go past before crossing the road. Sauntering, I spent a bit of time looking in shop windows, popped into a newsagent and straight back out, explored a few side turnings, doubled back, and generally exhibited that level of paranoia that keeps people in my business alive.

Back at the hotel, after quickly checking the car park, I picked my way over the vacuum cleaner lead, and then did a quick two-step back over the brush as the receptionist called me. The cleaner whined into quietness.

"Mr Grant."

"Yes?"

"A Mr..." She looked down at a scratch pad on the desk. "Rutherford called in. He said you were expecting him."

"That's right. Where did he go?"

"No further than the lounge."

I turned. Rutherford stood in the doorway, carrying a slim briefcase. "Barney. Good to see you again. And thanks for coming at such short notice."

We shook hands. He looked well. Fit. Relaxed. I thanked the receptionist and led the way upstairs.

Barney Rutherford was a Scot, like me. Same town. Different backgrounds. We had both been guided toward SIS by a teacher who had given us both extra tuition in German in our final years at school. I learned later he'd been an SOE agent and spent the immediate post-War years with SIS recruiting in East Germany. Why he'd opted for teaching in Glasgow after all that is anyone's guess.

Rutherford had ended up working in Berlin and East Germany running networks gathering low level economic intelligence – shopkeepers, wages clerks, that sort of thing. There had been rumours about the night the Wall came down, but the fact he was still alive meant they were wrong. In that part, anyway.

He had worked for JICIAID for a short while as well, before landing the top job with a small intelligence unit that most people had never heard of. Those that had heard of it only knew the rumours and dismissed them out of hand. Most of those rumours, however, are true. There really are sections of the intelligence community that investigate UFO reports and what is termed paranormal activity. Though not the ones you have ever heard of. If you want to know why, look back to 1938 and the Orson Welles broadcast of *War of the Worlds*. Although the panic was not as widespread as initial reports claimed, it made some people sit up and take seriously how effective mass media could be in manipulating populations. That is why Civil Defence set up a department in Room 9 of their Unit in the old Home Office building on King Charles Street to investigate the whole phenomenon. In these days of mass social media it always surprised me that Rutherford's department was still just a small group of misfits based in the wilds of Gloucestershire.

I unlocked the door and stepped into the muted atmosphere, indicating the only chair. Hotel rooms are strange places. They never have time to take on the character of those who inhabit them beyond the anonymity of living out of a suitcase. The vacuum cleaner was whining again somewhere downstairs, but the sound faded as the heavy door closed slowly on its spring.

I checked the bathroom, gave my other stuff a quick once over, and looked at the phone. Rutherford watched impassively. When I'd finished, he said, "Would you rather talk somewhere else?"

"No. Just habit I guess." He was still standing, so I waved him to the chair again and sat on the bed. "How's Gloucestershire these days?"

"Looking for a job?"

"Oh, please, don't tempt me."

He laughed. We'd had this conversation before. More than once. He hauled his case onto his lap and unlocked it, pulling buff card folders from its interior. I swear, I dream about the damn things sometimes. Piles of folders, endless shelves disappearing into the dark; never quite being able to find the one you want, always lost in the stacks.

"I brought the files you asked for. I think you'll be disappointed. I read through them last night. There's not a lot more there than you'll have seen from DS8, S4(Air), Sec(AS)2a, and RAF Rudloe Manor. It's all well before my time with CDI9." He handed them across. "There's some supplementary material there as well."

"Thanks. I wasn't really expecting too much. Just covering the angles, trying to get a handle on things."

"So what's happening?"

"You heard about Charlie Smith?" Rutherford nodded. "He was one of my probationers when I was at Thames House. I set him assignments. Assessed his work. I signed off on him." And he saved my skin, but that's a story to save for Georgie when he's old enough. "Anyway. At the moment, this all seems to centre on two skeletons – bodies that were buried in Rendlesham Forest in 1980 or thereabouts."

"And your system threw up the UFO incident."

"Along with other things, yes. Five bloody great files worth. I also looked at the Suffolk Police file which gave me nothing. So I went and talked with a Security Service man who was sent there to investigate. He said that as soon as your lot turned up, he was told to go home. Then CDI9 got written out of his report."

Rutherford smiled and relaxed back in the chair. No easy feat with hotel furniture. "It's not unusual. We aren't very popular, not even these days when Civil Defence is meant to be all the rage again. And the slightest mention of anything out of the ordinary, which is our official remit... UFOs in particular still send a shudder down the collective spines, such as they are, of our bosses."

"Now you know why I was checking for bugs." He laughed. "So what *did* happen in 1980?"

Shaking his head slowly, he said, "No idea. We used to run regional teams in those days, would you believe? Four of them. It was one of those that came out here. They dismissed the UFO thing straight away along with the story circulating in intelligence circles about a crashed spy plane."

"Why?"

"Which one?"

"Sorry. Both."

"Well, they discounted the UFO story straight away because of its source."

"Our Cousins?"

"Precisely. They've been spinning that nonsense since Roswell. It was one of their very first dis-information projects. Add to that the way it was handled. The procedure was all wrong. Despite official public pronouncements on the existence of aliens, most countries have had protocols in place for dealing with a genuine first contact scenario since the late 1940s. None of that was being followed.

"And the regional team also ruled out a crashed plane because there simply wasn't enough damage. CIA involvement would have meant a CIA flight. They occasionally flew one of their Lockheed U2s from Woodbridge, but they are biggish planes – 60 feet long, 100 foot wingspan. That would damage a fair bit of woodland if it crashed short of the runway on landing or ditched on take-off. Even something like a Cessna 340A which is 34 by 38 would tear a hole in the woods. All the CDI9 team found, after a lengthy covert search, was a couple of singed trees by one of the forest roads. And they only saw those from a distance because that site was crawling with Americans."

"There was other signals traffic at the time."

Rutherford shrugged. "The police had reports of lights. You'll have seen those. There was also a nearby air traffic control that reported unusual aerial activity. Which is no surprise because the Americans will have put planes in the air at the first sniff of anything untoward. And then denied it. But none of it adds up to much. And there's a psychology to these things. If you talk to people they always claim not to have heard about other things going on, yet there is always a weirdness factor at play. It's not easy to quantify. The guy who set up CDI9 in the late-1930s was a psychologist and he wrote papers on this. Low level hysteria infecting populations. Which is our main remit."

"So if the CIA didn't crash a plane and the Martians didn't crash a saucer, what the hell did happen? The Cousins were crawling all over that forest for days, putting out stupid cover stories, and upsetting the locals. There were flights in and out. Talk of large quantities of soil being removed."

Rutherford shook his head. "No idea. Sorry. In the end, it was all put down to Cold War hysteria. There were nukes on that base that the British population was not supposed to know about. And the CIA had a large operations base there. You know how they used to react to the slightest thing."

"Maybe so. But something happened to trigger all that and I need to find out what was so important about it that it's provoking so much interest forty years later."

*

We lunched in a local pub on a more than halfway decent ploughman's, savoured a fine local ale, and then drove out to Rendlesham Forest. I was still trying to get a hook on what could bring people back after so many years, so I took Barney along to where Charlie had parked his car. Perhaps he might come up with some bright ideas. They had certainly eluded me.

The afternoon sun was hot and we kicked about in the thin dirt at the edge of the field for a while. It didn't tell us anything. Neither did gazing at the line of trees. So we climbed back into the car and I took us on a little way further to what Barney wanted to show me. He checked a hand-held GPS against an OS map as I drove.

"This is it," he said after a couple of minutes.

All we had done was follow the road round three sides of the adjacent field, passing a few farm buildings on the way, until we came back to the edge of the Forest. The road then took a sharp right and we followed it further along. I pulled off the road onto a piece of ground still soft from rain. There wasn't a soul in sight.

I locked the car and we stood for a moment looking round. A house was just visible back the way we had come. Next to us an odd shaped field with a dirt track along one side.

"The lower end of the forest road has gone," Rutherford said, pointing to the field. "It ran along this side of the field and there's still a right of way."

The field looked small to begin with, but only because of a narrow clump of trees intruding at an angle. The further we walked along the edge of the field, the more of it that became visible. We picked our way through rough grass until a discernible track began to emerge, something wide enough for a truck or a fire engine.

After about four hundred yards, where the field ended, the road dog-legged to the right and we were suddenly on our own amongst the pines. We kept walking. The track was mostly packed earth, but there were stretches where concrete slabs had been laid. It was old and cracked and there were places where it had been torn out and replaced with rubble, crushed bricks.

"There's other paths and roads crossing through the Forest. They cut the plantation into blocks and serve as access for Forestry Commission vehicles and the Fire Brigade. Photos from the time show them to be much better maintained than this."

"It's a different world, as everyone keeps telling me."

Rutherford shrugged. "The airfield is straight ahead and over to the left a bit is the back gate."

"The infamous East Gate."

"That's the one."

We walked uphill a bit more.

"This whole area was clear-felled a couple of years after the incident and replanted," said Rutherford, his voice deadened by the trees.

"More grist to the conspiracy theorists' mills."

"They do grind long and incredibly fine."

We arrived at one of the side roads and Rutherford led the way off to the left. It was very quiet. No birdsong, no sound of children, just a light breeze pushing its way along the straight, level path.

"It gives me the creeps," said Rutherford. "Too much like my old stamping ground."

I knew what he meant. "I know what you mean. Perfect backdrop for the STB or the HVA. You half expect to come across a couple of Russian tanks parked quietly just off the road, the crew dipping black bread into pea soup and smoking those awful cigarettes."

We went on in silence until Rutherford pulled his map from his pocket. "It's back on the road we just left and along here somewhere that the so-called sightings took place."

"So basically the US Air Force was stumbling about the forest at night... For how long?"

"A couple of nights initially before it kicked off big time."

"And were they armed?"

"They claim not. The Air Force at least seems to have been playing by the rules. It wasn't until later, once the CIA circus was in town, that guns began to appear. We don't even know who authorised that or who was carrying them. Uniforms were mentioned by witnesses, but that doesn't mean anything, much. No one could describe them accurately."

There was a narrower road that carried on in the direction we had been walking. Still wide enough for vehicles, it was packed earth rather than concrete or rubble. The trees grew right up the edge. As we stood there looking round, he explained the bare bones of what had happened. Of how guards at the eastern end of the airfield had seen lights in the Forest and been given permission to investigate. They had eventually come this way.

After that, it's anyone's guess. As well as our investigations, there have been countless books, TV programmes, articles, and websites, all muddying the water. People have walked the Forest ever since in the hope of meeting aliens. It certainly had atmosphere. A chainsaw started up somewhere, the sound muted by distance and the direction difficult to judge.

"Did any of your people find any locals to talk to?" I asked.

"One or two, but I'm guessing there were more who never came forward for fear of ridicule. There were a few who popped up later when books were being written, but they added nothing of substance. I'll leave you the copies of the reports I brought down. It's all confidential, but there's nothing in there that's sensitive."

I still couldn't get a handle on any of this. It seemed surreal. Yet something happened, that's for sure. It upset the CIA at the time and it brought some of them back forty years later. What was worth protecting that far down the line?

"Any chance of talking to any of the original team?"

"Not unless you have a connection with the spirit world."

I wandered about a bit, not expecting to find anything. The chainsaw sputtered into silence. Rutherford stayed looking down at his map and said quietly, "I don't know about you, but I'm suddenly feeling a bit exposed here."

I walked across and looked down at the map as well, pointing at nothing in particular. "You heard it as well?"

In the silence that followed the chainsaw there had been a rustle where there really shouldn't have been a rustle. Add to that all the additional vehicular activity and the fact there were people happy to kill and then dispose of the body...

"Shall we go and look at some trees?" he asked. I thought it was a very good idea.

It is difficult to remain casual and keep a slow pace when every instinct tells you to run and hide. Rutherford folded his map and put it away. Then we wandered into the shade, getting closer to the trees. The ground was uneven, despite the thick layer of brown needles. Taking care not to trip we headed into a dense area and then assumed a defensive position, crouched low, backs to trees, watching and waiting.

"I was hoping you might say it was one of yours," whispered Rutherford.

"If it is, they're going straight back to Fort Monckton for a refresher course."

"And our Cousins?"

"That could be more of a problem. They trained in Vietnam and were posted here long enough to get to know every tree. On the other hand, we have years on them."

"Hmm. In which case, I don't think we'll go back to the car."

We waited a while longer in silence, but heard nothing more At the point cramp began to set in, we decided to head on up through the trees toward the airbase. The still air was stuffy and dusty, filled with dark shadow and smothering silence. The only life we encountered on the way were several huge anthills made of pine needles and crawling with brown and black wood ants.

Emerging onto the road I had been driven along before, we let a caravanette go by, crossed the tarmac, and made our way to the old East Gate of the airbase. There wasn't much to see. Rusty wire fencing. The cracked concrete road, mossy at the margins and along the joints between slabs. All that remained of the gatehouse was the brickwork base and some saplings.

We stared through. I was still trying to figure it all out. "What would draw a team of guards off a US Air Force base into surrounding forest? A forest they presumably knew well from having stared at it for months on end."

Rutherford turned and looked back at the trees and shook his head. "No idea. They were there to prevent people crossing the wire and getting on to the base. Anything outside was not their business unless it presented a threat."

"And given this place held US nuclear weapons, they wouldn't fall for some diversionary tactic. Would they?"

"The kids on the fence might. A long way from home. Bored out of their skulls. But I doubt their commanders would. Besides, the weapons store is way off at the other end of the base. It was in its own compound with its own guards. The planes had separate guards as well. As did the CIA compound, most of which was underground."

Someone had been doing their homework. I looked at Rutherford and he turned to me. "US bases feature a lot in our work," he said. "Layouts differ, but the basics are the same."

"So someone in there gave the go ahead for what? Jeeps? A truck? Armed guards? Technically that would be an invasion of UK sovereign territory." I had done my homework as well.

"Officially they weren't armed to begin with, but they certainly were later. I suppose they thought they would do whatever they had to do without anyone noticing."

"Got that wrong, didn't they?" No matter how deserted the countryside may seem, there's usually someone about. Even at night. Especially at night. Late drinkers. Poachers and other ne'er-do-wells. And if there had been lights in amongst the trees, locals would have noticed as well. There are farms and cottages all round the forest.

We headed back along the road.

"I just can't get a handle on this," I said, not for the first time. "Most cases, it's like being in a maze and knowing you have to work patiently to find your route to the centre. This. I can't even find a way in I don't even know if it *is* a bloody maze."

We managed to get a cab to pick us up at the camp site in the Forest and take us back to the railway station. I left Rutherford waiting for a train and walked up through Woodbridge to the hotel. It was overcast again and humid and I wasn't sure if the day had been worth it. The thought of a stuffy room was too much so I kept walking.

"I didn't pull you out of a meeting?"

"Just having a late lunch," replied Sally.

"Sorry."

"That's all right. What do you want?"

One of those nice pasta salads, I thought. Taking a deep breath, I said: "Someone to look over the car."

The phone was silent. She was either thinking or eating. "Not with you," came the reply.

Eating, I thought, assailed by the tea time aroma of a chip shop. Joining the queue wasn't an option, however. Not with what I was going to say next. "Possible IED."

There was a choking sound from my phone.

"What?!"

I moved the phone back close to my ear. "It's not certain. But we were followed into the woods. And it wasn't the babysitters you've stuck on me. Given the background of our Cousins..."

"Dear God, Alex, the ADG will go berserk."

"The ADG is an old maid. Never stepped foot outside an office. Does he really want to risk losing another operative? Or some local yobbo who fancies a joy ride? Shunt it across to TechOps and send the DDG a memo reminding him in capital letters that Charlie Smith is dead. I'm just dealing with the mess caused by whatever fuckwit sent Charlie out on a field mission. And it's no good telling me," I said before she could respond, "that it wasn't a field mission. People are covering their arses and redesignating the whole thing, but you know and I know that it was one, huge, cock-up. If Thames House wants me to deal with it, let me deal with it properly or not at all. Just get someone from TechOps down here to look the car over. I'll send the GPS co-ordinates."

There was another silence. I don't think Sally was eating this time.

"Look," I added. "I'm sorry. That wasn't aimed at you. I'm hot, going round in circles, and a good friend is dead."

"I'll get a team sent down straight away."

"Thank you, Sally."

I was just about to ring off. "Alex."

"Yes?"

"Please take care."

"I will."

The line closed and I felt like a heel. Sally was one of the few executive staff who appreciated what field officers went through. She had done a lot for me; not just visiting me in hospital after, but through the whole bloody affair that followed.

I looked round, found myself opposite the Fire Station and Police Office, so turned round and headed back to the Market Square. What I needed was something to eat, a shower, and a quiet time with those files that Barney Rutherford had left in my room.

"Fancy a ride?" I had one foot on the hotel doorstep.

Turning, I looked at the car that had pulled up outside. Laurie Fiquenet was leaning across the passenger seat. She looked cool and collected. "Now there's an offer," I said.

"Don't get cute."

"If it involves food somewhere along the way, I'm in."

She pushed the passenger door open and I climbed into the air conditioned comfort of a top of the range Cadillac SUV. Not the car she'd been driving earlier. I wondered for a fraction of a second if there was an opening for me in the US. Their federal agencies always seemed to have the money for this sort of thing. But then, no one in the US would touch me.

As a polite guest I decided not to say anything about the fact she had been driving a Citroen earlier in the day. I was still trying to work out how to fix the seat belt as she pulled away and swept round in a u-turn that somehow managed to miss everything in the narrow street.

Within minutes we were back across the River Deben and heading out into the countryside, back the way I had just come. Life's like that. As she drove, I struggled with the cellophane wrapper of the sandwich pack she had produced from a cooler. "I did – bloody thing – I did have something a bit more exotic in mind," I said, waving the pack before attacking it with a penknife. "Fish and chips, maybe." She snorted.

I was half way through the first sandwich and dreaming of an icy cold glass of ale when the car lost speed and pulled over onto a long, gravelled parking strip at the side of the road. I had no idea where we were. Fiquenet climbed out and I followed suit, bringing my other sandwich with me.

The car gave an expensive sounding chirrup as the central locking engaged. Starting on my second sandwich, I looked round. A country road with some cottages in the far distance, hunkered down beneath a sky that was deciding whether it could be bothered to become stormy. Not a pub in sight.

Beside us was a length of neatly clipped hedge. As I finished off my sandwich I stepped up to it and peered over the top. "Nice," I said. "Is this where you bring all the boys?"

She gave me a look calculated to shrivel me on the spot. When you've worked Internal Affairs as long as I have you become immune to that sort of thing.

I followed her along the length of the hedge and through cast iron gates that had long rusted in an open position onto a level. Just inside was a gravelled area with wooden seats along either side and several municipal litter bins. Behind one set of benches was a small, windowless brick building with a padlocked door that was in desperate need of a coat of paint. Attached to the wall beside the door was a tap that dripped into a wide grating.

Beyond all this was the rest of the cemetery, a large field that sloped gently away from the road. It was about three-quarters full, a recent burial on the far side marked by a low mound of fresh soil and bunches of wilting flowers. Everything was neat and bleak. I preferred the old, overgrown Victorian burial grounds where wildlife flourished and you could hear birdsong.

Here, the only sound was the gentle crunch of gravel beneath Laurie Fiquenet's expensive looking lace up shoes. She looked like she knew where she was going, so I followed, wondering how some people contrived to look fresh and cool all the time. Maybe she hadn't been crawling through the forest for most of the afternoon dealing with ancient fears. We cut across some grass toward the far end and then down a neatly mown path between headstones. Two thirds of the way down, she stopped.

"John James Pennyweather. 1958. 1981." I looked at her when I'd finished reading. She looked back. "So. You found your man."

"And?"

I shrugged. I really wasn't in the mood for guessing games. My feet hurt and my shirt was sticking to my back. Despite the sandwiches she had bought for me, I was still hungry. The prospect of stormy weather was starting to give me a headache. She pointed to the flowers.

"Is it normal to place flowers on a grave after all this time?" she asked.

I looked at them. Several days old. Past their best, especially after the rain we'd had. A bunch of assorted flowers, probably from a supermarket or filling station shop. The elastic band was still round the stems. It's the thought that counts.

"I still put flowers on my fiancée's grave."

"Oh. I'm sorry." She sounded sorry.

I smiled at her. "No need to be."

"When did she…?"

I took a deep and exhaled slowly. "Four years, fifty-six days…" I looked at my watch and did the math. "Twenty-one hours and forty-seven minutes ago." She didn't reply. I suppose it's enough to stop any conversation. It certainly gave me something to think about. "But you're right."

"Pardon?"

"Thirty-nine years and change is a long time. And they're reasonably fresh. When did JJ Pennyweather die?"

"January."

"And his birthday?"

"January."

I looked around at the cemetery again. "So maybe someone doesn't like the winter weather. Maybe they come when they can or more than once a year. And maybe, just maybe, they know why your civilian was in uniform just before he died."

Her slow applause was accompanied by a disarming smile. But I had no idea why she had dragged me out here.

"If you're hoping I'll show you mine if you show me yours," I said, "you're out of luck. I've got nothing."

08

(Thursday night)

Hotels in the evening have their own special atmosphere. They are full of displaced people. Some revel in the change to their normal lives, the escape, the sense of anonymity, the hope of adventure; others are wearied by the loneliness, the travelling, the sense of impermanence. None are truly settled.

The muffled clunk of doors and the passing of footsteps are mingled with the muted rise and fall of conversation. Air hangs heavy with the scent of polish and air freshener and that indefinable aroma of industrially cleaned carpeting. It was depressingly like Thames House.

Faint light filtered in from outside through the nets at the window and a line of light showed beneath the door. It was just enough to show a pair of feet at the end of the bed. I watched them, wondering about the sort of person who feels the need to leave his shoes on when he lies down for a rest, the sort of work he does, his prospects.

A car pulled into the car park and rolled into the empty space just below the window of my room, light swinging momentarily across the ceiling, shadows leaping for cover. The motor ran for a few seconds and then died. Not long after came the sound of the door opening and then closing.

Silence returned and I went back to thinking about those feet whilst a subconscious part of my mind was counting. By the time the sound of footsteps grew in the corridor, I had lifted those feet off the bed, grabbed my jacket, and walked to the door.

The tap was cautious. I opened up, keeping my eyes in shadow. Sally pushed her way in and switched the light on. She gave me a quick once over with tired eyes. "Going somewhere?"

I closed the door and slung my jacket over the back of the chair. "Old habits."

"Sitting in the dark? You still do that?"

"Me? I'm always in the dark." She smiled, but it was an old joke.

I stepped over to the laminate covered shelf as she looked round. "Drink?" She smiled as I held up the small bottle of Stolichnaya Raspberry Vodka.

"Any ice?"

By the time we had sneaked in some Chinese take-away, eaten our fill, and reduced the contents of the bottle, Sally was looking considerably less harassed. She was sitting stretched out on the bed, pillows piled up behind her back. I watched from the chair as she wiggled her toes to some rhythm in her head. Giving in, I slipped my own shoes off.

"Just like old times," she said.

"God, I hope not."

"You know how to charm a girl."

There are times I should pay more attention, especially to my big mouth. "So. Why are you here? It's clearly not for the vivacious and sensitive company."

Sally raised her glass to that and took a drink. I did the same, purely out of politeness you understand.

"I needed to get out of London," she said, holding out the glass for a refill. I topped it up. "A tour of Junior Ministers, heaven help us. I swear they only come so they can boast to their chums they've been inside the building."

"Are there any now that haven't?" I remembered those with equal loathing. We all kept to the back stairs while the politicians were shown the Atrium, Gym, and Staff Restaurant. Once they were safely ensconced with senior staff in the executive dining room, we would all crawl back out of our holes and get on with our work. I usually went down to the firing range and perforated a few targets.

"Anyway, the DDG was pestering for an update on this case."

"So you decided to come and see for yourself." I decided not to ask precisely when this had officially become a case, especially one in which the Deputy Director was taking a personal interest.

"It doesn't do to take an agent out of the field just to get an update."

"I'll drink to that," I said. I drank to that. Sally joined me.

A comfortable silence settled in the room. Laughter drifted up from the car park. I suppose it was a bit like old times.

"Well?"

"What?"

"Update."

"Oh. Sod all."

"Hmm. Might need just a bit more than that."

I looked into my glass, but there was nothing there other than vodka. "It doesn't make sense. What is worth protecting after forty... nearly forty years?"

"Assuming that we are barking up the right tree."

"Very funny."

She smiled that half-wicked little smile that always surprised me. I looked back into my glass.

"But are we?"

"What else is there?" I asked feeling very tired all of a sudden.

"Well, research has come up with nothing else."

They would be feeling the loss of Charlie. He had been well on the way to heading the department. A vision of his wet corpse, bleached by the halogen lamps, flashed in front of my eyes. I shook my head to make it go away.

"So. Something happened thirty-nine years ago. In that damned forest. And now..."

"Maybe it *was* a flying saucer." She grinned again.

"I can't see the CIA sending two superannuated desk men to sort things out, flying saucer or not. They haven't been in the field for years."

She looked at me over her glass. I knew what she was thinking so I stuck my tongue out. I happen to be in very good shape. For an old crock.

"Where are they, by the way?" she asked.

"God knows. I need people checking on hotels, holiday lets, caravans..."

More bad memories. Sally must have seen. She climbed off the bed and stepped across to where I sat. Her hand was light on my shoulder. I looked up at her and winked.

"It doesn't get any easier. Too many bloody reminders wherever I look." She squeezed my shoulder and I was all too conscious of her perfume, half tempted to take her hand. I kept a firm grip on the glass of vodka. "Get those two babysitters on search duty," I said.

"I don't want you exposed."

"They're wasting their time, Sally."

"That's not what you thought the other day."

"We got spooked. And it wasn't just me. Barney Rutherford was the same. Probably just the forest. It's full of ghosts and it's all too easy to think you're back in East Germany."

"Even so."

"I won't argue. The babysitters stay. But if you can chase up more people to do the basic research..."

"I'll see what we can do."

She began to pick at the food cartons.

"I was going to tell Rose first, but as far as I can tell from the police and pathology reports, Charlie's death was a stupid accident."

She stopped picking. "Go on."

"He followed Stan and Ollie—"

"Who?"

"Stefan Cichy and Oliver Navarro. Stan and Ollie." I gathered my thoughts, pushing through the vodka fumes. "He followed them. God alone knows why. Into the forest. They must have been going up to look at the site where the skeletons were found. Perhaps he overheard them talking." She went back to the bed and sat on the edge. I looked at her. "You know what Charlie was like. Always dropping stuff, shoe laces coming undone, inky fingers. How did he do that? He used a keyboard most of the time yet still managed to go home with inky fingers.

"Anyway, they would have heard him. Sooner or later. He ran, they probably chased. It was dark. He tripped and hit his head on a tree. Doesn't sound much, but that's what killed him."

I lifted my glass in a silent toast and drained it. Sally could work out the rest for herself.

"They didn't want a body found near the skeletons so they took him to the nearest river and dumped him. Bastards." She was genuinely furious.

"We're none of us pure in this game, Sally."

Bright daylight greeted me as I forced my eyes open. I pulled myself by degrees out of the chair wondering at what point in the night I had been run over. Someone had tidied away all the food cartons. The bed was made and an open overnight bag stood on the end. From the bathroom came the sound of the shower.

I poked around in my own bag and dug out fresh clothes. The bathroom door opened and released a cloud of scented steam into the room, masking the overnight odours of Chinese food. Sally appeared wrapped in towels.

"I hope you left one for me."

She smiled. "I asked the girl on the desk for some more."

"Bang goes my reputation."

The tip of her tongue appeared between her lips and I took my aching frame off to the bathroom. At the door, I said, "Would you mind taking me up to town? There's one or two things I need to do. You can have my flat for the day if you want to stay out of sight."

Nodding, she began to unwrap herself. I closed the door and turned on the cold tap.

09

(Saturday)

There was plenty to think about on the drive back to Suffolk. Not least was the ease with which Sally and I had slipped back into the tenuous tango of what might laughingly be called a relationship.

It had run true to form. After a quiet Friday with Sally working in my flat and me shuffling paperwork in my office, we had argued all through the evening when she caught me getting my gun out of the safe. Whatever was going on, it was being handled by CIA illegals. If they had gone to the bother of placing them into a 'friendly' country, it meant trouble. That put Sally in a bad mood. It didn't help when I also pointed out that I was still registered as a Firearms Officer and that she was no longer my boss.

Like all our arguments there was little heat in it and it was about work. If we could cut work out of the equation we might make a go of it. But we weren't in the sort of jobs that could be left at the office door at five o'clock. Not even when and if we ever retired.

Neither of us were quitters, either. I had come close. Once. But circumstances had forced me to change my mind. Now they would have to prise the job out of my cold, dead hands. Which is just what Sally was afraid of. Which is why I had decided to arm myself.

Then there was the business with the car. Tech-Ops had done their job, checked it over, given it the all clear, given it a wash and polish and handed me the keys. Then they handed me the paperwork. And the memo from DDG. I had it all couriered over to my boss, Jane Fortune. She would no doubt put it on my desk for me to sort out later on. And so it goes. The defence of the realm is accomplished mostly with official forms and reports. We will bring down the enemies of freedom with paper cuts.

The closer I got to Suffolk, however, the more I forgot the petty worries of bureaucratic infighting and the more I began to think of the case. The very fact that it was a case, with a file entry in Registry, meant it now had a formal reporting structure and was subject to operational review. I just hoped they had the good sense to let me get on with it. At least I knew I could trust Sally to act as a buffer.

Crossing the Orwell Bridge meant I was back in the weird and wonderful world of 1980 and the events in Rendlesham Forest. Sally and I had talked it round in circles over a late meal. In the end, we decided that the only things worth coming back for after forty years were the only things not likely to be there.

We know the CIA organised stay-behind groups from there, but the political situation in Europe was so different now as to make such groups redundant. Even the CIA thought so as the infrastructure had been completely dismantled and the weapons dumps removed. Other scenarios were too bizarre to contemplate. But I wasn't going to let it go and, thankfully, it seemed Thames House were of the same mind – paperwork and memos notwithstanding. We were supposed to have a Special Relationship with the US. When they started playing dirty in our back yard, when one of our own was found floating in a river, it raised hackles. Eventually.

I had slipped out of my flat early before Sally was awake, so the first thing I did when I reached Woodbridge was drop into the hotel and put my bag up into my room. Over a leisurely late breakfast, with rather too much toast and marmalade, I tried my hand at the Guardian prize crossword. Like most things, I would get it when it was too late.

And then it was back to work.

I spent five minutes matching the street atlas to the OS map and wondering whether I should have brought the SatNav. This was a tricksy landscape with nothing seeming to be in quite the place the maps suggested. Even the satellite images I had studied on Friday felt like they were of some other place.

In the end I did what I should have done at the start: climbed out of the car and asked someone. After that it was easy. I found the village and parked my car in the shade of a tree. A church with a square tower stood off to one side surrounded by lush greenery. Cottages lined the street. A small group of council houses clustered at one end. The place was empty, unless you counted the cat atop the lych-gate that opened one eye as I passed. A strimmer whined somewhere in the distance.

The house I was looking for wasn't difficult to find. A substantial double-fronted, brick-built villa set back from the road. In front, a roughly trimmed hedge of escallonia covered in red flowers screened the ground floor from the casual passer-by. A wooden gate, bleached to a silvery grey by wind, rain, and occasional sunshine opened on well-oiled hinges.

Wiry grass and a mossy path. The ubiquitous wheelie bins. Window frames in need of paint. A front door that had once been bottle green but which had faded over the years. It had certainly seen better days. Hadn't we all.

From somewhere beyond the dimpled glass of the door came the muted burr of a bell screwed too tightly to the plate. I waited a while, savouring the peace and quiet. And then I rang again. A door opened somewhere inside and let light into the hall, silhouetting the distorted shape of a person.

When the front door opened it was on a chain. I could see the face of a man in his mid sixties. Neatly cut greying hair. Pale blue eyes. "Yes?" he asked.

"Mr Bream?"

"Yes."

"My name is Grant. Alex Grant. I'd like to talk with you about the Rendlesham Forest Incident."

He looked me up and down and gave a quick, querulous frown. "I gave all that up years ago. I've nothing to say."

The door closed and I could see him walking away into the shadowy interior. I rang the bell again, but he kept going.

Fishing in my pockets, I pulled out my ID and my phone. Tapping in a number, I waited. The faint ringing of an old fashioned telephone could be heard from inside. It stopped and I spoke before he could answer.

"It's official, Mr Bream," I said and pushed my ID through the letter box. The flap snapped back with a loud clack, nearly trapping my fingers.

The connection was broken and I put my phone back in my pocket. By the time I had done that, Mr Bream had come back into the hall. He disappeared as he bent down and then reappeared. There were a few moments when he was looking at my card. I pushed the letter box open again and said, "You can check with the police headquarters at Martlesham Heath. I've been liaising with a Detective Sergeant Hopper."

There was a rattle as the chain was unhooked and the door opened. Mr Bream handed me the little folder and stepped aside to let me in.

Crossing the threshold was like going back in time fifty years. Pretty much like this whole case. Lavender and beeswax scented the air. Polished oak floorboards peeped around the edges of carpet. A mahogany coat rack with an oval mirror stood sentinel on one side of the dim hallway. Stairs led up to the first floor. Did everyone do this when they retired, I wondered? Revert to surroundings redolent of their childhood?

He led me through to the back of the house where the kitchen continued the theme. It was much brighter here. Clean, tidy, and untouched since the late 1950s. A blue and cream décor unsullied by the likes of a microwave. On the side next to a wooden bread bin was an old fashioned Bush radio.

"Would you like some coffee? I was just about to make some."

"Yes please." He began pottering and I sat myself at the scrubbed wood kitchen table. "What did you give up, Mr Bream?"

"UFOs. All that stuff."

I was happy to wait, enjoying the unusual calm that suffused the place. David Bream was much the same. Even if he had been wary to start with, he radiated a sense of geniality although I also sensed an underlying firmness. He pottered about the kitchen spooning real coffee into a cafetière before going on to discover biscuits in a large tin.

"It got silly in the end," he said as he set cups and plates on the table and we waited for the kettle to boil. "And I had other things to think about."

"I'm sorry if this is opening old wounds—"

He flapped a hand in dismissal. Having made up his mind to talk, having decided perhaps that he had no choice, he wasn't going to worry about it. "Amazing, isn't it," he said, "how it still attracts people after all this time." He used a tea towel to lift the kettle from the stove and poured the water with care. "I don't know what I can tell you, though. I told the police what I saw. I told that other lot..." he thought a moment, "...Civil Defence or something. Then I told the Americans. I expect it must be in a file somewhere."

I thought of the five hefty volumes Sally had supplied along with the bits and pieces Barney had brought. All locked in the hotel safe. "Yes. But why did all those people want to talk to you in the first place?"

"Do you know," he said, slowly pushing down on the plunger, "I never did find out. Not properly. In the end, I decided it was because I reported that maniac driver to the police. That was the second night of sightings I found out later. I've always assumed that because my report placed me by the Forest, they all came and asked questions." He poured the coffee. "That's how I got interested in the first place. Help yourself," he added, pushing the plate of biscuits across to me. I helped myself.

"Interested?" I asked round a well-dunked chocolate bourbon.

He looked a little embarrassed. "I didn't see anything myself, you see. Not in the forest. Apart from that car, which had nothing to do with it. But because I was there that night, and lived close by, I became fascinated. Spent years investigating it. I talked to everyone I could find. Locals, that is, people I knew, or who knew I was local, who would tell you what happened without trying to make a story out of it. But that was years ago."

"Did you keep notes?" I asked.

"Eh? Er. I might have." I could see he regretted even that half admission. "What's all the interest again?"

"Well, it's not exactly a secret. I take it you read the local paper."

We sipped coffee while he thought about the papers and I hoped against hope that this retired County Buildings Inspector had kept his research.

"The skeletons. That's the only thing to do with the Forest. Do they date from then?"

I nodded. "Yes. The Forensic Pathologist thinks they were buried around that time. But you didn't hear that from me."

"But there was no suggestion at the time that anyone... Oh."

"Go on."

"But it can't be that. It was all in the open. Police and everything."

I felt as puzzled as he looked. "What was?"

"I used to live up by Capel. This is... was my parent's house. I had a little cottage, one of a row of four. I was at one end. The cottage at the other end was rented by a young chap who worked on the Base. The Air Force Base. American, he was. Committed suicide. Shot himself. That was in the New Year. Place was swarming with US Air Force people, but they let the police handle it. I remember that, cos our local boy was off sick for weeks afterwards. Said it was an awful mess."

There are rare moments in this job when all three cherries line up and the sirens go off. "Do you have any notes on that as well?" I asked with my most winning smile, my fingers crossed under the table.

He looked at me over his empty coffee cup, weighing me up perhaps. "Let's go and see."

I grabbed another biscuit and followed him out of the kitchen into the hallway. With steady tread, he went up the stairs and I followed. The landing was large and light, all the doors bar one being wide open. He signalled to me to stop at the top of the stairs, went to a doorway and reached in. Despite myself I tensed, but he had grabbed a window pole which he pushed up at a loft hatch.

Having always lived in flats and out of hotel rooms, attics and roof spaces have always been a source of fascination. Despite that, I had no expectations. It was dark as he climbed up, and even when a light came on it was dim. I went up the ladder a rung at a time and found myself looking up at the underside of a table.

It wasn't until I had climbed right up into the attic and other lights had been switched on that I saw what the table was all about. That and all the other sections of board. A train whirred by.

"Sorry." I looked across the roof space. "I should have warned you. Power to the main lights feeds the set as well. I'll have to sort that out one day."

Magnificent. That's one word. Entrancing. That's another. I'd never seen anything like it close up. A huge train set. Main lines. Spur lines. Even a narrow gauge set-up climbing into a hilly region in one corner. Stations, roads, crossings, bridges, buildings. A whole town at the far end. Even a river.

"My sister made most of it when she was a kid."

"It's incredible," I said. And it was.

"Dad helped."

"And you?"

He laughed. "I used to work out the timetables. I was never good with my hands. Numbers and that sort of thing were more my line. I became a surveyor and building assessor. Margaret's the practical one, the engineer. She's in Africa these days." The pride was clear in his voice. "Switched to hydraulic engineering years ago and works as a consultant for various charities. Don't know how she does it. Went out there once. Heat. Flies. Heartbreaking poverty. But she thrives. And it's work worth doing."

He looked at the layout, perhaps remembering his childhood, certainly lost. I could sympathise. And if his sister was doing as well out there as she had done here, she was in the right place and the locals had, for once, got the sweet end of the stick.

"The notes?" I asked quietly as a laden goods train trundled by.

"Oh. Yes. Sorry. If you squeeze round..."

He pointed to a narrow space between the edge of the layout and the hardboard tacked to the inside of the sloping rafters. If you bent over a stretch of marshalling yard with its long lines of trucks, you could sidle your way along to the far end of the loft. It was there all the controls were set out on a table along with clip boards and stop watches. On the wall behind were framed posters, an old station clock, and other railway memorabilia all grouped round a large, metal station sign that said 'Capel Halt'.

A distinct absence of any notes was explained when he reached behind one end of the sign and there was a faint click. Part of the wall swung away to reveal another, smaller section of attic.

We ducked our heads and moved into the space. A workbench with a small vice doubled as a desk. There was a high stool tucked underneath at one end where an old, manual typewriter gathered dust beneath its cover. For the rest, it was three filing cabinets and an assortment of cardboard boxes. I watched as he began sorting through folders.

"Did you ever talk to any of the people who wrote the books?"

"Good grief, no. Steered well clear of them. And the television people, too. Fat lot any of them knew.

They all wanted a flying saucer. I just wanted the truth." He lifted an envelope folder and several scrap books from a box and then went through one of the cabinet drawers, pulling out two old, hard bound exercise books. Laying them carefully on the bench, he stepped back. "There. That's paper clippings about the suicide and my diaries."

"And all the rest of this," I asked. "That's to do with the incident?"

"Most of it."

It was a lot of paperwork. "Is it all right if I have a look?"

He gave me that weighing up look again. "I don't want my name mentioned."

"No one is going to get it from me."

10

(Sunday)

My head was still full of facts. At least, it was full of those that had stayed. David Bream would have given the archivists at Thames House a run for their money. Over a number of years he had collected and meticulously collated several hundred thousand words of information and had it all referenced to source material, cross-referenced, indexed along with maps, photographs, diagrams, transcripts of taped interviews, his original notes, diaries. He'd even assessed everything for reliability. And all of it done without a computer. I would have to ask him if he minded a visit from one of Rutherford's people. God alone knows what they could glean from it if it was put on a machine.

That was on the Forest incident. I had read it all. And even taking into account information overload, it still didn't make any sense to me. Even with a massive of influx of information you can generally pick out strands and patterns. These reports were garbled in a way I had never seen before. Any group of witnesses will produce minor contradictions in their statements, and they are often very revealing. But this was garbage. They might easily have been talking about completely different things. And despite Bream's attempts to assess the veracity of statements, there really was no way of knowing how much the statements had been tampered with between the event and their emergence.

So beyond the fact that terminally bored perimeter guards thought they saw lights in the forest on two nights directly after Christmas and then went out to investigate, there was nothing useful.

It's this very confusion that led to all the bizarre theories. And bizarre theories are very useful at masking the truth. Once they get into circulation, any denials or contradictory facts merely feed the suspicions of cover-ups and the wilder accusations of conspiracy theorists. Which is why, of course, the CIA, and every other intelligence agency on the planet, is happy to feed this voracious monster.

That's what disinformation is. A monster. And once created, it has a tendency to turn and bite the hand that first fed it. Like using money, material, and training programmes to create private armies to fight your enemies. Twenty years down the line you find they have turned their expertise and hard won experience, not to mention ordnance, straight back at you. Or that whizzy piece of malicious software that would sabotage your enemy's nuclear power plants. No way that couldn't escape into the wild and be modified by someone looking to create a little havoc of their own.

The stuff that Bream had collected about the suicide had been sparse. The usual newspaper reports, diary entries, and gossip. Whatever happened in that cottage had not been anything that prompted conspiracy theorists to start grinding their axes. But there had been enough to sketch an outline. Of course, whether it had any relevance was another thing altogether. What was very clear is that something important and untoward had happened back then in 1980 and the ripples were still spreading wide enough and wild enough to upset any passing vessel, tipping unwary passengers into the water.

I had read late into the evening, trying to absorb things that seemed relevant. David Bream had been kind enough to make a copy of the chronology he had produced of the events that had occurred in and around the forest. That, at least, could go into the Thames House file as an earnest of my field work.

Despite the late night, I went down to breakfast early. There was a lot to be done and I wasn't going to be doing any of it on Monday. Some of the Sunday papers were laid out on a table by the Reception desk. I glanced through the headlines. The world seemed to be heading to hell as usual without my help so I wandered into the dining room.

At first, I thought I had the place to myself, but when I turned after pouring myself a glass of orange juice, I saw Laurie Fiquenet sitting in a corner demolishing a full English breakfast.

She waved at the empty seat at her table with a piece of toast so I went across and sat down. "Girl's gotta keep her strength up," she said, grinning before getting to work on another sausage. I swear I could hear her arteries hardening. "You look like you were up half the night."

"And getting too old for it."

"Ha."

A sleepy waitress appeared at my side. "I'll have porridge please. A pot of tea. Wholemeal toast. Marmalade." She scribbled it down on a small pad and disappeared.

"Oatmeal? Yew."

"I'll outlive you if you keep eating like that." I sipped my orange juice.

"When in Rome..."

"Do as the Vandals." She laughed. My technique must be improving. "You're looking chipper. Despite the attempt to kill yourself."

She forked scrambled egg onto a corner of her toast. "Found out about my boy."

I waited until she was chewing. "Ah yes. Signed up young. Left under a cloud. Was allowed to work on the base as a civilian, so presumably not a very big cloud. A puff of smoke, maybe? Too ashamed to tell his dear mother, so he faked a few pictures for her benefit by wearing someone else's tunic. Committed suicide Saturday the third of January, 1981."

She gave me a hard stare. "You enjoyed that, didn't you."

"It's a mark of how sad my life has become." She finished her meal and started on the coffee. "So. Is that you finished? Back to the States?"

"No."

"Ah. Would that be the flowers on the grave or the reason for suicide?"

I was treated to another stare. "You have been busy."

As she spoke, my phone warbled. I made an apologetic face and pulled it from my pocket.

"Grant."

"DS Hopper."

"You at work?"

"'Fraid so. Something here that came in late yesterday you might want to look at. No hurry. I'll be here all day, somewhere under all the paper-work."

He hung up and I put the phone away just as my breakfast arrived. "You'd better bring more toast," I said to the waitress. "I doubt mine will be left by the time I've finished this." She smiled and flitted off to the kitchen.

"What worries me," said Fiquenet, buttering my toast, "is the method."

"He shot himself. Those were the only details I could find."

The stares not having worked, she narrowed her eyes at me over my toast. I spooned in some porridge. "Why," she asked, "are you interesting yourself in this?"

I shrugged. I had no idea, other than the fact I don't believe in coincidence. "It might be another way into my own investigation which, frankly, is as dead in the water as my friend Charlie."

"What? Never mind."

Interesting. That seemed like genuine ignorance to me. I wonder what she thought I was doing there, if she hadn't heard about Charlie. Maybe I should ask. Maybe it could wait. "So what about the method? Lots of people shoot themselves."

She shook her head. "JJ Pennyweather was a cook. He was a cook in uniform and then he was a civilian cook, working on the base. They don't get issued with side arms. Even if they did, they would not have been allowed to take them off base. That's a court martial offence."

"He shot himself with a Colt Automatic?"

I got the narrowed eye treatment again. Perhaps I was showing off. It was interesting to see just how much she was prepared to give me. "A Pistol, Calibre .45, Automatic, M1911A1 to be precise and official."

"Bet that made a mess." I thought of David Bream's local copper having to take time off.

"It also explains why he wasn't brought home. He was a civilian. He committed suicide. And he had dual nationality."

That stopped me for a moment. "Oh?" That meant we had something on him somewhere. Charlie would have found it. Someone else would have to do it now.

"His mother was a war bride. Married a flyboy."

"Who's going to break the news to her?"

"I don't know if there is any news to break just yet."

"Because of the pistol? It wouldn't be unheard of it, would it? For a kid to keep a sidearm."

"No. But it wouldn't have been that easy. If they thought one was missing from the base and he was connected they would have been on his tail until it turned up. Especially if he did leave under a cloud. Would he risk arrest?"

"Would he care if he was going to commit suicide?"

We made inroads into a fresh batch of toast and a fresh pot of tea. It gave the young waitress something to do. No one else came in whilst we were there, although one very pale, hung-over face did peer through the door for a few moments.

I knew I wasn't going to get away from the table without some sort of payback, so I was in no hurry. Hopper wasn't likely to be going anywhere and my own paperwork could wait.

She waited until the table had been cleared, embarrassing the waitress with enthusiastic thanks. Her eyes still on the kitchen door, she asked, "What about our disappearing Company men?"

"Stan and Ollie? The compass does keep swinging back towards them. Or, rather, I wish it did, cos I'm buggered if I know where they are just now. What did they do on the base?" She looked distinctly uncomfortable. "Suit yourself," I continued. "I'll find out sooner or later. It would be easier for both of us if it was sooner."

I put my head on one side and watched her. She didn't exactly squirm, but she wasn't making any effort to hide her discomfort. Of course, there was a chance they were working together, but I wasn't that worried. All they'd get from me would be the level of our ignorance. And then the penny dropped.

"Oh. Is it that bad?" I asked.

"What?" This time it was easy to see her ignorance was not genuine.

"My file."

"I've only seen a digest," she said hurriedly.

"Anti-American sentiments."

"How did you… Shit. I fell for that, didn't I?"

"I don't suppose it explained why."

"Look. We're not all—"

I held up a hand. "I know. But the reason I attend a quiet memorial every year for several members of my team is because they were murdered with weapons bought using money supplied to both sides of the conflict by Americans. Americans that the FBI, despite all the evidence supplied to them from us, was either too idle, incompetent, or biased to follow up on."

"I don't know."

Her strange response thankfully stopped me from blundering on about the other business that had kept me busy in recent years; embarrassing our masters by discovering how deeply we had been penetrated by right-wing groups funded from across the Atlantic

"Sorry?"

"What they did on the base. I don't know. It was a big set-up, lots of different operations."

I looked at her and she looked back. This time there was no telling. She was getting used to me very quickly. I bet she had an excellent arrest record.

"Can you find out?" I asked

"It will take time…"

"And set alarm bells ringing if they are here officially."

"I still have a couple of contacts at Langley who know how to be discreet."

I refrained from making a rude reply.

The CID office was almost empty. Two civilian support officers sat at a desk at the far end of the room, processing paperwork onto computers. A head emerged from behind a pile of folders, looked me over, and disappeared, calling something out with a muffled voice. Hopper appeared from a cupboard with a box of pencils. He saw me and waved me across to his desk.

I passed the detective who was hidden behind piles of files. He was pulling faces at a webcam and I could see a child giggling on the screen, a woman sitting in the background. Hopper yawned as I sat myself down and pushed a pile of folders to one side.

"Do you get paperwork like this in your job?" he asked, nodding at his desk.

"Oh yes," I replied. "They've given us trolleys so we don't hurt our backs when we move it from office to office."

"Straight up?" he asked. I nodded. "I suppose that's what we have CSOs for." He said it quietly, one eye on the two at the far end.

"What have you got?"

"The skeletons. Report came in late yesterday afternoon. Sorry I didn't get on to you before now. Saturday's are chaos and we had a series of arrests to process."

"That's OK."

"And there was something in from…" he opened a folder. "PC Crane."

Hopper pushed that across to me first. Crane had found the boat that had called in the sighting of Charlie's body. Local boys out for a night's fishing. They knew the run of the waters and reckon the body must have gone into the water at Boyton Dock, which is what Crane had suspected all along. There was a lot of other detail, plus Crane's suspicion that the fishing trip was less than kosher.

"Thorough."

"Yes. Bright lad. From out Capel way, so he knows the area like the back of his hand. Doesn't help you much, though, I suppose."

I got up and crossed to the OS maps on the wall. "Well, it helps tie certain events and people together. Not sure why." I stared at the map some more, perhaps hoping a pattern would leap out at me. It didn't. "What about the bones?"

Another folder was open and waiting for me by the time I sat back down. Forensic and archaeological reports. I had to look at the conclusion twice to make sure I'd read it correctly.

"In their eighties?"

Hopper stretched back in his chair. "I know. The whole thing gets more and more bizarre. Old folk don't tend to go missing without someone noticing. Especially round here. Less so back then. Two of them would be unthinkable."

"Will you be widening your search?"

He looked at me. I knew what he was going to say before he opened his mouth. Budgets. Work load. Chief Constable. I put my hands up in surrender. He grinned. "I'll do what I can," he said. "And I'll keep digging closer to home. So to speak. But my boss won't let it have priority."

"That's OK. Just keep it in the system. And you might want to look at what reports you have from the period. A Mr David Bream. Complaint about dangerous driving."

He scribbled it down on a square, yellow, post-it note which he stuck to the front of the report. When he'd finished, he said, "There is one other thing. The local paper has been on the phone wanting to know more. The governor said it was up to you lot."

I looked at the piles of paperwork and thought of my office. "I'm off to London shortly so I'll check at my end, but my instinct is to let them have what you've got as long as you keep me out of it. It might just prompt someone to remember something. Or try something. God knows we could do with that."

11

(Monday)

Sally and I stood side-by-side at the back out of everyone's way. As soon it was decent to do so, we left the packed chapel and slipped outside. Bright sunshine greeted us, gleaming on the big limousines that lined the access road. Drivers sat with the doors open waiting to leave, taking care to keep cigarette smoke and ash away from the spotless interiors. Babysitters stood around keeping a beady eye out for attack from the cemetery next door. There was even a watcher up in the tower, peering out from one of the verdigrised arches with a scope to his eye.

"Jeez," I said beneath my breath as we crossed the gravel turning space by the main entrance. "It looks like a bloody Mafia funeral. Did they all have to come in separate cars? How to win friends, influence people, and let the world and its dog know where you are."

Sally nudged me. "One of these days," she said, "that mouth of yours is going to get you into trouble. Oh. Too late."

I smiled my most withering smile, but Sally ignored it. Instead she pushed me off to one side as everyone else began to emerge. I know I should have been behaving myself, here and now of all places and times. This was Charlie's funeral. But the sight of the limos outside and the sanctimonious suits inside had riled me. Sally as well. She has better control.

"I'm surprised they all turned out," she said as we found a patch of grass in the shade of a tree from where we could watch proceedings unheard.

I nodded, remembering Lesley's quiet and very private funeral. It seemed like a lifetime ago.

"Someone made sure Charlie's death was top of the agenda at last week's JIC meeting."

"Oh? Someone? Who might that have been?"

I shrugged by way of reply. Given how far I had got elsewhere, it was the least I could do for my friend.

"So CIA Chief of London Station will have been there for the report."

"Yes."

"Don't go silent and mysterious on me. I wish you'd told me."

"I just did," I protested.

We watched as the gathering emerged and spread its way onto the top of the steps and down the ramp. Charlie was an only child, but he had several cousins, and there were a lot of research staff and analysts there as well. He had been the kind of person it was difficult not to like – helpful, patient, a wonderful father.

"That will have upset quite a few people, I would imagine," said Sally, interrupting my dive into mawkishness.

"I bloody well hope so. They're lucky I'm not pushing for a full Juvenal investigation."

Somewhere a little light began to flash in the dim recesses of my brain, illuminating my position in relation to the tent where a degree of pissing was bound to occur. It didn't surprise me that I had, yet again, been outmanoeuvred. They... Those people over there with their grave faces and expensive suits standing around outside the chapel door. They knew damn well that I couldn't do that if I was under their employ, no matter how temporary.

What did surprise me was that I simply did not feel like arguing about it. Sally would have realised, but she wouldn't have contrived such a situation. It wasn't in her nature. It's why, much as she would like the job, she would never get to the top floor of Thames House. And, I liked to think, she had a soft spot for me.

The DDG, Chandra Whickramasan, and one or two other senior staff stood in line with mourners who were filing past Rose. There were handshakes and long hugs from family members and friends. It occurred to me that George must be in that scrum somewhere, poor little sod, perhaps with Charlie's mother who stood just behind Rose.

If I hadn't seen what happened next, I would never have believed how neatly it was done. It was the sweetest snub and my heart glowed with pride. As the line brought the DDG to Rose, she turned away and picked up George. Rose's parents were suddenly between her and the senior staff and it was clear to everyone standing there that she had no intention of acknowledging their presence.

Sally and I kept very still. The DDG had the good sense to accept it and move away. He walked slowly down the steps and crossed to his waiting car. Whickramasan dithered and people began to look. He quickly got the hint and strode across behind the DDG's departing limo to his own car. The door slammed as he got in and the sleek vehicle crunched gravel on its way to the gate. By that time other senior staff had faded into the background.

"Doesn't look like Rose is planning to return to Thames House," I said.

"It's a real shame. She knows it was an accident?"

"Yes. But Charlie still shouldn't have been doing field work. I don't care if you lot are short-staffed and chasing your tails."

"I'm not the enemy here, Alex."

"Sorry."

She took my arm and squeezed it gently. I was glad when she didn't let go.

On the steps, Rose was talking with the Head of Registry, the one official representative of the Service she still had time for. His head was bent as he listened and he nodded. She hugged him and he looked embarrassed.

With the official cars gone and staff on their way back to work, family and friends began to drift off down the gravelled drive to wherever they'd had to park their own vehicles on the surrounding roads.

"I never really understood what they saw in each other," said Sally, watching Rose as she stood momentarily alone by the doors to the chapel.

"What, you mean a deskbound paper warrior and battle hardened field agent?"

Sally turned and looked me. I could sense her trying to read my expression, but I kept the covers well closed. She turned back to watch Rose. "She is hardly that."

"Rose is... was on the way to becoming one of the best. She has an instinct."

"You need ice in your heart for that sort of work."

"She has that." I remembered looking down the wrong end of her gun, knowing she would squeeze the trigger. "But it can melt, given the right circumstances."

"It looks like it can freeze again, as well."

I thought it might be a good idea for us to stop digging this particular hole. History had made it deep enough already. Stepping off the patch of grass, I headed across toward Rose. Sally came with me, still holding onto my arm. It felt good.

Sally let go when we reached the steps and I went up on my own. Rose looked like a child who has suddenly realised she can no longer see her parents. There was a sudden flash of panic in her eyes and then she saw me. I folded her in my arms as I had when I first broke the news.

I'm not sure she wanted me to let go. There was so much to face. Looking back, that quiet funeral when Lesley had died had been a real mercy. I wouldn't have been able to keep my cool in face of all those suits in the way Rose had just managed. That was the ice, at the exact moment it was needed and not for a second longer.

"How are you doing?"

"Coping. For George." I could see tears welling in her eyes. She pulled a small handkerchief from a pocket. "Stupid. Bloody stupid. So bloody stupid." She drew a deep breath and let it out slowly. "I suppose you saw me souse the bridges with petrol and drop the match?"

"They deserved no less." I glanced down at Sally who raised an eyebrow. "I think Sally wants a word. You up to that?"

Rose nodded. As Sally climbed the steps I went across to Charlie's parents and paid my respects before going in search of George. He stood with Rose's mother and let me pick him up.

"And how are you doing, young Georgie?" I asked quietly.

"I'm sad."

"Well, I'm not surprised. It's been a very sad time. How's your mum?"

"She's been crying a lot."

"She misses your dad. Bet you do as well." His face crumpled and I held him tight. "We all do, Georgie," I said, walking slowly off to one side where the trees grew. "We all do."

I did silly tricks, crossing my eyes, sliding the tip of my thumb up and down, things like that. George watched solemnly and managed a smile when I winked. Over his head I could see Rose and Sally talking. There seemed to be lots of nodding which I took to be a good thing. They had very little to do with each other professionally and I realized, as I watched, that it was very important to me that they got along.

When they finished, they hugged, and then came down the steps and across the gravel toward me and George. It looked like Rose had a friend on the inside, although I don't suppose she'd ever want to go back. Still, with her skills and background I doubt she would have trouble finding a well paid job with decent hours and no prospect of some lunatic trying to shoot her or blow her legs off. I wondered idly how she would cope with all the petty wrangling of Internal Affairs.

"We'd better go," said Rose. "My mum has everything organised at the house. And Charlie's mum and dad look completely lost. Will you be round? You are both welcome."

"Leave it for family," said Sally. "But thank you for asking."

"I might call in later," I said. "Are Charlie's folks staying with you?"

"Yes. They'll be here for a few more days. See you later, then." She kissed my cheek and then took George's hand. "Come on my love. Brave face for a little while more."

We watched them cross to the remaining cars and Rose made sure everyone was settled before climbing in herself. And then we were alone beneath the trees. Two attendants appeared from a side entrance and gave a quick sweep round; making sure the place was tidy for the next service.

Taking the hint, we headed off in the sunshine, dodging a learner driver on Brockley Way as we crossed over to Turnham Road and headed off in the direction of New Cross.

"Circles," I said as we strolled past the long, faceless blocks of flats with their new double-glazing.

"What?"

"We've come back to where we started." A gap on our right revealed a blue-fenced basketball court. Some of the ground floor flats had bars on the windows. Grey satellite dishes hung off the sides of the buildings like fungus. "And we've learned nothing," I added.

"Perhaps we *have* been looking in the wrong direction."

"What else is there?"

"Well..."

"I'm not sure I like the sound of that," I said, which was an understatement. One thing I had learned over the years, both in the field and in the endless meetings my latest post entailed was how to read someone's voice.

"There's a new player on the scene."

"What? Why didn't you tell me?"

"I'm telling you now."

"Touché."

"Besides, I only heard first thing this morning and I wasn't going to tell you during the funeral. And it's by no means certain."

"Out with it."

"A Russian."

"Oh, brilliant. Let me guess. Same vintage as Stan and Ollie?"

"Not sure. Head of the SOP simply said if you broke him open he'd have 'KGB' running all the way through. They're digging through the files as we speak."

"Alone?"

"He turned up at the Embassy last night with two of Putin's Pups. A flag was raised at Heathrow T4 when diplomatic passports were waved after the Aeroflot flight from Moscow landed."

"So he's official. How do we know he's anything to do with Rendlesham?"

"We don't, but you know what you always say about coincidences."

"This is rapidly turning into a three ring circus; a Saga outing for superannuated spies; a..."

Sally gave me a look that might just as well have been a condescending pat on the head.

"It's all very well looking at me like that, Sally Barrett, but I know damned well who they've put in baggy trousers and oversized shoes."

"Oh, but you do it so well."

We walked on in silence for a while. She's the only person I'd have taken that from. Which gave me pause for thought. Thoughts I didn't have time for just now.

What I really wanted to know was why this precise moment? Still, that's the Russians for you. They'll drive their tanks in front of the TV cameras with the crews giving a wave for their dear old mums at home, all the while saying, 'Nothing to do with us, tovarisch. Must be someone else.' And now it looked like they were manoeuvring a tank onto my front lawn. Cheeky bastards.

"Do you know where you're going?" Sally asked.

"Hmm? Oh. Like I said. In circles."

"No. Do you know where we are?"

"Of course. New Cross is that way." I waved my hand in the general direction of forwards.

"You're sure?"

"Stop worrying. We're following the railway. It's just over there." I waved my hand off to the right this time. She took my arm again. I gently disentangled her hand and put it in mine. She didn't take it away.

"Talk it through again," she said.

"OK," I replied, trying to isolate the relevant facts in the right order. "1980. Something happened. Just after Christmas. Forget all the subsequent nonsense the CIA were spreading about, drawing attention to their own presence on base. Idiots. All we know for certain is that on several nights, US Air Force personnel saw something that caused them to go off base and into Rendlesham Forest. Lights. Somehow, at about the same time, a couple of eighty-year-olds end up being buried in the same Forest, not far from where the US Air Force boys were chasing around."

"Maybe our ancient couple were out walking one night and got the fright of their lives when a lorry load of armed soldiers appeared?"

"No one was reported missing at the time and the CIA wouldn't get involved. And they put out a truly ridiculous cover story, one that was bound to attract the attention of every whack... persistent conspiracy theorist you could imagine. What's that all about? Why go with such a strange story?"

"What came first? The cover story or the gossip?"

"It's a bit fuzzy. It seems to have been described as a breach of security to begin with, but as soon as someone talked about seeing lights, that was it. I suppose the CIA decided to run with that. They are rather partial to a bit of disinformation. And they were very fond of UFO stories in the 70s and 80s."

"So, a story that would discredit anyone talking about lights."

I shrugged, but it seemed a sensible suggestion. "But what lights? That's what drew the perimeter guards out. So what were they? If it was a plane crashing, they'd surely know what it was. So would everyone living in the area. Everyone would have heard it. And seen the damage from the public roads. The only cover story needed would be to disguise what type of plane. I doubt it was Santa crashing his sleigh after too many sherries. And why, nearly forty years later, are two of the CIA personnel who were there at the time sniffing around? And why now are the Russians showing an interest? It has to be related to those bodies. That's where Charlie died. And nothing else has happened to draw attention to the place."

"Apart from all the books and documentaries."

"But that was years ago and they gave us nothing that hadn't already been put out in the original cover story. They just tried to provide a coherent narrative based on preconceived notions that themselves are based on CIA misinformation. And they certainly didn't get Langley in a lather back when they appeared, despite the claims of some."

"So the bodies are connected."

"They have to be. Otherwise why not leave Charlie where he was when he ran into that tree? Why go to ground?"

We turned right onto Jerningham Road. That was when Sally dropped her other little bombshell. "There is pressure from the top floor to let this drop now."

"Bastards." But I can't say I was surprised. "Have they set a time limit?"

"No, just dropped a few hints in the hope I'll close it down. But don't worry. I won't. Only if I get it in writing from the DG."

"Thanks."

"I also told them that Jane Fortune is likely to take it up if they try to bury it." She looked at me as we walked. "She would, wouldn't she?"

"Yes." I'd make sure she did although it wouldn't take much to persuade her. If nothing else, there had been a spectacular failure to observe standard operational procedure and she would want to make sure that did not happen again.

The traffic noise from New Cross Road was getting louder as we approached. We stopped at the corner, looking into the window of the estate agents.

"What does the US Air Force have to say about it all?"

"Nothing. Our Ms Fiquenet was, she says, sent over to do a background check on an Air Force personnel matter. She's using some old contacts to try to dig up more information on the CIA operations out of Woodbridge."

"I'm glad she's doing it," said Sally.

I laughed. "I can imagine the look on the faces at Langley if they saw my name at the bottom of an information request."

"It hinges on the CIA, then?"

"Unless we've all missed something else that was going on at the time, it has to. I know the base stored nuclear weapons, but I think if it had involved those we would have heard about it by now. No one has a nuke stolen and waits forty years to go looking for it." As we both knew only too well after the trouble with the Chechens and Ukrainians. "No one steals a nuke and hangs on to it for forty years, either."

"Perhaps they couldn't get to it at the time."

"No. This is silly. If you get a nuke over the wire you'd want to be away with it as soon as possible."

"Unless your contact doesn't turn up."

"With something like that you'd have transport laid on and a back up plan or three. Besides, the Air Force and the CIA went over that Forest with a fine toothed comb by all accounts. They took pine needles, soil, fallen branches, fallen trees, the lot.

By the ton. If there had been a nuke hidden there, they would have found it."

"Why the hell would they want to take the soil?"

It was a good question. It was a very good question. As usual, I had no answer.

When I left Sally I wandered into Peckham and caught the Overground to Shepherd's Bush. From there I wandered up Holland Park Avenue and on to a busy Notting Hill Gate. Up a side road opposite Kensington Palace Gardens is a nondescript door that looks like it might belong to a pub. It is, in fact, the highly secure entrance to one of the Security Service's Static Observation Posts, the one from which they keep a discrete watch on the comings and goings at the Russian Embassy across the way.

It looks like any other door in that part of London. Heavy and with electronic security. If you were foolish enough to waste time breaking in, you'd be confronted by a narrow stairway at the top of which is another security door. And then more stairs. At the top of that, if you were not meant to be there, you would be faced by a steel door and hearing the sirens of a police armed response unit making their way toward you. If you were monumentally stupid enough to persist at that point, you'd be gassed and have to take your chances as you tumbled uncon-scious down the stairs.

All I got, as I climbed the final flight to that steel door, was a bored, "Wotcher, Alex," from David Llewellyn, Head of Post.

I nodded at the concealed camera and the intercom squawked again. "Brought any doughnuts?"

I knew this lot of old. My late fiancée Lesley had been a watcher and done stints here, as they all did. As I stood getting my breath on the small landing at the top of the steep flight, I waved a Tesco bag. They let me in, locked the door, and relieved me of my burden.

"Had word you might be dropping by," said David, passing me a mug of coffee.

"How's tricks?"

"Same old, same old. Yesterday evening's excitement was almost a bit too much for some of the youngsters here."

Someone blew a raspberry. I grinned. David was a veteran watcher and a hard taskmaster, but all the watchers who passed through his SOP came out knowing every trick in the book for static watch houses. One of his secrets was that, boring as the work was, his team felt valued and he looked after them.

"Can't get the staff," he muttered and then beckoned me to follow him into his 'office'. The watch station was originally a three bedroom flat on the top floor of the building. Most of it was open plan now so that the high powered cameras and other monitoring equipment could sit well back from the specially glazed windows. The Russians no doubt knew it was there. Somewhere. There were decoy posts as well. And they probably knew that as well. But everyone played the game.

David's 'office' was a box room next to the kitchen. Big enough for a desk and two chairs. We sat. He turned the monitor of his computer so we could both see it.

"You back at Thames House permanently?"

I gave him a look. "No."

He shrugged.

"Here you are."

He tapped a couple of keys and a series of videos began to appear. They showed a car, from different viewpoints, pulling into the Russian Embassy compound and disappearing into the underground car park.

"And now the enhanced frames."

This time, in frames taken from the previous videos, I could see the occupants of the car. Even then they were a bit fuzzy. But the quality was good enough to match them against the pictures taken at Heathrow, which David called up to his screen.

"Do these hoods have names?"

"The babysitters are Leonid Khomitsky and Vadim Eskov. Boy Vadim is the one driving. They're often in and out. They've been attached to the Embassy for several years. Typical *Sluzhba vneshney razvedki.* They act as bag carriers, drivers, waiters..."

"I know the type." You'd pass them in the street without a second glance, unless you had a keen eye and noticed the hard, watchful eyes. "Anyone tried to get close to them?"

"Yes. No result."

"And the fly-in?"

"Meet Gennady Arbatov. Colonel, last we heard."

I stared at his picture. "KGB?"

"Dyed in the wool. I can give you his history as we know it."

"Just want to know where he was and what he was doing in 1980."

"1980? Bit before our time." He flicked through the file onscreen. "This is just a digest, mind. You'd have to get the full thing out of Registry."

I saw his expression out of the corner of my eye as he said it. A kind of scrunched up 'oh shit' of a face.

"Don't worry, David. I'm still allowed in if I can find a grown-up to hold my hand and make sure I don't leave half eaten sandwiches down there."

"Right. Yes. Sorry. So. Gennady Arbatov, born in 1949, blah, blah, blah, arrived in the UK in 1976.

Assigned the code name Flagtail. We'd run out of birds by that stage and were using shark names. Appropriate with this one. Anyway, Gennady already had experience in the field—"

"Where?"

"Vietnam."

Where else? I thought. "Go on."

"We didn't know much about him until early 1978 when he got into a bit of trouble. Student protests, that sort of thing, showing his hand a bit too obviously. That's when his previous activity was traced. We let him think he'd got away with it. His bosses, however, moved him away from that and set him to work watching US activity on Air Force bases in—"

"Suffolk."

David swivelled his chair to look at me. I stared back knowing I'd have another bloody file to request and read.

12

(Tuesday)

I seemed to be spending a lot of time in the vicinity of cemeteries and the dead these days. I'm not sure that sort of thing is healthy for an impressionable lad like myself. Mind you, there are a lot worse places to spend a warm, sunny day than a country graveyard – even a sparse municipal field like this one. I would have preferred to climb out of the vast car with its futuristic interior, stretch my legs and breathe air not scented with plastic, but I had no idea why we were there and didn't want to miss out on the treat that had been lined up for me.

Fiquenet seemed to have gone into a Zen-like trance. Absolutely still and absolutely quiet. The only movement I detected was her eyes as they flicked occasionally to the carefully positioned mirrors. I looked down past my crumpled jeans to the detritus that had collected around my ancient tennis shoes. It had been, I suppose, a childish experiment. She hadn't so much as glanced at the sweet wrappings, sandwich packet, and crumpled juice box. Too polite, maybe. Or too damned cool. If she really was that cool, it was just a little bit frightening.

We were in the Cadillac. Again. Which meant either that the US Air Force had an endless budget and didn't care how its agents spent it or my companion was worried to the point of paranoia. Mind you, she had chosen a black Cadillac Escalade with blacked out windows which stood out some-what in the Suffolk countryside, so maybe she just wanted something that was familiar in this alien land.

Birds sang. Insects buzzed. A gentle and cooling breeze eddied around the open window. I took another drink from the nearly empty water bottle and began to wonder where it was all going to go. The hedge around the cemetery was sparse apart from the stretch against which we had parked.

A sparrow set down on the headstone I could see through the leaves. How does a creature that small make so much noise? Before long it was joined by several young, wings aflutter, beaks agape. Kids. Always on the scrounge for food. I thought of Georgie. Of Rose. Cut off that distracting train of thought and stared back out the window.

There was nothing much else to look at apart from the burial ground. The neat rows of almost identical, municipally approved, headstones. The small brick hut, presumably once for a gardener's tools. The leaking tap.

The distant sound of a tractor grew steadily and I watched it approach along the straight stretch in front of us. It bounced and bumped, a monster machine with a high, enclosed cab. Its shadow flicked over us as it passed and a cloud of diesel fumes and dust settled as it faded into the distance behind us. Could we stand the excitement?

"'How long have we been sitting here?'"

She didn't move, her eyes still on the mirrors. "I didn't think you were the impatient type."

"It's a quote. A game we used to play."

"Who is 'we'?"

"It's the first line of a book. Two characters sitting in a car."

She was silent for a while. "No idea."

"*Berlin Game.* Len Deighton."

This time she did turn. I met her puzzled gaze with a smile. "You read spy novels?"

"Where else did you think I learned those snappy one-liners and all that field craft?"

A narrow eyebrow flicked up. "In Czechoslovakia and Northern Ireland."

"Oh. Someone sent you my full file. So you do read spy fiction."

"Very funny."

"Yeah. I bet it was a laugh a minute."

A cyclist whirred past at a leisurely pace and free-wheeled up to the gates. He stood and swung his leg over the saddle, finishing the journey standing on one pedal. By the open gates he stepped off and swung the bike round to leave it resting against the hedge. It was good odds he'd done that more than once before.

I turned to Fiquenet as the man removed his bicycle clips from well worn corduroys. She was staring toward the gates.

"You look like you've seen a ghost," I said.

She drew her eyes away from where the cyclist had gone through into the cemetery. "I'm not sure I didn't."

A piece of paper landed in my lap. I unfolded it and saw a colour printout. The cropped, slightly fuzzy photograph at the top showed a young man in uniform smiling at the camera. Behind him was a poster for a dance. The date on the poster was December 1980.

It was her case so I stayed in the background, standing in the shade of the little brick hut as she made her way along the path and then down the grassy row of headstones. John James Pennyweather was in his late fifties now and kneeling by the grave that bore his name. We watched from our different perspectives as he cleared away the old flowers, tidied away a few weeds, and placed the new bunch of flowers he had brought by the headstone.

It was quiet and I heard her voice, distinct if faint. "It must seem strange."

Pennyweather turned and then stood. Colour really can drain from someone's face. I'd seen it before, had no doubt it had happened to me once or twice.

He watched her as she spoke again, eyes fixed intently, perhaps wondering who she was. "What's it like putting flowers on your own grave?"

It was an impressive turn of speed from a standing start. Must be all that cycling. He leapt several graves and was almost at the gates when I stepped out and put myself between him and his bike. Gravel pattered against my legs as he skidded to a halt.

"We just want to ask some questions," I said as gently as I could.

Fiquenet arrived at the same time as the car. We all turned to look as an elderly man clambered out. He passed us clutching his flowers as if we might try to mug him. I suppose social gatherings are not common at the entrances of rural cemeteries.

"Here," said Pennyweather after the old man was out of earshot. He nodded to one of the benches. "In the open."

"Fair enough," she replied.

We didn't move.

I shrugged. "Feel free."

"You're English."

"After a fashion."

"Who is in the grave?" she asked trying to keep things on track.

"You're American."

He had a great line in witty repartee and probably had his Henry Higgins badge from the boy scouts, but it wasn't going to get us very far. Fiquenet produced her ID.

"Air Force?" asked Pennyweather.

"Expecting someone else?" I asked in return.

Pennyweather looked from Fiquenet to me and back, considering an answer. "No." It was a lie. Of sorts. While he stood thinking some more, I had a chance to look at him properly. He was well preserved for a corpse although on the thin side, draped with work worn corduroy trousers, flannel shirt, and carrying an old waterproof jacket. His face was lean and tanned in a way that comes from working outside a lot, topped by cropped hair that was greying and nervous eyes that wouldn't settle. He was still coiled up for flight as well, although it was clear we weren't going to let him go anywhere just yet.

"What do you want? I haven't been in the Air Force for a long time."

"Not since 1978. I know." She searched his face, perhaps looking for the same things I was. "Your mother is dying." Nothing like breaking the news gently.

"And AFOSI sent someone to find me?" He didn't much sound like he believed that. But then, it's not the response I would have expected. Neither did Fiquenet, by the look of her. The momentary softness in her face was snatched away.

"Not exactly. Your mother wanted to know why the Air Force didn't bring you home when you... well... died."

The news was beginning to hit home. He clutched the back of the nearest bench for a moment, then sighed. "I thought she was already dead," he said quietly. "A long time ago."

He stepped away to the brick hut staring into his own past. We both moved quietly toward him.

"Your private life is your own," I said after giving him a few moments, "but we do need to know a few things."

"And can you guarantee I'll—"

He turned to me as he spoke, but he didn't finish. Chips of brick and mortar exploded from the side of the little hut beside his head just as the whipcrack sound of suppressed shooting reached our conscious brains. Fiquenet had already started to react and executed a perfect tackle on Pennyweather, shielding his body in the process. Like something out of a television show. I didn't hang around to admire her technique. I heard them hit the ground as the vehicle outside the gates roared away along the road.

By the time I got out there, all that was left was a rank cloud of rubber smoke. The vehicle was a dark shape receding in the distance. Never a tractor blocking the road when you want one. Although given the happiness of their trigger fingers, I'd guess that was no bad thing. Shaking my head, I put my Beretta away and went back to inspect the damage.

Fiquenet and Pennyweather were untangling themselves from one another and climbing to their feet. On the far side of the cemetery the old man was glaring at us with open hostility.

13

(Tuesday)

Safe houses. There must be a buyer's instruction manual somewhere detailing the precise level of grot and late 1970s ambience required before such a property is considered, acquired, and then allowed to die slowly. I'd used a few myself and they were always depressing, certainly not places you'd really want to hang about in. Maybe that was the point.

This one, however, was different. Not only had I never been there, I didn't even know it existed. Given the décor, I suspect it was kept especially for when Thames House needed somewhere to 'entertain' the Cousins covertly so they didn't feel too much like they were being made to slum it.

The location was perfect. A three storey Victorian villa next door to a hospital. There were several ways in and out and lots of people moving backwards and forwards twenty-four hours a day. You could even bring someone in round the back by ambulance without it looking out of place. Sling on a white coat and you could disappear in full view.

On the ground floor were offices which were not only cover, but provided security. At a casual glance, a passer-by would probably think it was part of the hospital, right down to the faded, hospital style sign by the front gate that simply said 'Administration. Private'. The only thing that put me off was that faint smell of boiled food and disinfectant that permeated the place from its busy neighbour.

Despite the constant movement outside, indoors was quiet and calm. I stood on the first floor landing next to one of the baby-sitters and watched through an open door as the doctor finished his examination. Pennyweather began to button his shirt whilst the medic packed his bag and said a few last words. The long dead American touched his face where chips of cement and brick had been removed. As he finished dressing, the doctor came out and looked at me over the top of his glasses.

"I'm done," he said quietly. "No physical harm apart from those nicks on his face. Stunned rather than shocked. He's had a mild sedative, but nothing that's likely to impair his ability to answer questions. Just don't push too hard."

"Thanks."

The doctor from Thames House left and I heard the downstairs door being locked behind him and put on the chain as I went into the room where Pennyweather sat. It was large and overlooked the ambulance drop-off point. Heavy blast nets over the armoured glass prevented anyone looking in. Other doors opened and Sally came in trailed by the flying Ms Fiquenet.

"Would you like anything to eat or drink?"

Pennyweather looked up at me and then at the others. "Sorry?"

"Food? Drink?"

"Oh shit. Work. I haven't... Will I be here long? It's my day off today, but..."

"What do you do?"

"I'm a chef."

So much for my theory about him working out-doors.

Sally said: "Write down the details. We'll sort it all out if needs be."

She pointed to the pad and pencil on the coffee table.

Pennyweather looked dazed. "Just like that?"

"Just like that," I said.

"I've already ordered food, by the way, and coffee's brewing," said Sally.

And there was me thinking she'd been on the phone to Thames House. "I hope everyone likes Chinese," I said quietly.

Sally gave me one of her school teacher looks and then spoiled it with the lightest flicker of a wink.

Fiquenet wanted to get started straight away, but Sally had the good sense to hold her off with talk of getting the coffee. By the time they had sorted that, bags of aromatic food filled the large coffee table. Which suited me better. I wanted J. J. Pennyweather relaxed and comfortable.

Of course, what I want and what I get rarely co-exist. We were hardly half way through the spring rolls when Fiquenet started.

"Mr Pennyweather." She caught my expression and that eyebrow shot up again. "John..."

"Philip Ingleton. I'm Philip now. Have been for a long time." He looked at each of us in turn. "Everyone calls me Phil."

"Phil". I said. "You're here for your protection. We'd like to ask some questions, but you're not in any kind of trouble."

I watched the noodles in his chopsticks where they hovered halfway to his mouth. He sat back and dumped the food into the foil tray.

"Someone shot at me. In a cemetery. And you say I'm not in any kind of trouble. Just how do you define trouble?"

I saw Sally suppress a smirk.

"We just want to help," I said, anxious to get the conversation on track.

Pennyweather picked up his chopsticks again and poked at his food. "It's a bit late, isn't it?"

"What do you mean?"

He stirred the noodles but seemed to have lost his appetite and put the tray onto the table. Whatever tale he had to tell he had kept to himself for nearly forty years. You could see in his face he was struggling, trying to decide whether it would be better to keep quiet or finally unload the weight to which decades of deception must have chained him.

We all sat still, Sally nursing a mug, Fiquenet watching him with a predatory glint. I hope she had the sense to stay silent for now. I knew she wanted to get back home with a simple resolution. But it wasn't going to happen. It never does.

"Philip Ingleton."

He had decided to talk.

"Yes?"

"That's who's really in the grave."

"And who was he?"

Pennyweather sighed. "A friend. A good friend. The best. He died for me. Let me hide all this time."

His hands were shaking and he gripped them tightly in his lap, looking down at them as if seeing them for the first time.

"What happened?"

He looked up at my question, eyes narrowing. "Do I need a lawyer?"

"We're not the police. Unless you stole a nuke or killed someone..."

"Was that meant to reassure me?"

I held my hands up. "Sorry. As others here will tell you, my mouth is inclined to run ahead of my brain. You don't need a lawyer. We really are interested in your story and in protecting you. Nothing else."

He thought about it for a bit as he looked at his hands again. "OK," he said. "What do you want to know?"

"Start with your time on the base. Why did you leave the Air Force?"

"It was good there. Not a bad life, even if it wasn't quite the exotic location I'd hoped for. But I was an idiot. A kid. Trusting." I let myself sit back in my chair, giving him space to talk. "I worked in the commissary," he continued. "Enjoyed it. Cooking. Worked with a great crowd. Still do. Anyway, I was often off base picking up supplies. A lot of stuff was flown in, but we bought vegetables and meat locally. Part of the deal, apparently. Keep the boys on the base happy with familiar brand names on the stuff in packages; keep the natives happy by using local stuff that didn't need labels."

He was back there. A kid again, on an adventure. A safe adventure in a foreign country with all the comforts of home. Not a care in the world. Perhaps he had never really left.

"And?"

His eyes focussed on Fiquenet. "I went out in a van so some of the guys would ask me to pick up stuff from the shops. Spares for their motorcycles. LPs. Tickets for local dances and concerts. That sort of thing. I'd earn a few shillings each time. It mounted up."

"And I suppose you didn't ask questions."

He smiled and gave a rueful laugh. "I didn't think to. Oh come on, don't look at me like that. I was a kid. I only joined up cos dad and my big brother had been Air Force. I thought I was going to travel, see glamorous places." That put another smile on his face. "In a way, I was glad I didn't. I like it here. I liked my work on the base."

"Until?"

"I thought she was the one meant to be asking the questions," he said, nodding at Fiquenet.

"Hey, I'm happy to sit and listen," Fiquenet replied. "We're all headed in the same direction."

"And I'm not in trouble? Not arrested or anything?"

"Guilty conscience?" asked Fiquenet.

I winced, but our friend J. J. Pennyweather seemed to have regained some of his confidence.

"Stuff was found," he said, picking up his story. "Dope. It took AFOSI about three seconds to work out who was bringing it in. It took a lot longer to persuade everyone I hadn't known.

"You weren't cashiered, though."

"That was Colonel Conrad."

"Base Commander," said Fiquenet for our benefit, although I already knew from those huge files Sally had given me.

Pennyweather nodded. "He believed me. Let me resign. Even made sure I got my old job back on the base as a civilian. But there were strict searches after that; on and off the base. I wasn't even allowed a bag."

"Were you in...?" I struggled to remember.

"Crag Cottage," said Sally.

"Thanks."

"Number four," said Pennyweather.

"Nice place?"

"I guess." He took a different journey back, this one with shadows. "Until..."

"It's OK. Take your time. You were working on the base as a civilian."

"Yeah. Nothing much to tell. I cooked." He looked at the remains of the Chinese food on the table. "Usually the early shift. I liked that. Bakery and breakfasts. I started college as well. Catering."

It was clearly a time he had not revisited much, unless he was naturally a dreamer. But I suppose when something derails your life you either go over it until it drives you mad or you lock it away until some mad sods turn up and start trying to prise answers out of you.

"What about the winter of 1980?"

Most people would have to think about a question like that, do a bit of maths, and work out where they were. Especially after such a long time.

"I went up to Norwich," he replied. "Had saved up some leave. And some money. I was going to spend it with... a girlfriend." He raised his eyebrows and shrugged. "We had a bust up. I didn't fancy hanging around so I spent a couple of days with a cousin of mum's. Span the old story. The rest of the time I was in a cheap hotel, didn't want to waste the holiday. I had a good time, actually, despite the bust up. Went to the castle museum and the cathedral, places like that."

"So where does Phil fit in?"

"He was a friend." He shook his head then took a deep breath. "A bit of a drifter, but a nice guy. Genuine. He used to go round to music festivals and things and do catering out of his van. Vegetarian stuff. He didn't have anywhere to go over the holiday period, so I let him have the cottage while I was away."

"Go on."

"One of the reasons I stayed on in Norwich was because I'd arranged a lift back and I had no way of contacting the guys without causing trouble. It was strictly against regs, but I knew a lot of the drivers on the base. They always came in at odd hours for food, so you'd get talking."

I could see Fiquenet perk up and wondered why drivers on the base would be of interest. Perhaps we'd find out. Pennyweather seemed to be thinking about his story, picking his way carefully into the next bit. Perhaps not wanting to get anyone else into trouble. Even after all this time. Which shows how wrong you can be.

"Some of them were working over the Christmas period. They'd been real busy since Thanksgiving. They were going round picking stuff up from other bases or something. I didn't ask. They wouldn't have said. But they were using those big, black armoured trucks."

Fiquenet perked up even more. I caught Sally's eye and she gave a very small nod.

"I mentioned I'd be in Norwich and they said they'd pick me up. Bring me back."

"Do you remember any names?" It was Fiquenet who asked, very casual. No one took notes. It was all being taped.

"Oh. Er. Don't suppose it matters now. The driver was Jack Lincoln. Leastways he was driving when they picked me up. There were three others. Mike Lang... Langham, Langlands, something like that. Lasky. Don't know his first name. Laskowski. Everyone called him Lasky. Donny Smith. Two in the cab and two in the back." He looked round as if for approval. I nodded for him to continue. "Well, I met them like we'd arranged. Late evening. A pub car park on the outskirts. The Ipswich Road."

"Any idea where they'd come from? I know you said you didn't ask, but any ideas?"

"It's all tied up, isn't it?"

"Wha—" It was Fiquenet, but I cut her short with a gesture. I had no idea what all this had to do with Philip Ingleton, but there was only one way to find out and that was to let him tell the story his own way. And if Fiquenet hadn't done her homework, I didn't want her blundering about just now. She gave me a sharp look but settled back in her chair.

"It's all right," I said. "Go on. Any ideas?"

"I couldn't tell you why, but I've always had it in my head they'd been to Birmingham or somewhere like that. I knew a lot of crews were on the road over that Christmas."

"OK. So what happened next?"

"We drove down through the night. Took it steady. Didn't stop anywhere. It wasn't the main road, though. They left that not long after they picked me up. And for some reason they were going in by the back gate at Rendlesham, so they dropped me off just before the Forest."

"This was the Tangham Road was it? Off the Woodbridge Road?"

He shook his head. "No. That was the odd thing. Well. One of them."

"So... Where?"

"We came off the main road at Butley." I tried to remember the geography of the site as he spoke. "Cut through The Clumps to the eastern end of the Forest and the start of the Night Road. One of the forestry roads. It wasn't that far from Crag cottages, so I didn't mind. It wasn't too cold and after being in the cab with the others I was looking forward to a bit of fresh air, stretch my legs.

"Lasky got out with me and I remember he unlocked the gate. More of a barrier really, like a single bar across the road. Jack took the lorry through. I cut across a field toward home. I don't know how far I'd gone, but I heard the lorry move away up into the trees. It was really quiet in the dark. Then I heard the engine racing for a bit and then there was, like, a second of silence and then a muffled crunch.

"I couldn't work it out, but I ran back cos it seemed odd. Part way up the forest road... well... off the road to the right, actually, was the lorry. On its side. It was dark in amongst the trees so I couldn't really see, but after that first... it's not even a turn, just a slight kink... anyway it's a straight concrete road after that. I couldn't work out what had happened. Jack had a broken arm. Everyone else was OK, but they were all shaken. They told me to clear off as they had radioed in to the base for assistance. I went. Didn't want trouble for me or for them."

He sipped the remains of his coffee. It was cold and he pulled a face. "When I got home, I could see lights in that part of the forest, a faint glow, you know? I guessed they'd put up arc lights and were clearing up. Didn't think much of it. They were the best people to handle the job. I was just grateful I hadn't been in the cab when it happened.

"I still had a few days holiday left. Did all the things you do. Shopping. Watching TV. Kind of patched things up with... my girlfriend. It wasn't till I got back on base... I asked after Jack. No one had seen him. I went across to the base infirmary to ask how his arm was after the accident." He looked at us one by one. "Stupid. I know. I mean, how was I supposed to know he'd been in an accident. Anyway, no one had seen him. Or any of the others. And I mean no one. I couldn't work it out. In the end, I got taken aside by a senior officer I didn't know. He told me that Jack had shipped Stateside and I was ordered to stop wasting people's time."

"Ordered?" I asked.

"Oh yes. In no uncertain terms. Pissed me off, I can tell you. I was just asking after a friend."

"Had you not heard any of the rumours?"

"Well... I'd been kind of occupied. Didn't get out much those days between getting back and starting back on base. Anyway, it was all bullshit. All that stuff. How anyone could mistake a crashed lorry for a flying saucer... Next thing I know, these CIA types are looking for me."

Fiquenet produced a couple of small photographs from her jacket pocket and, pushing aside some cartons, lay them on the table. They were old ID photos, taken a long time ago, but I recognised them. Pennyweather leaned forward and looked at them.

"Shit. Was that them? This morning?"

"We don't know. What did they want back then?"

"Nothing. They weren't the guys looking for me on the base." He sat back in his chair and you could see the tiredness eroding him. There was something else there as well. A look of desperation, the look of the person who knows you can't go back but wishes it had all been different, that they had done something about it. I'd seen a face with that look before. In a mirror, every time I shaved it.

"We really need to know," I said quietly.

"I slipped out at the end of that shift. It wasn't difficult." He shook his head and frowned. Maybe he was thinking what I was thinking. 'Not difficult' can easily translate as 'too easy', especially with hindsight. At the time, though, it will rarely occur to you. "Anyway. That was a Saturday afternoon. The Saturday afternoon. I went home thinking it would all be forgotten by Monday morning. Phil was packing. He was off in the early hours to go stay with friends in Brittany. He wanted to see all the standing stones there. It was one of his things. I even helped him pack all his stuff in the van. It was up the other end of the cottages. Some bloke who worked for the Council lived there and there was like a parking bay he let Phil use. I had a bath, said goodbye to him, and went out."

We waited in absolute silence, willing him to go on. Well. I was. It had all the horrific attraction of a car crash in slow motion. You could see all the parties converging on that point. A sheen of sweat stood out on Pennyweather's brow and he looked for some more coffee, gulping down cold dregs from one of the mugs.

"When I got back..." He slumped. Sat up again and took a deep breath. "When I got back, maybe eleven that night, the place was crawling with cops. Lights flashing. There was an ambulance as well. I don't know why, but I played the drunk and kept walking until I was back in the dark. Doubled back along a field behind the hedge. Just beside the front door. That's when I first saw those two." He pointed at the photos on the table like he'd just seen cockroaches in his kitchen. "They came out. Said something about how he'd shot himself. The police asked if they knew who it was. John James Pennyweather, they said. Bastards. I couldn't believe what I was hearing. I actually stood up. Was going to shout out they'd got it wrong. But another car pulled up and out got the CIA types who'd been looking for me earlier. So I ducked back down again. Didn't know what to do. In the end, I went back up the field behind the cottages to where Phil's van was parked. Broke in. Hid."

"How did you know these people were CIA?"

He looked at Fiquenet and then back at me. "The Company had a big, fenced compound on the base. And I mean big. A base within a base. Their own buildings, offices, quarters, commissary, lots of underground levels, their own planes, vehicles, guards, the works. You soon learned to pick them out. I'd seen the ones who were looking for me earlier in the day. They didn't seem in a hurry."

"What about our boys in the photos?"

Pennyweather shook his head. "I may have seen them about, but it wasn't till they came out of the cottage..." He wiped his fingers across his brow and flicked another glance at Fiquenet. "See. It didn't hit me at first. I mean. What were they all doing there? Local police wouldn't have got in touch with them, wouldn't have had any reason to. And even if they'd been in touch with the base, it would have been AFOSI who came out. And when I realised it was Phil that had been shot... It wasn't a suicide. Couldn't have been. There weren't any guns in the cottage and he was too laid back, too happy, looking forward to his journey."

"And what did you do?"

"Next day, when it was quiet, I drove off in Phil's van. Silly sod kept the keys on a magnet under the dashboard. I always said someone would steal it. I just kept going. All his stuff was in there. Everything. Even his passport. So I grew my hair, stopped shaving, became Phil."

It was dusk when we emerged, that time when the city gets its second wind and starts to light up for the night, that time when hospitals clear the decks for the casualties of that second wind. A siren whooped nearby and an ambulance pulled out into the heavy traffic, its blue light flickering down the street as the driver pushed his foot down.

We had gone back over Pennyweather's story, asking lots of questions, but he could give us nothing more. Not that we hadn't shifted from fuzzy blundering in the jolly mists of unknowingness, a state with which we are much accustomed, to an overdose of information in one interview. There would be plenty now for the researchers to get their teeth into – on both sides of the Atlantic. Once the poor sods in the attic had produced transcripts from the recordings.

Laurie Fiquenet had made her excuses and disappeared as soon as was circumspect. If what Pennyweather's story implied was true, then CIA operatives had murdered a UK citizen in the belief he was a US citizen. I suspect as the sole representative of the US and one time employee of said agency, she didn't much want to be around for any conversation that might follow. She'd want to be talking to her legal people on an encrypted line.

Sally and I cut through the backstreets and made our way down to Cheyne Walk and ambled past the houseboats. "I want him out of that house straight away," I said as we came up to Battersea Bridge. "Put him somewhere the Cousins don't know about. And don't tell Fiquenet if she comes asking."

"Do you seriously think they'd try something?"

"Someone was happy enough to shoot at him in a cemetery this morning. In front of witnesses. And even if it wasn't our CIA chums, they may have contractors on stand-by."

"It's a bit..."

"Louche? I know. You just can't get the staff."

She dead-armed me with a vicious jab of her knuckles. "I'll get him moved. But if Fiquenet goes through official channels there's not a lot I can do."

"That will take weeks. Pennyweather has dual nationality and is, in any case, officially dead. They can't extradite Philip Ingleton as he has not committed a crime against the US. Well, not that I'm aware."

"Don't worry. We'll run a background. What do you make of it all?"

"Sweet FA. It just raises a load more questions. Mainly, what were the CIA doing at Rendlesham and why were they involved with this lorry?"

"And here's another one to ponder."

"What?"

"Where are you taking me to dinner?"

14

(Wednesday)

Wednesday morning was wasted in presenting reports to a Parliamentary Intelligence Committee that could just as easily have been handled by one of my team. They were interim reports on procedures to ensure better sharing of intelligence between agencies and feeding it all to JSTAT, especially the increasing number of units set up by politicians and run out of the various Ministries. They were a serious pain in the posterior, but at least we could curb their enthusiasm by snowing them under with bureaucratic flim-flam. It didn't stop them wanting me in the chair. Partly out of revenge, I suspect, but mostly to get me to summarise the reports so they didn't have to bother reading them. Everybody was at it these days.

Any thoughts of getting away by lunch time were scuppered when a JICIAID investigation I thought I'd wound up months ago developed a 'complication'. Could I pop into the office, wondered my boss, Jane Fortune? Did I have any option? I suspect it was a ploy to pump me about progress in my little caper into Suffolk. So I slogged across town from the awful Home Office building, up to Perkin's Rents and along to St James's Park for a breath of fresh air.

JICIAID is just off St James's Square on the other side of the park in a piece of real estate that would probably fetch several million pounds if it were put on the market. It wouldn't sell to the sort of person prepared to pay that much as the only views at the front are of windows of offices across the street. At the back, where my office is, you get to look at brick fire escapes and a brutish looking hotel tower.

On the street, a discreet, unnumbered door was the entrance. It was squeezed between an art gallery and a shop selling rare and antique books, and contrived to look like every other anonymous door along the street. Indeed, it looked like it might belong to the bookshop. It didn't.

I buzzed and was let in, climbed the stairs to our secure lobby, nodded at the secretary on desk duty, and went on through to the hushed domain wherein those who watch the guards go about their daily business.

"Ullo stranger," came a voice from a small room. "Shall I take some coffee up to your office?"

I peered in. Daphne was of indeterminate age, but definitely long past retirement. She 'did' for us. Cleaned, made perfect coffee, and guarded the stock cupboard with all the guile one would expect of an experienced primary school teacher. Which was, I suppose, appropriate. "No thanks, Daff. Won't be here long."

On the top floor was the usual Sunday afternoon atmosphere. It didn't matter what day of the week it was elsewhere, here it was always Sunday afternoon – that curious mingling of calm, security, and certain knowledge of all the dull, boring, and sometimes unpleasant things you later had to do in the outside world.

As I suspected, the 'complication' was nothing more than misrouted paperwork, which took about ten minutes to track down. I then allowed my boss to pump me about what had happened. She listened. Made a few notes and then took me to the café across the road and treated me to a salad sandwich. She was a good boss, a pleasure to work for. And due to retire. Given the current propensity for politically motivated appointments, I dreaded to think who they might get in to replace her. At the same time I prayed to any gods listening to anyone with a soul as sullied as mine that no one had put my name forward.

It was late afternoon by the time I got back to Suffolk. During the drive I had come up with a whole new bureaucratic spanner to throw in the works of those ministerial intelligence units. Which put me in a good mood. They were a waste of money and resources and caused no end of trouble with their petty wrangling and hoarding of information. It was true that most of it was useless, but on several occasions we'd had to haul SPADs in front of a JIC tribunal and read them the Riot Act for screwing up investigations. Lives could have been lost because some elected yahoo wanted to use his unelected chums to play spy games.

The hotel had moved me to another room so that my stay could be extended. It made little odds to me. It was pretty much the same as the previous one with just a different view of the car park. When I had finished settling in, I read the local paper. And then I went to the pub. It's a hard life.

Early evening and the heat was gradually going out of the day. It was warm enough to be pleasant and ideal for sitting outside with a pint and plough-man's. I had the pub garden to myself and when I had taken the edge off my thirst I phoned Sally.

"Sounds very tempting," she said when I told her where I was.

"Maybe, but there's no way you're coming down here again. Not till this is over."

"You are a misery guts."

"I don't care. You made me case officer. And as senior field agent as well, I'm telling you to stay away. Quite aside from the DG having a fit if he found out one of his department heads was in the field, I want you well out of harm's way."

"So who's going to look for Stan and Ollie?"

"Let Fiquenet think she's heading that up. Using her own resources. I don't want the Americans knowing we are interested. Well, any more than they already know. If this is 'official' I want to catch those two with their pants round their ankles. If it's not, I want it dealt with so we can dump the bodies in Nine Elms on Chief of London Station's doorstep. Nice present for Woody Johnson as well."

There was a moment's silence.

"I sincerely hope you're speaking metaphorically."

"Yes, Sally. Metaphorically."

"And the genuine bodies?"

"Hopper is still working on that. And the team you sent down – for which many thanks – are working their way through every caravan and camping site and holiday cottage in the county."

"Sounds like everybody's busy. What about you?"

"Me? Oh, I thought I'd take a couple of weeks off and go up to—"

"Very funny."

"When I have finished here I'm going to talk to a name on the list that our inestimable Mr B provided. One that no one else seems to have approached."

"OK. Let me know how it goes. And watch yourself."

"I will. Bye."

I rang off and put my phone in my pocket. As I finished my food, a young couple came through from the bar, seemingly shy in each other's presence, and settled themselves at a table with drinks. I took my empty plate and glass back inside and chatted a while with the landlord. He was happy for me to leave my car parked out the front so I strolled the short distance down the road, turning my head like a tourist until I arrived where I had been headed all along.

It was a brick built cottage that looked like it had turned round several times before it had settled comfortably into its patch of garden and lay sunning itself in the evening light. Half lowered blinds in the small, dusty windows added to the impression that the cottage dozed. The gate opened onto a well worn brick path bordered with delphiniums. It sheered off to the left where a more recent extension skulked behind the original building.

The front door swung open a couple of inches when I knocked. "Hello?"

There was no reply. I slipped my left hand in under the back of my jacket and rested it on the grip of my Beretta. With my right, I knocked again and called louder.

A faint voice drifted to me. "Leave that on the hall table. I'm in the garden."

I doubt the voice meant my handgun, so I left it where it was and followed the path past the newer addition with its frosted glass window, squeezed along beside an overgrown hedge, and found myself looking onto a long, narrow garden laid down to flourishing vegetables. Half way along, a woman was slicing at weeds between two rows of cabbages with a long-handled hoe.

"Sorry to bother you," I said. "I'm looking for Grace Sparrow."

The woman straightened and leaned the hoe against a cane wigwam. "Who are you and what do you want with her?"

She took my ID and looked at it thoroughly. "Home Office. Is that the police?"

"Not necessarily."

"Hmm. Have trouble enough getting someone from the Council to come round. So why does..." She looked at my card again. "Alex Grant come all the way out here from London?"

"To look for Grace Sparrow."

"And what does the Home Office want with her?"

"Nothing she need worry about. But I would like to talk with Miss? Mrs? Sparrow. About what happened in the Forest in 1980."

It didn't look like a reply was forthcoming from within the fortress of folded arms and a stare every bit as stony as the path on which I stood.

"It is important," I added.

"Well, you're out of luck." I took back my proffered ID card. "She died several year ago. Left me... everything."

"I'm sorry." And quickly removing my foot from my mouth, added, "That she died."

We did a two-step on the path and I followed her back toward the cottage. She pushed through a curtain of plastic strips hanging over an open back door and disappeared into a large kitchen. I stayed outside on the step. Water began to run.

"How'd you get her name?" she asked as she scrubbed her hands. "And why turn up now? That were coming up for forty year ago. No one was interested at the time. Only that chap from Crag Cottages... Course."

The water stopped and she re-appeared, drying her hands on a towel, watching me as she did so. "You'd better come in," she said finally.

I stepped up into the kitchen where it was cool, the plastic strips rustling as they settled back into place.

"I'm Sandy, by the way. Sandra Brockwell. Do you want some tea?"

It was good tea. Strong. Lots of it. Shared in a living room that had the same comfortable air as the exterior. Books filled the wide alcoves on either side of a working fireplace to which ancient, sagging and very comfortable arm chairs were drawn. Everybody seemed to have them except for me. One of these days I was going to ask just where they came from.

"You said outside that no one was interested at the time. What did you mean?"

"Just that. I was young and didn't push. Should have."

My look of confusion must have been obvious.

"My aunt was a bit touched, some would say."

"But not you."

"No. Eccentric, maybe. But she was kindness itself. Thoughtful. Bright." She sipped tea, another one taking a decades-long trip into the past. "She looked after me a lot." And I could see that was part of the story I wasn't going to get. I sat back and waited for the bit I would.

"She loved it round here. Born in this cottage. Lived here all her life. Knew the countryside inside out. Every day she'd walk, for miles, no matter what the weather. All the same to her. Collected herbs. Sorted out any sick animals she found. And a few humans. Every day she'd write down where she'd been, what she'd done, what she'd seen. Spose in the past she'd be thought a witch." A private smile came with the observation.

"Wrote things down?" I asked as casually as I could.

She pointed to the alcove beside her. The lower shelves carried a large number of identical books. I looked at the one she passed to me. A black hard covered artist's sketch book, with a number on the spine. Inside, the pages were ruled with faint pencil lines and filled with passages of neat copperplate handwriting that were separated by the most exquisite colour illustrations.

"It's beautiful," I said.

She smiled. "She made her own ink. Used a dip pen for the writing. The pictures were all done with coloured inks and a fine brush. I used to sit and watch."

As I flicked through the pages and read of people and flowers and herbs gathered and weather experienced and wildlife observed, she searched along the shelf and took down another volume. She waited until I had finished and passed it across, already open at a page.

"She was the kind of lady who saw fairies and thought nothing of it." I took the book and looked. Not the twee, sentimental Victorian things, but what my mother would have called the Good Folk, though what experience she might have had of them next to the ship yards in Govan is anyone's guess. I looked up. It was easy to see loyalty fighting with scepticism in Sandy Brockwell's expression. "I showed you that for a reason. Didn't want to hide anything."

"Go on."

She took a deep breath. "Grace liked to walk in the woods at night. She wasn't keen on the plantation, but said that the trees and all the creatures there were deserving of our respect."

I didn't understand what she was getting at. She passed a third book.

"Toward the end. She spent a lot of time in the Forest around then."

It took a moment, flipping through the pages, and then I saw a date. Winter 1980. Yet more wonderful entries with coloured pictures of moonlight on the pines, of starry skies, of hares, of the lacework of winter hedgerows, of pale ghostly shapes amongst the trees.

The change was as dramatic as it was sudden. One page exquisite, headed with the date, 25

December 1980. The next page... No more neat pencilled lines. No more beautiful handwriting. Gone was the love with which everything had been recorded, replaced with an urgent, anguished scrawl. The writing was erratic, spidery, disjointed and made no sense to me. The pictures were abstract nightmares. I couldn't begin to guess what had caused this.

"What happened?"

"I have no idea. To this day it's a complete mystery. At the time, I thought she'd gone mad. She was raving, angry. Like a two-year old having tantrums. Lots of things to say, no way of saying them. I got the doctor and he wasn't much help. Said it wasn't a stroke and that was that." I looked down at the badly creased pages that someone had later smoothed out. "She was like it for days. Weeks. Frightened me, I can tell you. Frightened me silly."

"I bet."

"No one else wanted to know. She'd always been viewed with suspicion. I took time off work and nursed her. Eventually, she began to calm down. It wasn't till late February that she began to get close to normal. But she was never the same after that. Never the same. Like there were shadows in her life. She started walking again, but never left the garden after dark. Was always back inside the gate afore the sun went down. She writes about it a lot for about a year, especially after that chap came. Then it's like she tried to forget it."

I took another book and turned the pages, watching the tremble disappear from the hand and the light come back into the pictures little by little. But there was a lot of soul searching in the text and the joy seemed to have gone out her life.

"What's this all about, anyway? You never did say. Is it those skeletons?"

I could have left it that. Should have, I suppose. Secrets are meant to be my business. Sometimes, though, honesty and openness really is the best way. "A friend of mine," I said. "He died in the Forest. I'm trying to find out why.

15

(Wednesday night)

Sheet lightning flickered far away to the west as I strolled back to the car in the dark. It filled the distant cloud with vast flashes and flickers of light, a spectacular free display. The pub garden was full, people sitting and talking quietly, watching the sky. Thunder rolled over us as I unlocked the car door. It growled lazily away toward the sea, echoing back and forth across the flat landscape. A dog began to bark in the village, the sound echoing across the flat landscape.

I turned off the main road and made my way back to where they had found Charlie's car. After reversing in, I stepped out and perched on the boot, watching the storm approach. A few hundred yards ahead of me, in the dark, the bulk of the Forest sighed as a light breeze sprang up. Jagged treetops were silhouetted against the sudden flashes of light. It was a backdrop any sci fi movie director would have killed for.

I now had three people on the spot at the time and not one of them had claimed to have seen a flying saucer. True, Grace Sparrow had seen fairies, but she had always seen fairies, and she was emphatic that she didn't see them that night. She experienced something altogether more disturbing and was never able afterwards to articulate what it was that had happened in amongst the trees.

Yet something had drawn her back on successive nights. There was a hint in her diaries. Those ghostly figures she had seen in amongst the trees during the nights before. Distorted trees. Odd colours that she gave up trying to paint and describe. Comprehensive as her books had been, even during that period of disturbance, they were no guide to precisely where she had been. Yet I couldn't help thinking that it was not very far from where the 'late' J. J. Pennyweather had seen the lorry on its side, part way along what he had called the Night Road.

Perhaps what Grace Sparrow had seen had also been seen by the lorry crew after Pennyweather had left them, making them crash. Perhaps they too were so disturbed that they had been shipped Stateside for treatment as quickly as possible to keep them away from the rest of the base personnel. The last thing you wanted was a nuclear base crewed by people with the jitters.

And what of Mr Bream? The retired, mild-mannered building surveyor who had missed all the fun at one end of the forest whilst witnessing erratic driving at the other. All that information he had gathered over the years with obsessive patience without once falling for any disinformation. Keeping himself to himself and working discreetly. He had come up with nothing to back up a story about a crashed UFO. All it amounted to in the end was lights in the Forest. An old lady going mad. And a car driving erratically. A car the police never traced.

Whenever you listen to someone you have to try to understand the story from their perspective and get back beyond what they tell you they have seen to what actually happened. That's not always easy, especially when you collect testimony from such diverse sources and from such a long time ago. It took me back to my training, to lectures about relative chronology, motivation, confirmation bias, how to avoid being sold a pup, how to avoid being drawn into a trap. That, at least, was unlikely to be a scenario here. People don't set traps on the off-chance they'll catch someone out forty years down the line – although they are still clearing landmines from decades old conflicts.

On top of that, there were also my increasing suspicions. Not about the people I had encountered or the history I was unearthing, but about the whole operation. What were the motives of the great and good of Thames House? Why had I been so readily loaned back to them? True, they would want to know what happened to Charlie, just as I did. Maybe for them it was a case of morale. Everybody in Thames House and the Service's various out-stations, not to mention members of its sister services and the wider intelligence community would have heard in one form or another of what had happened to an analyst sent to do fieldwork. I had made absolutely certain of that. For the sake of morale at a particularly difficult time, the boys and girls of Millbank would sleep better and work better for knowing that their sorry carcases would be wept over.

But I am not a policeman. I grew up in the business and my instinct is to get to the source of information without letting anyone else know and then exploit it. Or hand it on to someone who can. If you make arrests or close things down, you lose the advantage. Because new channels will open else-where of which you know nothing. It is a risky business, and when it goes wrong everyone calls for your head. The public, fed on a diet of gung-ho TV shows and films along with braying headlines in an ill-informed and politically biased press, don't under-stand how it works. Neither do the Americans who seem stuck in some weird vision of themselves as a white hat gunslinger in a border town. And the trouble with that approach is that you end up being outgunned or with situations that blow up in your face. Sometimes literally.

So what, I wondered, was going on here. Some importance was placed on this case by someone. Somewhere. Important enough to follow two super-annuated Company men when they fly into the UK unexpectedly. And who, just who had kept them on a list all these years? And why? I didn't know the answers to these and a dozen or more other questions. The fact that the questions existed and that money was being thrown at something I would have considered important but of low priority did nothing whatever to make *me* sleep easier.

I wandered part way up the track that Charlie must have taken, thinking as I went that he would have been the ideal person to analyse this mess. And there was another paranoid theory to tuck away. Near the top of the field I stopped and watched the Forest. The breeze had died, but the trees still moved in lazy fashion, creaking and sighing. My skin crawled as I stood looking at the sinister tree line. Lightning painted sharp images on the darkness. It was the only genuine illumination I was getting.

The storm hung around overhead as I drove back into Woodbridge. The hotel lobby was a bright refuge, though it felt no less surreal than the rest of the evening. Right down to someone sitting in the chair in the corner hidden behind a newspaper.

"Have you been there long?" I asked.

The paper lowered to reveal DS Hopper. He folded it neatly and laid it to one side on the small table beside an empty plate and cup. He dragged back the cuff of his shirt and looked at his watch.

"About an hour. Your phone's off."

"You could have left a message."

He shrugged. "I would have had to turn out any-way. There's still time."

"Something interesting?" I asked as he stood and lifted his jacket from the back of the chair.

"Just another piece of the puzzle, but I though you ought to see it as soon as—"

"I thought I recognized the voices." We turned to see Laurie Fiquenet standing in the entrance to the bar. "I have some... information for you."

It's turning into my lucky day, I thought. "Mind if she tags along?" I asked Hopper.

"Be my guest."

"Where are we going?" she asked.

Hopper smiled. "A little mystery tour."

Lightning still flickered in a half-hearted fashion as we drove. It painted surfaces with pale electric blue and then let the dark shadows snap back into place. Thunder grumbled across the sky and echoed in the narrow streets as we stepped out of the lobby onto the pavement.

Fiquenet sat up front with Hopper and I sat in the back, watching, glad there had been time to slip up to my room and change my shirt, check the things one likes to check. For example, if anyone knew where the Russians had gone. Which they didn't.

I shifted in my seat and watched a phone box go past. For the second time. "When you said a mystery tour..."

Hopper chuckled. "You noticed, did you?"

"Yes."

"I thought we were being followed. So I made an illegal turn and came back round the town again."

"And?" I had better sense than to turn round and stare.

"Now I know we're being followed."

"Cheeky sods."

"Is it—?"

"Stan and Ollie? No idea."

"Must be daft, trying it round here."

"Or desperate," added Fiquenet.

"Is this the lot that took a shot at you this morning? Do you want me to call for back up?" There was now an edge of concern in his voice. His pleasure at spotting a tail had suddenly scraped alongside what it meant to go from hunter to hunted.

"And how long would that take?" I asked. "An armed unit."

"Oh, god," he groaned.

"Stop thinking about the paper work."

"I'm not sure I could convince anyone. I'm not even sure who the on-duty AFO is. Not much call for it round here."

"Never mind. Technically, I'm the nearest AFO." I'm not sure he found that reassuring but I had other things to think about. "You know the town. I need to be able to get out somewhere without them seeing. Somewhere they have to stop. A quiet junction so I can get behind them and then vanish. Nothing obvious."

"This isn't going to be legal, is it," he said, glancing at me in the rear view mirror.

"A couple of flat tyres," I replied with a smile.

"How?"

"If you're worried about legal," said Fiquenet, "you probably don't want to know."

"Anyway," I added cheerfully, "your DI said 'all assistance', didn't he?"

I watched the mirror and saw the ghost of a worried smile flit across Hopper's face. "OK," he said. "Hold on tight. You'll need to get out my side."

He kept his speed steady, took us into a series of back streets, then along a narrow straight road. There was a car park on the right, rear access to shops on the left and an even narrower section of road ahead. He braked by the car park and I slipped out into the shadows of a recessed loading bay, slamming the door as he pulled away into the narrow lane.

His brake lights flared and I saw him take a left just as another car coasted by me, close enough to see Stan and Ollie. It stopped at the end for a moment, which was all I needed. I put a bullet in each of the rear tyres. As the car slumped down, I ran back past the car park, ears ringing from the shots.

At the next junction, Hopper's car was waiting for me. He pulled away as I was closing the door and I sat in the dark blowing gently on the palm of my right hand, more to get my breath back than anything else, before slipping the brass into my pocket. It had been a long time since I had done that.

It was a short journey. Through the town and along more back streets, turning finally into a large yard where security lights blazed. Hopper parked off to one side and got out. We followed suit, looking round at the high bricks walls topped by rotating anti-climb spikes and the great double doors.

"What is this place?" asked Fiquenet.

"A funeral director," Hopper replied.

"Nice. I bet you bring all the girls here."

Hopper grinned and crossed the yard to the double doors. He pressed a button on a sturdy looking intercom.

A rasping sound was followed by an echoing voice. "Who is it?"

"Detective Sergeant Hopper. I spoke to a Mr Jefferson earlier."

The intercom went dead. After a short while a wicket gate opened and a small, round, jolly looking man in his late sixties peered out. He was wearing a cardigan over more formal trousers, shirt, and waistcoat. "I'm Eric Jefferson," he said.

Hopper showed his warrant card. "These are my colleagues. Ms Fiquenet and Mr Grant."

Jefferson smiled. "Well, come on in then. That storm finished yet?"

"Looks like it," I said glancing up at the sky.

"Rain, you see," said the undertaker as he closed the gate behind us and checked the lock. "Mucks up the finish on the cars."

We stood in a large garage where two hearses were parked, their paintwork like black mirrors. Sidling round them, Jefferson led us into an office. Several desks and chairs were arranged by a barred window with frosted glass. There were several other doors and, beneath the window that looked out on the garage, a sink and a draining board with upturned mugs.

"Come on in. Plenty of room." He watched as we trooped in, managing to be avuncular and funereal at the same time. No mean feat. I closed the door. "So. What can I do for you?"

"Thanks for waiting, Mr Jefferson." said Hopper. "1980. The winter. Last few days of the year."

Jefferson looked from Hopper to me and back, smiling at Fiquenet on the way. "I'm not sure I understand," he said.

"Did you bury anyone?"

He pursed his lips, catching the lower one between forefinger and thumb. "That's going back a bit. Hang on."

Unlocking the drawer of the desk with a key he took from his waistcoat pocket, he slid it open and removed another key. With unhurried movements he crossed to a steel key cabinet and unlocked that. Another key was selected from one of the hooks and taken to a heavy door. When this was opened it revealed a space like a pantry with shelf upon shelf of ledgers and file boxes.

"All on computer these days," he said as he began searching. "My granddaughter does all that. She's doing some of these older ones as well. From when we started. 1847. Can't think why." He emerged with a heavy ledger and closed the door. "These books'll last longer than that machine of hers." He nodded at a computer on one of the desks.

We continued to watch as he sat down and put on a pair of glasses with the same unhurried care he gave to everything else. The ledger was filled with entries in a meticulous hand not unlike that of Grace Sparrow. Perhaps the same generation. Perhaps the same school.

The heavy pages turned and Eric Jefferson nodded to himself as entries caught his eye. "Ah. Here we are. December 1980. Last few days you say?"

"That's it," said Hopper.

"Do you have a name?"

"That's what we are after."

Jefferson looked at us one by one then back down at the book. He turned it toward Hopper and stood. "There you go then. Help yourself. I'm going to finish off in the chapel. Just through there." He pointed at the garage through the window. "Let me know before you go so I can lock all this up."

He shuffled out of the office and across the garage, disappearing through a wide door on the far side.

"Care to explain?" asked Fiquenet as we watched the undertaker. I sat on one of the desks.

"We had two skeletons," said Hopper. "From the period we believe the bodies went in the ground—"

"Late 1980," I added.

"There were no reports of elderly missing persons."

"So?"

"Round here, you can't go missing without someone noticing. And even if you did, someone would eventually wonder where you were; start asking around, even if only for a bit of gossip. They might never be found, but if they disappeared it would be on our books. Back in 1980 it was... even more close-knit. Most elderly folk drew their pensions from the local post office. Milk was delivered to the door. The Postie was a local and knew everybody. He would see if mail wasn't being picked up from the mat."

Very neat, I thought. "So the question is: how can two elderly people go missing without anyone noticing."

"Exactly," said Hopper with a smile. "And the answer is if everyone thought they knew where they were."

Fiquenet found the flaw. "Assuming, of course, they were locals these skeletons of yours."

Hopper shook his head. "We have to make that assumption otherwise it's just too complicated."

"It's a working hypothesis," I added. "We can test it. See what happens."

"Fair enough," said Fiquenet.

"And there's only one place you can be certain a person is without actually being able to check."

We all looked out at the hearses parked in the garage.

"But what's the connection? I assume you don't suspect Jefferson of devious practice."

"No."

"So why would anyone in their right mind want to do something like this."

Hopper was enjoying himself watching us trying to work it out. And it dawned on me that I knew something they didn't.

"There are two questions there," I said. "The first one is 'why?' and the second one is 'were they in their right minds?'"

They both looked at me.

"Meaning?" asked Fiquenet.

"I was reading a very interesting diary earlier this evening. Someone who was in the Forest the nights of the... incident. Someone who all the original investigators missed."

"And?" Fiquenet looked sceptical.

"I'm no expert, but whatever happened in there sent her out of her mind. She was fairly eccentric to start with. Used to walk a lot at nights, visit the Forest to see the fairies and so on. But her journal is coherent and very matter of fact up to the night of the lorry accident."

Hopper looked surprised. "What accident?"

"I'll fill you in."

"And what was she like afterwards?" asked Fiquenet.

"Her mind was all over the place, like she was skirting something dark she didn't want to think about yet desperately needed to talk about and didn't have the vocabulary to describe. Neat handwriting becomes a scrawl. The whole thing breaks down. She seems to me to be trying to describe hallucinations."

"How could you tell? You say she claims to have seen fairies."

"Which she had always previously described as if she was going to visit a friend down the road for a cup of tea. Nothing otherworldly about it. From that night on, though, it's different. It improves after a few months, but her niece tells me she was never quite the same afterwards. Not paranoid, exactly, but always wary."

Hopper shrugged. "I'm not sure I see the point."

"If Stan and Ollie were in the Forest that night, perhaps they had been affected in the same way." It sounded thin.

"OK. But what would induce them to steal two bodies and bury them? That's what you're getting at isn't it? Some whacko ritual?"

It was my turn to shrug. "No idea."

"And why this place?" She had no shortage of questions.

"That one I can answer," said Hopper. "In 1980, Jefferson's had four establishments. See the code in the column there?"

He pointed to the ledger and we went and looked.

"H," he continued, "is for Hollesley. Which is very close to the Woodbridge base and to Rendlesham Forest."

He ran his finger along the line and there were the details of two funerals. Two people in their eighties.

"If that's them, and it's a big 'if', we now know where they got the bodies," said Fiquenet as Hopper copied the details into his notebook and then took a photograph with his phone. "But we're no closer to knowing why."

A mobile phone began to ring. It was Hopper's. He walked across to the far side of the office as he listened.

"Perhaps it wasn't the bodies they wanted," I said, watching Hopper. Something serious. He turned and looked at me.

"The coffins?" asked Fiquenet. "But what use would they be? They got buried next day."

"With something in each one, otherwise the good gentlemen of Jefferson's would have noticed."

Hopper put his phone away. The worried expression was still there.

"Something up?" I asked.

"A patrol car found a vehicle abandoned at the junction of New Street and Thoroughfare."

I nodded. "Stan and Ollie."

"They also found a corpse. Shot."

Fiquenet came out with an unladylike, "Shit."

"OK," I said. "We'll do this slowly." I raised my hands and placed them on my head with fingers interlaced. Turning my back on Hopper I said, "If you reach in under my jacket, Sergeant, you'll find my gun. Left handed draw."

After a few moments, it was lifted from the holster and I turned slowly. He was wearing blue latex gloves and was holding the pistol between finger and thumb. After checking the safety was in place, he laid it on the desk.

"Now what?" he asked.

"Would you?" I asked Fiquenet.

"And get my prints on it?"

Hopper produced a second pair of gloves and she put them on. She picked up the gun and dropped out the magazine, ejecting the round already loaded in the chamber.

"That's a Beretta PX4 Compact," I said. "Tell him the magazine capacity, please."

"Fifteen 9 millimetre rounds," she said.

"Count them please."

She emptied the magazine with practised fingers and lined up the rounds. "Thirteen."

Lowering my right hand with exaggerated slowness I fished in my jacket pocket and pulled out the two spent cases. "That," I said as I put them on the desk, "makes fifteen. One for each tyre. That's a full magazine."

"No spares?" asked Fiquenet.

"So kind," I said. I pulled the other two magazines from their belt pouches. Fiquenet picked them up and emptied them as well, standing each round upright in two more rows. "Fifteen in each."

Hopper nodded, staring at the row of bullets before coming to a decision. He took a picture with his phone and then said: "OK. But for Christ's sake don't tell my DI you're armed unless you have to."

"I am an AFO," I reminded him as I loaded up the magazines. I pushed the one with thirteen rounds into the gun and pulled back the slide to put one up the spout before engaging the safety. The other two magazines went back into their pouches on my belt. "But if you're that worried," I added as I reholstered the gun, "I'll get my boss to do it."

I took my phone from my pocket. Sally was going to love this.

16

(Wednesday night/Thursday morning)

Even at this late hour there were onlookers lined up at the blue tape as well as local press and television. The mob by the car park was being kept at bay by a couple of youngsters in uniform who looked like they should still be at school. Whatever happened to the beat bobbies I remembered from childhood? They were built from girders, like the ships my dad worked on, and had faces as stony and red as the tenement we lived in. Mind you, some of my school-mates had looked like that.

Beyond them you could see the shimmering white of a great tent that filled the end of the alley, billowing lightly in the still warm breeze. Even under the halogen arcs, it flickered as flash guns went off inside. Ghostly white SOCOs with blue, latex hands were swallowed by it and re-appeared, reverently bearing gifts that they took to their van to be logged. Others walked like alien astronauts, making strange obeisance in their slow search of the surface of the road and pavement.

Stifling a yawn, I climbed out of the back of Hopper's car and trailed the others as they walked along the street. We passed police cars and vans, pushed through the gathered crowd, and ducked beneath the blue and white tape. Our names went on the list and we moved away from prying eyes and ears to stand and watch as the circus went through its grim routine.

"My DI," Hopper said from the corner of his mouth as someone wearing a suit and sour expression emerged from the ruck of uniforms and approached.

"Sergeant."

"Laurie Fiquenet, United States Air Force Office of Special Investigations and Alex Grant, sir. They've been with me."

Fiquenet flashed her ID. I smiled.

"Detective Inspector Gardner," he said, introducing himself. It came out sounding just a bit like a threat. He turned to Hopper. "Any particular reason I would want to know that, Hopper? In the frame otherwise?"

"The shooting of the tyres," I said, "is not connected with the shooting of the man."

Gardener's gaze returned to me. "And you would know this because?"

"I shot the tyres. I'm an AFO."

"And I take it there were bloody good operational reasons you would discharge a firearm in a public place in such a way?"

"Yes, there were," I said. Two could play at the terse politeness game. "May I see the body?"

Gardener looked round toward the tent before answering. "When SOC have finished." He turned to Hopper again. "Sergeant. Care to do some work?"

Hopper made himself scarce.

"Any word on the second occupant of the car?" asked Fiquenet.

Gardener was very good. That slow, deliberate air of his was giving him time to react with calculation. "You see? This is why I am not a happy man. I do not—"

His cell phone began to ring. He answered straight away. We stood staring at him as he listened. After a while he put it away. I was about to speak, but he lifted his index finger, clearly enjoying the moment even if he wasn't wearing out the smile he must surely keep somewhere about his person. My phone began to ring and I went through the same routine, listening as the other two stared.

"At your convenience, Detective Inspector," I said when I'd put my phone away.

"What the hell was that all about?" asked Fiquenet.

"The great and good of the Home Office. They were not happy being disturbed late at night with such news so they were making sure us minions know who pays our salary, with a threatening reminder to play nice."

Gardener looked back at the tent again. "I've no idea how long we'll be here. I just hope no one is trying to start a war on my turf because, Cabinet Secretary or not, I won't be very happy."

Turf? I thought that sort of talk went out with Dixon. "Once I've seen the body and told you who it is, I suggest that Ms Fiquenet and myself go back to our hotel and wait there."

"I warn you now; it's not a pretty sight."

I sighed. "It won't be my first. Not by a long chalk."

Call it a sixth sense. Call it intuition. Call it a trained eye coupled with experience. Call it what you like. They have fancy words for it at Fort Monckton. I call it knowing exactly where I left things and setting a few traps.

Since the invention of the Polaroid camera, teams have been able to photograph places they turn over so they can put things back just as they found them. These days, with digital still and video cameras built into phones it is so much easier. No packets of film to carry and pictures to drop, images sent instantly to a computer waiting elsewhere and erased from source, rooms scanned in minute detail without the need to touch things.

This lot had been good. You had to admit that. Very good. But everything is so high tech these days that there is a tendency for those brought up with such technology to overlook tricks from the days of a dinosaur like me.

There are some things you can't put back exactly as they were, no matter how hard you try. Moving them alters them randomly. As long as you know to check them before you go out, you can tell if someone has been going through your things.

On the key ring of my keys is a little toy. If you open it up you'll see it generates a random eight digit number every time you move it. Lifting the keys is enough. And keys are always such a temptation. Especially complex looking ones like these. Not that they open anything. They're just bait. Like the memory stick. Well, anyone stupid enough to fall for that one deserves the virus they get on their computer. And it's a very effective sound activated recorder as well.

As I said, this lot had been good. They hadn't touched any of the toys. But someone had moved the phone. Those traces of talcum powder had gone. Which made me wonder. Who the hell bugs a land line these days? We use mobiles with a sophisticated scrambler kicking in on certain numbers. Unless it was meant as a diversion.

More to the point. Who? Stan and Ollie had been following us until they got a couple of flat tyres. And then Stan was getting a bullet in his head whilst Ollie was... what? On the run? Lying in an alley yet to be found? Sitting on a plane with a black bag over his head and a one-way ticket marked GTMO pinned to the lapel of his orange jump suit?

So who had been in my room? The Russians? I wouldn't put it past them, but I wasn't going to find out by standing in the middle of it, staring at the bed. Leaving as quietly as I could, I locked up and sauntered along the corridor to Fiquenet's room. When she opened to door I put my finger to my lips. She frowned, grabbed her room key, and followed me.

Overhead, the strips flickered into life, casting a ghastly light across the hotel kitchen.

"Sandwich?" I asked.

"What?"

"Do you want something to eat?"

She looked as tired as I felt.

"You didn't drag me down here—"

I opened the huge fridge and looked inside as the motor kicked in. Fiquenet joined me. "Someone was in my room this evening while we were out. They were bright enough to leave my toys alone and then stupid enough to tamper with the phone."

"Toasted cheese and tomato."

"Ah. Yes. That sounds good. It's unlikely they got to the kitchen as it will have been too busy."

She shrugged and wandered off looking for coffee. By the time I had rustled up the sandwiches, the scent of coffee filled the air. We leaned ourselves against one of the preparation benches and let the cheese cool enough to eat without taking the roofs off our mouths.

"You said earlier this evening that you had some information for me."

"After a fashion. Langley is locked down tight. My source was nervous. He didn't want to be logged doing anything out of the ordinary."

"Not just hiding the corpses from the forty-five administration?"

"I doubt it. They've been doing that for too many numbers to get into a panic about it."

"Panic? Really? Langley in a panic?" I picked up my sandwich and took a bite, trying to imagine what it must be like to see the Company in a flap.

"It is a bit of a scary thought, isn't it. But at the moment they are a political soccer ball in a game where no one is playing in gentlemanly fashion."

"I'd say so," I said, thinking to myself it was something of an understatement. "That'd be twice in a decade. How quickly did they reach the shelters when they heard the Pentagon had been hit? Before or after they put out an official denial?"

"That was a cheap shot."

"So what's got them in a lather this time? Apart from the White House."

She turned and I watched as her forefinger traced two letters on the worktop. S. M. It's one of the digraphs that the CIA assigns to a particular country. To be specific, SM is the digraph for the United Kingdom.

"Oh, that's just wonderful. Stan and Ollie, I presume."

She shrugged again, spilling some of her coffee on the worktop and scrubbing it away with a wad of kitchen roll. Paranoia is catching. "This is getting beyond me and my remit. And my pay grade, come to think of it. I found who I was looking for, but I can't now report back for fear of compromising whatever else is going on."

"So you don't think Stan was down to, say... the Russians?"

"Are you serious?"

I shrugged.

"Just a thought."

"Don't muddy the water. Besides, my contact didn't mention them and you can rest assured if Langley thought they were involved, word would get out. No. This is domestic. Our squabble in your backyard, and frankly I don't want anything to do with it. That's why I joined the Air Force, to get away from this sort of thing."

I had some sympathy. If the CIA were prepared to protect something here by taking out its own people, it could get very messy. But that sympathy only went so far. Like DI Gardener, I didn't like people fighting their wars on my turf. Not least because I had a nasty feeling it was to protect something that shouldn't have happened here forty years ago.

"What are you going to do?" I asked.

"Pay a visit to Providence Court."

That suited me. While she was in London saying 'Hi' to the good folk of the fortress-like AFOSI head office, I could do some digging of my own. In more ways than one.

17

(Thursday)

The heavy cleaver stopped on the upswing and the face of Mr Yao squinted through the steam. When he realized it was me standing in the doorway, a broad smile lit his face and he put the cleaver down. Wiping his hands on his apron, he called, "Wotcher, cock," above the clattering of pans and waved me toward his office.

It was marginally quieter in there and a lot less steamy. "Big pile of mail for you," he said.

I lifted it from my personal tray on top of the filing cabinet. "Thanks, Harry," I said, flicking through the wad of fliers, junk mail, and begging letters. "How's business?"

"Terrible," he said.

I looked out through the window of his office into the kitchen. "Is that why you've got more staff?"

"Cousins. Who'd guess I had so many. Till they all started losing their jobs elsewhere. You want any-thing to eat?"

"Not today, Harry."

"See, even my best customers are deserting me," he moaned with a wide grin. "You bring that nice lady down someday soon. We put on a treat for you."

"Stop match making."

"Don't need me for that."

His grin broadened and he went out laughing. I threaded my way through the kitchen to a door at the rear. A small hallway had one door onto a store room and another onto a services cupboard. Opposite the store room was a steep and narrow flight of stairs. I climbed them up to a landing. More stairs climbed up to a service hatch that gave onto the roof of the building.

Round a corner that didn't look like a corner until you were right on it, the landing gave way to a long corridor. At the far end was a door to more stairs that led down to the main street. At the near end were more stairs down to the side entrance of the restaurant and just beyond that was the door to my flat. It was always good to have different ways in and out. Feeding my paranoia, some would have said. Only the living can be paranoid and that suited me fine.

It had once been the flat for the manager of the cinema next door. That was now a multiplex and the manager worked out of the back of the ticket office. In its heyday, however, it had been a single auditorium with more corridors and access points than you could shake a stick at. Quite a few of those were still there, tucked away behind the panelling used to divide it up. And the door into the cinema from the original manager's office was still there as well. Which was my little secret.

After a long shower and the simple pleasure of fresh clothes, I filled the washing machine, made some tea and went through the mail. As I sipped the brew and nibbled at some chocolate gingers, I paid some outstanding bills, succumbed to the appeals of a couple of charities, declined the opportunity to buy garbage made in some Eastern sweatshop, decided I didn't need another funeral plan or any more life insurance, and fed everything I didn't want to keep to the shredder.

My phone woke me. I untangled myself from the blanket and picked up the handset by the bed.

"You need a louder doorbell."

I yawned and, with the blanket wrapped round my shoulder, padded through the flat and down the stairs to undo the heavy locks on the lower door.

Sally took one look at me and raised an eyebrow. I yawned again and followed her back up to the kitchen, watching as she emptied the brown paper carrier bag.

Shrugging off the blanket, I peeled potatoes and sliced beans as instructed and then watched as she put together a cottage pie. It turned into the best meal I had eaten in days. The company helped. And when we had finished and washed up, we stood side-by-side at the living room window with glasses of red wine and watched the rain.

It was there I dropped my bombshell.

"What?"

"Exhumation," I repeated.

"God. Don't we have enough bodies to deal with already?" she asked, wiping wine from the window sill with a tissue.

I fetched the bottle and topped up her glass then made myself comfortable on the settee. "If I'm right, there won't actually be any bodies."

Sally perched herself on the arm of a chair. "What *will* there be after forty years in the ground?"

"That's what I want to find out. But it needs to be done formally. Through the proper channels. With approval."

"In case you're wrong," said Sally as she slid down into the chair and took a sip from her glass.

"In case I'm wrong. And it needs to be kept quiet."

"Any relatives will have to be informed."

I nodded. I already had someone in my office seeing if they could trace anyone and contact them. "And I need to go on a paper chase."

Sally raised an eyebrow. "And you wonder why nobody upstairs loves you."

I said something extremely rude about the people upstairs. Sally didn't have time to respond as my mobile rang. I listened and then thanked the person at the other end. "Thames House," I said. "I asked them to look through the stuff that had been in the hotel room when I had a visitor."

"Did they find anything?"

I shook my head. "No."

"Are you sure there was someone in there?"

I gave her my most withering look.

"Are you feeling constipated?" she asked.

"Someone had been in there. Not sure what they hoped to find. Maybe it was just a way of letting me know they were there and could get to me."

"A body in a car wasn't enough? That must have been seconds after you shot out the tyres."

"I know." I knew. I played those moments over and over in my head and there was never anyone there. Whoever it was, they were good. It still gave me the shivers. "Yeah, well that was probably the other part of the message. 'Let us clean up our own mess'."

"You're such a comedian. Since when did the Company care about cleaning up their mess?"

"When it prevents compromising an operation."

Sally sat up a little. "What operation? On British soil? And, we keep saying it, it was forty years ago."

"So. What was happening forty years ago?"

"Before my time, dear," she said with a smile.

"And the rest," I said. "We were both at school in 1980."

We stared at each other for a while. "I'll get some-one to produce a briefing paper for the morning," said Sally eventually and looked at her watch. "I'd better phone for a car." She fished her phone out of her pocket and spoke briefly to the transport section. "Are you going back?" she asked me when she had finished.

"To Suffolk? Yes."

"I meant the hotel."

"No. If they think I've come back to London perman-ently, I don't want to disabuse them of the notion. I'll phone Hopper and ask if he can sort something out."

Sally finished her wine and began looking for her shoes. I pulled them out from under the sofa. That was when she dropped her own little bombshell. "Top floor are definitely making noises about pulling the plug."

"Bastards."

"I did point out that JICIAID would probably step in with their own investigation if they weren't happy with ours."

"I bet that made you popular." She shrugged. "And?"

"I think they'd rather still have you inside the tent just now. But you'd better get Jane's backing."

They went back a long way, the pair of them. I've no doubt they had already discussed it, but it wouldn't do to let me in on things otherwise I'd be getting ideas above my station.

"Have the Americans been leaning on people, do you think?"

"Undoubtedly."

"Bastards."

The big double-fronted Edwardian town house with its neat front garden seemed to be in darkness, but I rang the bell and waited. The security was discrete. So discrete I couldn't see it. No doubt, someone inside was checking me out as I stood in the open porch. A door opened somewhere inside, casting pale light into the hallway. It was eclipsed moment-arily as someone left the room and moved toward the door.

Light flooded the porch and the door opened. "Hi, Alex, come in."

I stepped into the hall as the heavy front door was closed and locked and then followed my boss, Jane Fortune, into one of the darkened front rooms. She lit a standard lamp and I closed the door. From somewhere nearby came the muffled sound of a television.

"Sorry to break in on you like this," I said.

She waved me to a seat and I perched on the edge of the settee while she stretched out in a large armchair and waggled a pair of hedgehog slippers. Her jeans had seen better days and the sweat shirt she was wearing had the faded logo of a rock band.

"Relax," she said.

I didn't. "Sally tells me that she's under pressure to close down the Charlie Smith investigation."

"I know."

"I haven't finished."

"Technically, you have. You were asked to find out what happened to Charlie and you discovered it was an—"

"Accident. I know. And they seriously want to close it down on that basis? Surely they realise it is an accident that would not have happened if the Americans hadn't turned up; if some..." I took a deep breath "...idiot at Thames House hadn't sent Charlie into the field."

"And?"

"There's too much going on to let it drop."

"Based on what evidence?"

"You want it dropped as well?"

"No. Of course I don't. Charlie was your friend. He was family. And Thames House dragged you into this, presumably to stop you launching an official Juvenal investigation. Because the incompetent sods are trying to cover their bare arses. But I need something concrete that I can take to the Cabinet Office. Something they cannot argue with. The Security Service has received an informal request from Langley to back off. Chief of London Station took the DGSS to one side at the end of the last JIC meeting."

"I don't suppose you heard what was said?"

"No. But the DG was far from happy."

"So why not stand up to the Cousins? Unless he wants someone else to do it for him. And, more to the point, why the pressure from Langley in the first place?"

"Your guess is as good as mine. I have a feeling that other levels of pressure have been brought to bear."

"Special relationship," I said quietly. "Someone this side of the Atlantic confusing craven kowtowing with a partnership."

"Exactly. So I am going to need—" She stopped as the door opened and the main light came on. We both turned to see a man in his late twenties.

"Oh. Sorry, Mum. Didn't realise."

"That's OK, Martin. Did you want something?"

"It's all right. Button came off my jacket. I was just going to..."

Jane Fortune reached down on the far side of her armchair and came up with a wicker sewing basket which she held out. Martin, her eldest, took it from her hand, nodded to me, and left, closing the door quietly.

"He's got an interview tomorrow. Not sure how he and Flick will afford London if he gets it."

There was a moment's silence while we picked up our own thread. "Like I said, I'm going to need something concrete, Alex. Something to preempt unofficial pressure."

I shrugged. "I'm not sure anything will do that if the Americans become insistent enough. I do have a British national in a safe house. He was shot at, probably by a CIA employee. Until that CIA man is found and out of the country, I suppose we can invoke the Security Service charter. A British national has been terrorised. The Security Service exists to frustrate terrorism."

"Hmm." She knew exactly who I was talking about and knew I was stretching it. J. J. Pennyweather held dual citizenship, and under his assumed identity was born and brought up in the UK. "Muddy the paperwork. Blame it on having to work out of Thames House under severe restrictions. It will buy you a few days."

"It might be enough. I'd rather have more."

"I'm sure you would." She looked thoughtful. "I'm retiring soon." I sat back into the settee, relaxing a little now I knew Jane Fortune would fight for those few extra days. "You don't look surprised," she added.

"I'm an Intelligence officer. We tend to spot things."

"On the one hand, it means I can afford to push things just a little more than normal. And I will. On the other, I don't want to do anything to prejudice my choice of successor. It's taken a lot of manoeuvring to get the candidate I want rather than some political appointee who couldn't empty a bucket if you told them the instructions were printed on the underside. At the moment, everyone on the selection board who matters agrees with me on that. And most of them agree with my choice. So neither of us wants to rock the boat. Which is very awkward just now as we are both being pulled deeper and deeper into this mess. And the spite of Civil Servants and politicians knows no bounds."

I felt an enormous sense of relief. I was Jane Fortune's deputy and some would assume first in line to the throne. And if her preferred candidate had been me, she would have said there and then. But she knew I didn't want the job.

"OK," I said. "A few days. Thanks. And I'll make sure it all comes back to me if there's a problem."

Jane Fortune nodded.

"There's some stuff on my desk you should take a look at before you head off back to the wilds of Suffolk with that exhumation order in your pocket." I must have frowned. "Apparently your American friend was unable to persuade her chum in Langley to go rooting in the cupboard where they keep their skeletons?" I nodded. "I pulled some of our own material from Registry," she continued. "From the section they don't let you into. Be a good chap and don't get caught reading it, and for God's sake don't leave it on a bloody bus somewhere."

I gave a Boy Scout salute. "I promise to try not to rock the boat."

Jane Fortune smiled and shook her head at the same time. "I think you are incapable of keeping any boat steady, Alex. It's why you are so useful."

I hesitated on the edge of my seat, not sure whether this was the right time or place to mention it. "Um... There's... No. It can wait."

"Rose Smith?"

This is why Jane Fortune is worth working for and why I really didn't want to rock the boat if I could help it. For all our sakes. I gave a sheepish grin. "She is an excellent investigator," I said. "Bright."

"A field officer."

"So am I. Or was. But she has Georgie now."

"And she has no experience of committee work."

"Neither did I."

"Are you sure you're pitching this properly?" She said it with a barely concealed smile. I could tell she was enjoying this.

"Rose would be perfect for Juvenal. She knows her way round. Would have no problem dealing with the Friends. Did a stint at Cheltenham. Is great with people."

"And could be said to have every reason to be biased against anything Thames House does."

"Like me."

"She's young. Has little George to think of. Can be impetuous. Dropped a few points on her latest fire-arms assessment—"

"You've been reading her file," I said accusingly.

"As any prospective employer should."

I walked straight into that one.

18

(Friday afternoon)

Paperwork. The lifeblood and the hunting ground of the modern Intelligence officer. I hated it. Especially all that formal Civil Service stuff that contrives to fill pages with nothing worth mentioning. The pedantic corrections that get your reports sent back to you for re-writing when you should be out in the field. Endless talk without decisions being made. Endless assessments and reviews that are a complete waste as you know they are a substitute for action and will be repeated on an annual basis ad infinitum.

It was a relief, however, to read the stuff that Jane Fortune had dug up for me, even if some of it was only on the fringe of what might legitimately be called intelligence work. It was certainly an eye-opener, and a clear indication that someone had decided to keep a close, if not altogether productive, eye on the CIA base at Rendlesham.

It was even more of a relief to get to Thames House and read through the historical briefing documents that Sally had got one of their probationers to put together. I'm not sure most of it wasn't a cut and paste job straight off the internet. The fact that 1979 was the start of Lego's golden age was hardly of relevance, but they had at least had the good sense to add detail to anything relevant to the UK political scene and provide references to texts in the library.

And what a couple of years '79 and '80 were. I was still at secondary school. Having learned to avoid the bullies by merging with the background and studying their methods, I was beginning to realise I was quite good at languages. And that's where it all began, the long trail that started with German, followed by more German and Czech at University, the Foreign Office entrance exams when I graduated. I had no more ambition than some vague idea of translation work or the heady heights of diplomatic service.

Someone had been watching me, though. Even today, word gets passed on from people who used to be in the Service to people who are still there. Talent is monitored. Although talent is probably stretching the description in my situation. Whatever the case, I found myself doing some strange courses and assessments, being encouraged to take up hiking, gliding, that sort of thing.

When it finally dawned on me that I had been recruited into secret service I was quite excited. It soon gets knocked out of you. Which is just as well. It was a long hard road after that and it had led me to this desk with this report. Alive, despite the scars. Going round in bloody circles.

After a quick glance through the list of deaths, I went over the main report and highlighted a number of entries. I then wrote a note of thanks to the researcher and asked them for more detail on the events I had highlighted, to be forwarded to me via Sally Barrett.

Before I left the building, Sally wondered if I would like to have lunch with her. She wanted a word. I wasn't going to like it, she said. Over a pasta salad, which she paid for, she eased me into it by telling me off about my expenses claim. She even helped me fill in the new form. I knew it wasn't that because I'd never put in a claim in Thames House that hadn't been challenged by accounts. When she had done all that, she hit me with the news.

One of the clever children at Thames House had begun to check second homes in the Woodbridge area, the sort of property that stands empty eleven months of the year and doesn't appear on holiday home registers because they are never let out. The list, doubtless incomplete, went out to the PBI in the field and they had slogged from address to address using some innocuous cover story to get a look at whoever answered the door and see if buildings where doors stayed firmly closed were as empty as they appeared.

Sometimes foot slogging pays off. Navarro was spotted in a cottage. Just outside Tunstall. A watch was set. The plan was to pick him up this morning once reinforcements had arrived.

It was at this point in the narrative that Sally stopped.

"Please don't tell me he spotted our watcher."

"OK. I won't. He didn't."

"Points for that watcher."

"She was on her own."

I sighed, leaned back in my chair and folded my arms. "Have the stupid buggers in this building learned nothing? Please don't tell me she was a probationer."

Sally kept quiet for a moment. "The first she knew anything was happening was about two thirty in the morning when someone jumped the hedge she was camped in and ran across the ploughed field behind her."

"I hope to God she had the sense to stay put."

"Yes."

"More points for that watcher. Go on."

"Moments later a van roared up to the front of the property and waited while two figures lurched out of the kitchen door. One looked in a bad way. They more or less fell into the van which sped off. Our watcher called for back up."

"Fuck," I said, staring at the remains of our meal.

Sally shooed me out into the real world with a promise of a full report. It didn't much cheer me up. All our hard work fouled up by whoever had gone blundering in on Navarro. A phone call just as I was passing under the M25 on the A12 did cheer me up. Relatively speaking.

The Russians had turned up outside London. In Ipswich of all places. Who would have guessed? I made my wishes known in no uncertain terms and put my foot down. And being in an official car I switched on the blue lights and watched everyone else suddenly remember the speed limit as I sailed by.

I parked behind the Sir John Mills theatre and took a moment to compose myself and bring myself up to date. The Russians, it seems, had been wandering about the city and were now not far from where I had parked. One of the watchers had sent the co-ordinates of the theatre car park to my SatNav. Before I tackled the Russians, however, I read the preliminary report on the cottage where Navarro had been staying.

It made for interesting reading. If you like that kind of thing. Other than a rumpled blanket on a sofa, Navarro seems to have left the place tidy. Up to the point he fought off two attackers and legged it over the adjacent fields, that is. One attacker clearly came off worst as there was a lot of blood and a discarded kitchen knife. No prints and no DNA in the system.

Whatever Navarro had been doing there, it wasn't his base. He'd been travelling very light. So, wherever he went, it wouldn't be far. You get to a certain age and surviving in the field in a foreign country is really no longer an option, no matter how good you are, no matter how friendly the natives. You need a bed, a kitchen, and a bathroom. At least, I do.

I stuck in an earwig, made contact with the team on the streets, locked the car, and followed the instructions that were whispering in my ear like a trapped mosquito. Left out of the car park and then right onto the Bramford Road. My man was standing on the pavement a few hundred yards away opposite a furniture shop.

You couldn't miss him. Colonel Gennady Arbatov was straight out of central casting from behind the door marked 'KGB Spies – Old Style'. Solid and unmoving with a face that looked like a tank had run over it, he had his hands in his pockets as he stood contemplating the other side of the road. Everything about him said he was waiting and would continue to wait. In fact, the only way he could have been more obvious was if he'd been holding a banner that read: 'Let's talk'.

I strolled up to him and stood beside him. "I see the pizza place up the road is looking for drivers. You after a job? Or maybe you are looking to retire?"

"Defect?"

I shrugged.

He took his time, as if he was giving the idea some serious thought.

"I never had you people tagged as optimists."

"Nice place there," I said and turned my head to the sheltered housing block behind us as his two minders came out through the metal gate. "Company?"

Within seconds you could hear the sound of sliding van doors and the crunch of booted feet. The street by the furniture shop became busy with a bunch of handy looking types who didn't much seem like they wanted a new three piece suite.

"Prikhodite k kablukam, rebyata. Pust' vzroslyye spravyatsya s veshchami." The Colonel growled out the command without looking round and his pups came to heel as ordered.

He sighed and shook his head. "Did they really think someone as senior as you would be wandering around without protection?"

"Me?"

"Don't play games, Mr Grant. You are a power in this land."

It was news to me, and I dreaded to think what Sally would have to say about that when she read the transcripts, but if that's what he wanted to think I had no intention of disabusing him.

"A shame the same respect was not accorded to Charlie."

"Da. Da. A bad day. Tell me. Smith?"

"Yes. That was his real name."

Arbatov nodded and then we stood silent for a bit gazing across the street. I shook my head at an enquiring glance and the babysitters that I had requested ambled off round the corner to their van.

"Two people nearly had it away with a bit of merchandise from under our noses last night."

This time he did turn. "Lyuboy iz vas, idioty, znayet ob etom?"

They shook their heads.

"Nu, zabludilis'. Vam ne nuzhno eto slyshat'."

After a moment's hesitation, they headed for the pizza parlour. Perhaps they were going to jack it all in and buy a couple of mopeds.

"You do know I speak Russian?"

"Da. They probably don't though."

I kept my counsel on that as we went back to gazing across the street at the furniture store.

"Ice cream," he said.

I knew.

"Back in old days," he said, laying on the accent good and thick and then grinned. "We had a small shop on the corner there and our yard was out the back. I had a whole string of vans. I still hear those bloody chimes in my dreams. Who was going to look twice if one of those was parked in a lay-by by an Air Force Base while the driver had a quick smoke? We got all sorts of pictures. Not just of the bases and aircraft, but all the personnel who lived round here."

He nodded to himself, remembering the old days.

"Made a good profit as well," he added with a chuckle.

"I heard it could be a rough business."

"We never had any trouble."

I could believe that.

"I don't suppose you have any files?"

"Anomal'nyye yavleniya? Bug-eyed monsters? Little green men?" Arbatov doubled over, laughing, before stepping back to the nearby lamppost. He leant himself against it till he regained his breath.

I turned to him, hands in pockets. If he thought that was funny... "I meant on the CIA base at Rendlesham."

Arbatov sobered up. "You really are an optimist."

I shrugged. It didn't hurt to try.

In a much quieter voice, he said: "I'll ask my people. But don't hold out any hopes. Your government is not being very nice to my government at the moment."

I could have said the same, but I was after something, so I just nodded and smiled.

"So it was all just passive surveillance? No access agents? No active measures?"

"We had nothing to do with those bodies, if that's what you're asking."

I was asking and I wanted to be sure he understood that.

"Just remember," he rumbled on. "Where there were bodies in the past there will be bodies in the future."

"Is that a threat or an old Russian saying?"

"Who are you calling old?"

"Gennady Mikhailovich Arbatov, born Friday 3 October 1952 in Ulyanovsk. As a child lived near the soccer stadium. Did well at school and went on to—"

Arbatov grunted. "Do you have a good memory or is that coming over your earpiece?"

"You think they give me that sort of back-up?"

"I know we are outnumbered, even if my baby-sitters haven't woken up to the fact yet. But it was meant as a friendly warning, not a threat. All sorts of deadly creatures lurk in the forest at night. Most of them human."

I knew that and I knew I wasn't going to get any more out of the Colonel, which left me with all sorts of questions he would never answer.

"Well," I said. "This is going to be an interesting contact report to write."

"Oh," replied the Colonel, beckoning his heavies, "I expect someone has already written it for you."

And that was that. He seemed to shut down in an indefinable way, so I gave a little nod of the head, said: "Bezopasnoye puteshestviye," and wandered off back to my car via the pizza place, wondering what the Russians would want in return.

The same thought had occurred to Sally. She must have been fed into the comms, because when I got back to the car my phone rang.

"What the hell did you do that for? They'll want something in return."

"Really? I thought that nice Colonel Arbatov—"

"Flagtail."

"I thought that nice Colonel Flagtail might offer the file out of the goodness of his heart."

There was the silence of a restrained curse.

"Look," I said. "They clearly have an interest otherwise they wouldn't have hauled the good Colonel out of whatever passes for retirement in his leafy Moscow suburb and shipped him over to Suffolk with two SVR minders. It sure as hell wasn't to update their files on the UK's ice-cream trade. Arbatov is the same generation as Stan and Ollie. He knows something. Possibly. Or he's just sticking his oar in to see who trips up. Whatever the case, if we can tie him up in his own red tape for a day or so, I'm not going to complain. Besides, the chances of that bunch letting us see anything they have are way beyond remote.

"And they must be nervous about something to pull a stunt like that, if it's genuine. There may be something current going on in the area or, more likely, they've taken an opportunity to sow seeds of doubt to get us twitching at our own shadows."

I could almost hear Sally's smile. "Nice try, Alex. I'll get someone to look into it. Someone senior. But, face it, you're just making this up as you go along, aren't you?"

"Sally, you have no idea."

Come to that, neither did I.

By the time I got to the police headquarters at Martlesham Heath, it was late afternoon and the inside of my car smelt like a pizzeria.

"Afternoon, sir," said the desk sergeant. He looked pleased to see me. Which was something of a novelty. "DS Hopper's not on duty just now, but the DI asked me to let him know when you came in."

He picked up a phone and I stood and waited. Gardener soon appeared and led me up to the familiar office.

"We've given you a desk," he said.

"Ah. That must mean paperwork. My joy is un-confined."

He grinned. A little too fiercely. "Various reports on the shooting. Plus some other stuff you might find of interest."

I thanked him. Everyone was short-staffed and on a tight budget. This was something of a hole in his working day, not to mention a huge operational mess, and it did no harm to acknowledge that. Even if the desk was just a trestle table against one wall of a small conference room. It had a substantial pile of folders and a reading lamp with a wobbly bulb. "You're spoiling me," I said.

The grin was a little kinder. "DC Matthews will help if she can. This is her desk," he pointed to a small table just outside the conference room. "Not sure where she is just now, but till DS Hopper is back on duty, she's your liaison."

"What's she done wrong?"

He grunted out a laugh. "Nothing. Thought the experiencee would be good for her."

"Do you know anything about the accommodation Hopper was fixing up for me?"

Gardener shrugged. "Eric might know."

"Who?"

"Sorry, DC Matthews. Erika. Eric."

I nodded and went to my 'desk', sitting in the plastic chair. After seeing if I could fix the wobbly bulb, and giving up before I electrocuted myself, I switched on the lamp, pulled the top report toward me and began to read. It didn't tell me much that I didn't already know. Stefan Cichy had been at the wheel and had died as the result of a single shot to the head. Where Oliver Navarro had been at the time and where he was now remained a mystery. As a possible suspect, he was being sought by the police. I wished them luck.

The second report brought me up short. "Eric!"

A pixie appeared in the doorway. Short, slender, with an elfin face and close cut hair. "Sir?"

"My name's Alex. Are you happy with Eric?" She looked back at me with all the expression you'd normally associate with a brick wall. "OK. Erika. Please take me here." I pointed to the open folder, closing it once she had seen the address.

"I've got a set of keys for you, sir. Alex."

"Oh?"

"DS Hopper found a place for you to stay."

"OK. We'll sort that when we get back."

I knew what it was going to be before we got there. The clue was in the name. The Sands Caravan Park. But the sight of all those tin boxes in long lines in a field did not fill me with nostalgia for the family holidays we had near Girvan when I was a young child. They just reminded me of the blood bath in Wales. There was getting to be altogether too much of those sorts of memories in my life.

DC Matthews parked up by the site office, a prefab, flat-roofed block with metal-framed windows and a forced seaside cheeriness painted across the concrete façade that depressed me even further. I was pleased that she had backed into the space, even more so when she said she'd go in search of the manager.

A flock of noisy children went surging round me as I stood in the sunshine and squeezed their way in through the door. I stepped to one side and was safely out of the way when they re-emerged minutes later armed with ice cream cones. A trail of multi-coloured drips marked their passing along with sticky handprints on the wing of the car. Young

George could do with some of that, I thought. And Rose. Me too, as long as it was somewhere a bit less flat than this. Scotland would be good. Oban, maybe.

Not long afterwards, DC Matthews came out. In her wake, a sallow stick of a man in an apron. He treated me to an easy smile.

"Did I win the lottery?" he asked.

I heard DC Matthews sigh.

"Why do you ask?"

"Well. You lot normally send round a couple of uniforms in a motor if we have trouble. Her and that other one yesterday. Now I got another chap in a suit."

DC Matthews pulled a face at me from behind his back. "This is the owner," she said. "Mr Sands."

"Ah. That explains it."

It was his turn to look puzzled. "We're miles from the sea," I said.

He grinned again. "Oh. That were my dad's idea. Good isn't it."

Depending on your definition of good. Erika Matthews pulled another face. "So where's this caravan that's got us all excited?" I asked.

"Hang on."

He went back in through the door and I could hear him call out to someone. When he came back out, he'd lost the apron.

We fell in behind him and walked along a concrete path past a single-storey red-brick shower block, weaving our way between children in various stages of being scrubbed up for bed or an evening meal. The smell of food hung on the still air, drifting out through open caravan doors.

The path led to a concrete road that ran up the gentle slope of the field. Most of the caravans were ranged neatly on either side. Part way up, the road branched. "That's all new up that way," said Mr Sands proudly. "Might be a pain, but it beats farming. Killed my old dad, that did. Dropped dead in a field late one night. Took us hours to find him. Not happening to me."

We carried on up the slope to the very top. The field narrowed here, with a coppice of trees beyond, crowning the top of the hill. Mr Sands stopped by the last caravan on the right. He folded his arms, watching me as if I might pull a rabbit out of my pocket or a golden coin from behind his ear. I got the idea that DC Matthews was expecting pretty much the same.

"Keys?" I asked.

"Lock was bust," said Mr Sands handing me a shiny, new key attached to a big plastic sheep. "I had that repaired cos I didn't want anyone else helping their selves."

"Everything else left as it was?"

He nodded.

I looked round. It was a good spot to be holed up. Clear view of the approach, cover for an escape to the rear. Lots of people about to raise the alarm if anything untoward happened. I shivered.

"Sir?"

"Hmm?"

"Sorry. Do you want to go in?"

"What did the local boys find when they turned up?"

"Not a lot."

I slid the key into the lock and turned. The door swung open on well oiled hinges, releasing a gentle waft of baked air.

"What's that smell?"

"That'll be lavender," said Mr Sands. "My missus insist on that in all the 'vans. Keep them fresh."

Despite the large windows, the interior seemed dark. But once I had climbed up inside everything was clear. Even more clear after a cursory search was that the caravan was empty. All the cushions, blankets, and other bits and pieces scattered about came with the caravan. It was a mess. Certainly not methodical. Not the Russians. Sands would never have known. Not Stan and Ollie, either.

Sands pushed his head in through the doorway. "When will I be able to get in and tidy?"

"When was this one last let?"

"Only been empty the week. Someone cancelled."

So that had been a waste of time.

"Could have let it though. Those Americans. One of them offered to take it so I wouldn't lose custom. Couldn't work it out."

"What Americans?" I asked, as casually as I could. Perhaps it wasn't going to be a waste of time after all. "Family was it?"

"Oh, no. Couple of older chaps. There's another van up round the corner here in an odd bit of the field behind them trees. They took that in the end." He waved his arm off toward the end of the caravan as I stepped back out into the late afternoon and locked up, handing back the key. "You have to know it's there, see. I reckon they was at the base when it was open. We get quite a lot of them. I suppose I should do a proper little package for them. We used to get all sorts when I was a lad as well. My mum did B&B in the farmhouse. All from the last war they was. Not all Americans are wealthy. And there must be a fair number who was here up to when it closed."

I let him prattle on as he led us around the caravan that had been broken into and along a grassy path. A casual glance showed no break in the fence ahead of us, but if you went right up to it, as we did, there was a new wooden kissing gate leading into a sheltered area beneath the trees surrounded by thick hawthorn hedging.

"Old sheep fold. Used to allow tents up here. More trouble than it was worth. Always meant to put a couple more vans in here, for older folk. Somewhere quiet. One day."

The old sheep fold contained one caravan. It stood fairly close to the gate at the near end, shaded by trees and looking down over the hedge onto a field of flax.

"Is there anyone here?"

"Didn't notice their car as I came up," said Sands. "Looks all closed up."

Which meant nothing as the Americans' car was in a police compound somewhere and Ollie had last been seen running across a field. "OK. Thanks, Mr Sands. Probably best if you go back down to your office." I made sure he had gone before turning to DC Matthews. "Stay here. If there's any trouble—"

"Trouble?"

"If there's any trouble you leg it as far and as fast as you can. No heroics."

It wasn't far, but some walks cross larger spaces than the physical. There was no cover and no time to call in the sort of team you properly need. So I crossed the open ground with my flesh crawling and the old wound in my right shoulder aching.

When I got to the corner of the caravan, I stopped a moment and took several slow breaths. Now I was out of sight of anyone inside I eased my gun out and kept it close by my side. Another step took me to one side of the door. I knocked. The door rattled, but I could hear nothing else. I knocked again.

"Mr Navarro?"

Still nothing. Perhaps he really had gone. I raised my hand to knock for a last time. The door burst open. If I hadn't had my arm raised I would have taken it full in the face. As it was I went over, rolling in time to see a pair of legs make off round the far end of the caravan.

"He's heading into the woods!" called DC Matthews.

"Stay where you are!" I called back as she began to squeeze through the gate. She hesitated then took another step forward. I lifted my gun so she could see it. She froze.

Dusting myself down, I walked to the end of the caravan and peered round. Navarro had disappeared. I didn't mind that much. It was preferable to some stupid shoot out in a caravan park full of families and a young police woman in my immediate background. And he wasn't going to get far as he was running out of places to stay.

Happy that he had gone, I beckoned DC Matthews.

"Nobody told me anything about guns," she said accusingly.

"Take it up with your DI. He should have briefed you better. No. I'll do it." Ignoring the look of relief on her face, I continued. "No one goes in there until I have a team of my own secure it."

Sally was already answering my phone as I spoke.

19

(Friday evening)

We had picnicked on the grass at the bottom end of the old sheep fold with fish and chips covered in generous amounts of ketchup and vinegar, piles of bread and butter, followed by sticky buns and builder's strength tea, while the bomb squad checked the caravan for booby traps. As an encore a police forensics team went over it inch by inch looking for all the things that forensics teams look for. DC Matthews enjoyed herself thoroughly, especially as I insisted she act as my liaison. I got to put my feet up and she got to tell everyone what to do. How she managed to organize such an elaborate meal out here is anyone's guess. She would go a long way.

DS Hopper dropped by to get himself up to date and scrounge some food. He seemed to be happy as well, perhaps because I had caused his bosses such grief. When he had finished, he took off again to check on the search for Navarro. The CIA man was armed, dangerous, and probably desperate. People kept interrupting his rest with malicious intent.

We wanted to prevent him getting to any of the usual exits if we could help it. Bus, rail, boats. If he got to one of those he could easily disappear. Not that the surrounding countryside wasn't full of convenient hiding places. Convenient if you were young and not too desperate. Had plenty of ready cash. Navarro, however, was in fear for his life.

Despite that, I had a feeling he wouldn't want to be too far from what was going on. Perhaps he was counting on us and whoever shot Cichy getting in each other's way. Perhaps.

Sally had done a great impression of having a fit down the phone, although I suspect that was more for the benefit of the top floor than for me. She could truthfully tell them she'd read me the Riot Act. I didn't envy her. Having to deal with the top floor of Thames House was bad enough. Having to deal with me as well... Jane Fortune was considerably calmer, and happy that things had developed so that we could keep the case alive.

I wouldn't, in normal circumstances, have called a raid on a caravan a development. Especially as all we seemed to have achieved was picking up Navarro's dirty laundry and Cichy's effects. Still, if it kept me on the road, I was content.

It was a great deal later in the evening when the stars were sparkling in the sky that Sally phoned back with news that the Home Office had granted permission for the exhumations. She must have been at home as she was a lot friendlier. I asked DC Matthews to keep the Suffolk Police Family Liaison Officer in the loop, insofar as there was a loop to be kept in. After that, once everything was quiet and the two uniformed officers had arrived, to watch the caravan overnight, I got her to take me back to Woodbridge Police Station.

My new base was a tiny cottage in the grounds of a bed and breakfast establishment east of the River Deben. It was a cosy little billet with its own access to the road and a view of the Forest. There was food laid on at the main house if I was around. Hopper had done me proud.

Once I had unpacked and familiarised myself with the place, its garden, and the surrounding fields, I drove back into Woodbridge and parked up behind the hotel where I had been staying.

"Hello, sir," said the receptionist as I entered. "I thought you'd checked out."

"Yes. Back to London for me," I lied. "Just dropped by to see if Ms Fiquenet was still here."

I received a coy look for my trouble and a nod. "Do you want me to ring up?"

"It's all right," I said. "It's late. I'll drop by tomorrow before I leave."

Barely concealing her look of disappointment, she smiled again and I wandered out through the front entrance. As I strolled down the pavement I flexed my right wrist. It was still tender from where it had taken the full force of the caravan door.

It wasn't too long before I heard footsteps behind me and I turned to see Laurie Fiquenet. Waiting for her to catch up I had a good look round, but it was just another Friday evening in a provincial holiday town. Police parked up side streets waiting for the pubs to empty, cars cruising, laughter.

We wandered on down to the quayside. "Thought you might have been recalled."

"I was expecting it," she said. "I'd found my boy and could explain why he hadn't been brought home. But then I had to explain why he couldn't go home now."

"I bet your people loved that."

"Not exactly. But it did stir them up."

"Oh? Anything interesting float to the surface?"

I sat on a bench by the Tide Mill. Fiquenet stood looking out over the river. There wasn't a lot to see in the dark. Shapes of boats, a glint of light catching a ripple. Perhaps she was looking to see what might float to the surface here. I'd already seen enough of that.

"It seems there has been a... history... between the Air Force and Cichy and Navarro."

"Go on."

"There isn't a complete profile. But there have been run-ins in the past."

"Criminal?"

"Nothing proven. Never enough evidence. Just suspicions raised and noted by OSI Agents."

"Such as?"

"It's a long list. These boys started in Vietnam."

"With the CIA?"

I already knew but it doesn't do any harm to check.

"Yes."

We both knew what that meant. It was a black ops playground fuelled by drugs in industrial quantities. And that, in its turn, went toward financing all the fun and games in South America – another source of drugs that financed the shenanigans in Russian occupied Afghanistan. And so on. The boys at Langley were a one policy party.

"Woodbridge must have been a bit of a come down for them after that," I said. "Especially when all their buddies must have been heading south of the border."

It was clear there were things she was reluctant to talk about. Orders, perhaps. Who knows? I'd just have to live with it.

"So what sort of things were they suspected of?" I asked again.

"Drugs."

Squeezing the stone. That's what I'd once heard it called. Extracting information from someone who had conflicting orders or loyalties. After all, Fiquenet was ex-CIA. And for all I could tell, she wanted to help me more than she was allowed. I knew all about that. I'd been with SIS before being moved into the Security Service. They might be on the same side, but they constantly watched each other like a pair of un-neutered tom cats meeting in a dark alley.

Tiredness hit me. I had become used to regular hours, a safe office, working within a short train ride of my home, putting my feet up on a Saturday evening. All this running around, colliding with caravan doors and being shot at in cemeteries... Which reminded me.

"I have to go," I said, suppressing a yawn. "I have bodies to dig up and I'm going to need my sleep."

That caught her attention. She turned away from the dark river and looked down at me. "What?"

"Hopper's graves are being opened. I need to make arrangements. No point in your being present at the actual lifting. We want to keep that as low key as possible. But you are more than welcome to the party at the path lab afterwards."

"Gee. Thanks."

I shrugged and stood. She was looking back out across the water again so I left her to it. She'd tell me what she knew in her own good time. Or not. We had resources of our own, when they could be spared.

I'd only gone a few steps when I turned and said, "By the way. We found where Navarro had been staying."

She caught up with me at the level crossing.

"Hell of an afterthought."

"Well I wasn't sure you were taking part in the conversation any more."

"Screw this. Stan and Ollie." For some reason, she cracked a smile. "They were suspected of being into drugs – which went with the territory from Vietnam onward. That didn't make them popular with the Air Force there because too many of their boys were picking up bad habits. But they ran up against OSI at Woodbridge as well. The office there didn't like them and made no secret of it in their reports. But they were always able to hide behind the wire of their own compound and claim that whatever they were up to was clandestine."

"They were legals?"

"Yes, but you know as well as I do that means nothing."

"And the CIA has clammed up in recent days?"

"Big panic. Except my contact doesn't know why. Doesn't want to know why, either."

"So would we be safe in assuming that an operation is in danger of compromise?"

"Geez. That's a big leap. Look. Sorry about earlier. I've got used to being a Special Agent. I like it. Police work. Tracking criminals and getting them put on trial. I found myself back in that limbo... Sent out blind with no one telling you the whole picture. It always did and still does feel like being the sacrificial goat chained out in the open to see what predator takes the bait. You can only do it for so long."

"I know," I said. I knew.

We reached the hotel as the receptionist was closing up. "Just ask yourself," I said quietly, "what kind of operation would get Langley in a panic after forty years? What kind of operation is worth protecting with a hit squad after forty years? Because that's what we've been asking and not coming up with any answers."

She looked at me and frowned, before nodding. "That is just a little scary."

"That doesn't come anywhere near to the nightmares I've been having. Sleep tight," I said and walked on up to the entrance to car park.

20

(Monday)

I had an altogether agreeable weekend in my little country cottage. Plenty of good food courtesy of the main house and my own company, which says a lot about how easily I am pleased. The weather stayed warm and I was able to sit out in the small private garden. It made a pleasant change. I caught up on my sleep and had time to work on easing the stiffness in my right wrist.

It wasn't all fun and games. I re-read the pile of briefing papers that Sally and Jane had put together – a fact that told its own tale if I could have been bothered to think about it. Actually, the thought did cross my mind, but I let it go and shut the door behind it. I didn't feel like spoiling the moment by chasing chimera into shadowy Byzantine byways.

Sally phoned from her office after lunch on Saturday and we spent an hour talking. We went through the arrangements for Monday morning, although it was too late by then to make any changes. And then she got me to explain all over again why I was happy for Navarro to be on the loose. He wasn't going to be able to get out of the country and he would be running out of places to hide before very long. That would give us all a few day's grace because when we went looking for him, I knew that the CIA would be on my tail in one form or another, and I wanted to give it all my concentration.

By Saturday evening I had completed the prize crossword in the paper, which left me feeling what would have been insufferably smug had there been anyone there to be smug at. After that, I had another superb meal, which was something I could get very used to, waistline notwithstanding. Then, with the French doors open and the sweet, warm country air filling the room, I put my feet up and watched *The Thin Man* before turning in.

Sunday was even lazier. I resisted the temptation to go back over the briefing documents. I had the feeling I was missing something, but I knew staring at sheets of paper didn't always make it spring out at you. That was my excuse, anyway, and I was sticking with it. Instead, I went for a slow walk along country lanes and across fields, always conscious of the dark line of the Forest on the horizon. If nothing else, it convinced me that if I was being tailed they were so bloody good, or using a small drone, it wasn't worth me trying to avoid them.

Having worked up an appetite, I went to a pub for a full Sunday lunch. Roast beef with all the trimmings and a very fine glass of ale. After that there really wasn't very much to do but sit down with a copy of *The Mind Readers*, the book I had brought with me. Not much of it got read.

As evening drew on and the light faded, I sat on the step for a while to give myself a chance to wake up properly from my afternoon doze and watched some bats hawking across the garden. When the moths started heading for the lamp in the living room, I closed the windows and pulled the curtains. In the small kitchen, beneath the glare of the neon, I spread out one of the Sunday papers on the table, opened my kit, and cleaned my gun.

They had already started when I arrived on Monday morning. A diaphanous mist haunted the fields and hedgerows, clinging in pale streamers to trees that stretched up into the dawn light. A dove grey sky grew paler above us, the coming heat of the day nascent in the still air. I parked and walked along to the gates of yet another cemetery. It is as well that I am not an imaginative man.

Having eyed the discreetly placed armed policemen with satisfaction and exchanged a few quiet words with DS Hopper, I stood out of the way beneath a youngish tree and watched the proceedings. I could have stayed in bed. There wasn't a lot of point in me being there, but as I was the one that had requested these burials be disturbed, I thought it was the least I could do.

Over the weekend the graves and their surrounds had been subjected to a discreet geophysical survey, courtesy of Suffolk Archaeology. I had hoped they might be able to say for certain whether the graves were properly occupied, in which case I would have called off the exhumations. As it was, the results were inconclusive. So here we were.

One of the junior staff at JICIAID had done wonders putting together information on the two people whose skeletal remains we assumed had turned up in the Forest. The woman had no living relatives that could be traced. The man had distant cousins in Canada. They had been contacted and I bore witness on their behalf.

The exhumation team worked in silence apart from the mini digger which clanked and growled, blowing blue exhaust into the pristine morning air. Its yellow cab matched the overalls worn by the team who stood at a respectful distance around it as it removed the soil from the grave, acolytes at a bizarre ceremony.

When the digger stopped, the silence was momentarily oppressive. It certainly had me looking over my shoulder and along the lane that led past the cemetery. Nothing moved, not even the two policemen at the gate. By the time I turned back, one of the yellow clad men was in the first grave clearing away loose soil, working slowly around the edge of the coffin.

I wondered how much of it would remain after all this time. I wondered if there would be anything at all to see when it was opened except perhaps for a heap of stones. Or human remains. I wondered how long I would keep my job if that turned out to be the case.

While they were preparing the cradle to lift the coffin, one of the team walked quietly to their van and opened the double doors at the rear. I shivered. It was altogether too much like the one that had come to collect Charlie. Perhaps it was. I looked at the number plate, but it meant nothing to me. It should have. It's the sort of thing I was trained to notice. But I'd been a bit distracted at the time and a few years out of the field.

The man in yellow removed a trolley, a sturdier version of the sort used in ambulances, and set it up. This was followed by a long, plain box into which the contents of the grave would be lowered. He fixed it in place with care, double checking everything.

I didn't see the next bit. Once the trolley was alongside the opened grave, they pulled the screens right round. DS Hopper, as an official observer in the event this became part of a criminal investigation, moved himself to a position where he could see what was happening. The engine of the digger started, revved, and then the arm lifted before swinging very slowly to one side. It dipped as its load was lowered into the box.

There was silence for a while. I assumed they were checking to see that the grave contained nothing but soil. The screens shook and were lifted back to reveal the yellow-clad team forming an honour guard around the box.

They escorted it to the van with all the care they would have accorded someone recently deceased.

Although I doubted it, the coffin may have contained someone's mortal remains. Somewhere close by a blackbird began to sing.

The roseate hue that had grown along the eastern horizon burned suddenly with fierce yellow and long shadows lay themselves across the misty landscape. With them came a light breeze with just the faintest tang of sea air. The exhumation team were already at work on the second grave.

There was a long pause after the screens went round and Hopper re-emerged. He looked round, saw where I was standing, and strolled across to me.

"This coffin's in poor condition," he said. "It will take a bit longer to lift it."

We turned and watched a tractor go past, the driver in his high cab craning his neck to try to see what was going on. Hopper shook his head slowly and wandered back to the screens. I found a bench by the hedge and sat down, enjoying the early morning, watching the mist vanish. A little while later the tractor came back.

"Yes, sir," said the uniformed policeman when I wandered over to the gate and asked. "He's a local. Lives just across that way." He pointed across some fields to where a set of barns and sheds were grouped round a house. "Just nosy, I expect."

"OK," I said. "But you see anything or anyone you don't know, you sing out. Loud."

His brow dipped in a quick frown before he nodded.

I went back to the bench and sat down just as the digger started up again and the arm appeared above the top of the screens. As it turned, I took out my phone. I sent a text to Sally, thought about letting Fiquenet know, but put it away. It was early yet, and despite what I'd said, I wanted first look at whatever was on offer.

We went in convoy all the way up the A12, through Lowestoft and on to Gorleston. One armed officer was in the point vehicle, the other rode in the rear. At the hospital we drove round to the back of the buildings and parked up by the Pathology block. It was more like an industrial estate round there – loading bays, pipes, tanks, scores of large yellow bins, and containers. There were laundry trucks and decorator's vans and people standing round in small contemplative groups smoking despite all the No Smoking signs.

As they unloaded the crates containing the coffins, I relented and phoned Laurie Fiquenet. It rang for a while and I looked at my watch. It wasn't much past seven. I let it keep ringing.

"Sorry," she said when she answered. "I was in the shower."

"We've just arrived at the James Paget Hospital in Gorleston. Pathology. They're taking the contents of the graves inside now. It'll be a while before they get started."

"What's the drive like?"

"Straight through. It'll probably be busy in Lowestoft by the time you get there, but it's easy enough otherwise."

"See you soon."

I went in search of Hopper. He was making sure the armed cops were deployed.

"Are they really necessary?" he asked.

"For now. Don't forget that Cichy and Navarro tried to burn this block down. Come on. I'm OIC on this, so stop worrying. I'll buy you some breakfast."

We upheld the finest traditions of policing and intelligence and got lost somewhere on the ground floor. A frighteningly young and frighteningly tired looking doctor pointed us in the right direction. We joined a queue, surveying healthy food as we shuffled along with our trays.

"I miss the old police canteen, sometimes," said Hopper. "There are times when a fried breakfast is the perfect treat."

Over tea and sandwiches we yawned and chatted until Hopper's phone warbled. He listened intently, made a few cryptic remarks, and then switched it off. "Got to go," he said. "Some poor bugger's just found a couple of bodies in Ipswich. As we've got four of their men here, I've to go and assist. Keep me posted."

He made his way out eating the last of his sandwich as he went. A moment later I saw him heading back the other way and he gave a wave and a grin. I took my time. They would only be doing paperwork to begin with.

When I did finally make my way back upstairs to Pathology, the place seemed deserted. The armed policeman had found himself a convenient alcove and watched me for a moment with impassive eyes and then went back to scanning the corridor while I went through the door. Inside it was silent.

Double doors with round windows gave on to the scrub area for the autopsy room. Other doors had plastic labels I didn't understand. Just one was ajar and I knocked.

"Come in."

I went in. That is I stepped through the door and had to stop because there was nowhere further to go. A young woman with strikingly green eyes looked up from the desk. "Can I help?"

"I'm looking for Dr Khurana. My name's Grant," I said, proffering my ID.

"Oh. They're your boxes."

She gave my card the once over and tapped something onto the computer.

"If you mean the exhumations..." She nodded. "Then, yes. My boxes."

"I'm Tarala Khurana." She handed back my little folder and fished around for her ID on its lanyard. "I'll be starting soon. I just have to finish all the preliminary paperwork. I'd offer you a seat."

"Not to worry."

"Won't be a moment." She looked back down at the screen and began typing and using the mouse. I stared at nothing in particular for a couple of minutes. "There. All done. Will you be observing?"

"Yes. If that's all right."

"I'll get you a gown and mask organised."

"A colleague will be here soon as well."

"OK." She smiled and picked up a phone. I wandered back out into the room with all the doors and peered through into the autopsy scrub room again.

"Come on," she said, sweeping through the swing door. "We'll get you fixed up. I'm afraid your colleague will have to join us whenever they get here. I've lots to do today so I'd like to get started."

"Suits me," I said.

An orderly appeared from somewhere on cue. My old flak jacket was put on a hanger and placed in a locker. A moment of awkwardness ensued when my Beretta was noticed in the small of my back and I had to produce my ID again along with my AFO card. When I had finished scrubbing up I was dressed in a gown and mask, cap and goggles. The gloves were held out for me as we went through to the inner room. I felt a complete idiot. I probably looked it as well. So no change there.

"Seems a bit excessive," said Dr Khurana, "but we don't know what we're dealing with and we need to make sure any evidence..." she looked at me and I shrugged. Her eyes narrowed. "Hmm. Any evidence stays uncontaminated by us."

The room was all hard surfaces, tiles and stainless steel, and it sounded a bit like being inside a cutlery drawer. Set out on their trolleys next to adjacent tables were the two boxes containing whatever had been lifted from the graves earlier that morning. The lids had been loosened but left in place.

"If you go over there," pointed the orderly, "you'll be able to see better."

I went over there, out from under the feet of the people doing the work. There were two steps up to a raised section of floor with a metal barrier along its edge and I could see better.

A second orderly appeared. They lifted off the first lid and carried it out of the way. Next, they unclipped the sides of the box and lowered them like some stage magician's trick. I half expected them to turn the trolley through 360 degrees just to prove they weren't hiding any doves.

In the event, it was an unlikely reveal. No glamorous assistant in sequins, just a plain, oak coffin with all the bronze furnishings intact. Forty years in the ground hadn't done it any favours, but oak and bronze are durable.

Dr Khurana measured the coffin and spoke quietly into a small microphone attached to a headpiece. While she worked, one of the orderly's took photographs. The other one had gone, but probably not very far.

Watching them work was an education. They were calm and exact, recording everything and taking nothing for granted. If something puzzled either of them, they stopped to discuss it until they were both happy.

Once the initial descriptions had been recorded, they started cleaning away soil and bagging it. This was also a slow and meticulous process. It put me in mind of the two archaeologists in the Forest. I admired such fortitude. Me, I just wanted to take a crowbar to the lid and see what was in the box.

Laurie Fiquenet turned up just as the orderlies were removing the last of the screws from the coffin's lid. I caught a glimpse of her face peering through one of the round windows in the door from the scrub room. She watched a moment and then disappeared. I asked Dr Khurana to hold on until she came in.

"You made good time," I whispered as she settled beside me at the rail. "Pick up any speeding tickets?"

It was difficult to make out any expressions behind the mask, but I'll swear she scowled. "With no thanks to you," she said.

There was a crack as the lid was prised away from the rest of the coffin and we both leaned forward. Dr Khurana did the same, but she had the advantage of being directly beside the coffin. She looked in. Her head turned from left to right as she scanned the contents. She stood looking into the coffin for a long time before she turned to us.

"What were you expecting to find?" she asked.

"Anything except a body," I said.

"OK. Well… It's anything except a body."

She cocked her head at the coffin and we stepped down from behind the rail and crossed the floor of the room to stand either side of her. We looked down into the long box. I straightened up and looked at Laurie Fiquenet who looked at me in return. It would have made a good comedy routine. Which was just as well as it might have to be my new career.

Laid out neatly along the bottom of the coffin were five packages, more or less filling the space to a depth of about twelve or fifteen inches. Each was wrapped in tarpaulin. There was a heavy, damp stink of oil from a sticky residue that had soaked into the coffin's lining.

Dr Khurana looked at each of us in turn. "Any idea what this might be before we go any further?"

Laurie Fiquenet shook her head and I shrugged. "I doubt it's drugs," I said. "It would be too far degraded to be of any value and not worth all the fuss."

"Explosives?" asked Fiquenet very quietly.

Dr Khurana stepped back so she could see both of us. "Is that a serious proposition?"

"I bloody well hope not," I said. "If it's C4, it's still potent. There's... what... 8 stone. About 50 kilos. Possibly the same in that one." I pointed at the other box.

"C4 is stable," said Fiquenet. "You'd need a proper detonator."

"After forty years," I said, "it tends to be cranky. Ask any Cambodian widow."

"When you two have quite finished." We both looked at Dr Khurana. "If there is the slightest risk that this is explosive we need to evacuate the building. Now."

"It's highly unlikely, but if you want to be certain."

I'm glad I wasn't the one that said it.

Dr Khurana turned on Fiquenet. "Oh, no, it's all right. I'll just go poking around in there with a pointy stick to see what happens, shall I?" She spoke quietly, but the sarcastic edge to her voice was powerful enough to strip paint from steel and polish the bare surface to a mirror finish.

"It's not explosives," I said, with more certainty than I felt. "No one's going to bury that for forty years and then get in a flap about it being found by the authorities. Besides. We've just hauled it out of the ground, bumped it along gravel paths and driven forty miles along British roads. We're all still here."

Nobody said anything.

"You can all go outside if you want."

Nobody moved.

"Shall I?" I asked.

Dr Khurana looked at me for a moment. I tried to exude confidence through my mask. She took a deep breath and crossed to a two-tier medical trolley which she wheeled back alongside me.

When it was in place, I reached slowly into the coffin and eased my hands down either side of the package that rested in the shoulders of the box. There was more room there for me to get my hands all the way down. A bead of sweat rolled into my eye. The salt was sharp and I blinked.

With my fingers curled underneath, I began to lift. Laurie Fiquenet was on the other side, her head low, using a bright torch to look for wires or other obstructions. She shook her head. I lifted some more.

Whatever it was, it was heavy and awkward to hold. The tarpaulin was sticky and dragged against the package on either side. For a moment it stuck and although I was certain it wasn't going to blow up in my face, I could feel my heart hammering in my chest. Just as well I was in a hospital, I suppose.

With a bit of gentle lateral wiggling, the box worked free and slid up. I was able to lift it out and lower it onto the trolley.

We all breathed a bit after that and I tried to moisten my lips. There was nothing to damp them with. Before I lost my nerve, I eased my fingers in under a fold and began to unwrap the oilcloth. It was stiff and sticky, but I managed to unravel it without too much effort, peeling back the overlap to reveal the dull, pale metal of a case.

It was a pilot's case. Made of aluminium. One of those large boxes where the top third is split and the two halves are hinged to swing right back. The lid seemed to have rubber seals. There were heavy duty draw snap-catches securing the lid and a chain with a lockable wrist cuff. On each side of the handle there was a combination lock.

Laurie Fiquenet leaned over the case, looking at it carefully. "Shit."

She said it very quietly and I moved my hands away from it as if it had burned me.

"Sorry. It's OK. It's not explosives." I sagged. "It's something way more dangerous. I recognise the case. They were standard issue. Still are for all I know. For transporting documents."

"Dental records?" Sally sounded like I still felt.

"That's what I said."

"As in brown card envelopes with white card inserts printed up with a diagram of teeth?"

"Yes, Sally. From a dentist. Next appointment, two-thirty. Or, judging by the different handwriting, several dentists."

I stared at the wall in front of me through the silence, conscious of Fiquenet carefully pulling the slightly damp cards apart and peering at the faded handwriting.

"How many?"

"No idea. We've only just got one case open. There were four more in the first coffin. The other coffin's being looked at now."

"And they were in CIA document cases?"

"Well. Cases similar to those used by the CIA. They don't have 'Property of the Central Intelligence Agency, if lost return to Langley, Virginia' stencilled on them."

There was a knock at the door as Sally lapsed into silence again. Fiquenet stood and sidled round the table. Outside there was one of the orderlies with a trolley.

"Four more," said Fiquenet to me.

"Are you alone?" asked Sally.

"No."

Fiquenet gave me a look and I shook my head, pointing to the phone with my spare hand.

"Bring them in. All the boxes. As they are. Lose the American if you have to."

"Bit drastic."

"I want to know what the CIA thought was worth all the damned fuss. Dental records don't sound right to me. The other boxes—"

"OK. I get the picture."

The orderly was bringing the boxes into the small room. As he left, Dr Khurana appeared.

"I have to go, Sally. It's getting crowded here and there's still stuff to do. I'll phone back."

Without waiting for a response, I put the phone away. The orderly left and I looked at the pile of metal cases, the pile of dental records. Despite the relaxing weekend I was beginning to flag.

"So what now?" asked Fiquenet.

"Well," said Dr Khurana, "I need to know what you want me to do in the absence of bodies."

"Can you take this?" I pulled the rest of the records from the opened case, closed the lid and handed it to Dr Khurana. "Test it for... blood... anything."

The Doctor looked at me. She was being very patient. "Anything?"

I held my hands up. "I'm making this up as I go along. I have no idea what you might find. Drugs. That sort of thing. If there's anything to find after all this time. Same with the soil samples, inside of the coffin..."

"All right," she said with a slight shrug. "And I suppose you want the results yesterday."

"To DS Hopper at Woodbridge, please. Send the bill to the Home Office using my number. My department will pick up the tab. And thank you."

She nodded and left pushing the trolley with the case still on it.

"Don't look at me like that. I'm just trying to cover all the angles. What sort of car do you have?" Fiquenet looked at me as if deciding whether to argue the point. "Technically," I said, "these records are the property of the British NHS. You might be happy to tackle MI5, but you really don't want to go up against them."

She grinned. "It's still the black Cadillac Escalade. Parked out front somewhere."

"That big thing still?" She nodded. "Blacked out windows?" She nodded again. "OK. We'll get this stuff back to the police headquarters at Martlesham Heath, if that's OK?" She nodded. "But first, a cardboard box and then something to eat."

We boxed the loose records, locked everything in a steel cabinet and then locked the store room door. I wasn't happy about leaving the stuff. It intrigued me. But I needed food.

The cafeteria was full, as was the rest of the front of the hospital. I went for a time honoured combination from my homeland – macaroni cheese and chips. Plus a bowl of apple crumble and custard.

Fiquenet looked at it in mock horror and then shrugged, choosing the same.

Half way through the meal, I began searching in the little bowl in the middle of the table. After a while I gave up and said, "Can you see if they have any ketchup on the next table?"

"What?" She looked at the bowl. "There's some—"

"And while you're doing that, take in the table on the far side about your current eight o'clock." I kept smiling as I said it.

Fiquenet looked at me for a moment and then turned in her seat, leaning across to the person nearest her at the next table. She turned back to me after a few seconds with a sachet of ketchup, which I mangled before extracting a red dribble.

"Langley boy?" I asked, watching him from the corner of my eye. Big. Close cropped hair. Neat pointy beard. Sunglasses hanging from a cord round his neck.

"Or worse," she said quietly.

She looked at my raised eyebrow. "I did two tours of duty at Balad," she replied. "He looks like military to me. Or ex military. Kinda sticks out here doesn't he."

I couldn't help thinking a bloody great Cadillac SUV with blacked out windows was also a bit of a giveaway, but I didn't mention it. It seemed to pale in comparison with this development. Ex military confirmed what I had feared, that we were dealing with one of the many arms-length private firms used by the CIA. Mercenaries. Completely expendable. Completely deniable. Completely ruthless.

"If he sticks out," I said as I pushed my plate away, "it means he's meant to. And it means the others don't."

I moved straight on to the apple crumble.

*

There was a queue at the cash machine and I did my part to make the queue longer, maxing out three cards as I ignored the tutting of the pair of wiry elderly ladies behind me. Bundling the cash into my pocket and stowing the receipts, I wandered back through the hospital toward Pathology. I didn't need anywhere like as much cash as I'd drawn, but it made it look like I might be planning to go on the run. If it tied them up trying to second-guess my moves all to the good. It wasn't much, but all I could think of at the time.

Stopping at his alcove, I had a quiet word with the armed policeman there. He nodded and I left him to it while I went in search of a trolley. By the time I had found what I was looking for and loaded it, Laurie Fiquenet had driven round to the rear and backed up as close as she could to the mortuary service door.

We loaded the Cadillac through its rear door and I went round to the driver's side and made a fuss of climbing in. Once inside, I slid between the front seats, scrambled over the load, and dropped out the back door as Fiquenet swung it down. By the time she had climbed in the passenger's side and eased across to the driver's seat, I was tucked away out of sight behind a large wheelie bin.

Not long after she had pulled away, the two armed policemen appeared through the door. They stood by the bins, chatting quietly. It looked casual, as if they had been stood down, but they blocked any view of the door and I shuffled through it in a crouch as it closed. So far so good.

A quick word with a passing cleaner had me going in the right direction. I kept my eyes open as I went along the corridor and up some stairs. A radio, cheery whistling, scattered dust sheets and the smell of fresh paint told me I was in the right place.

It took a bit of convincing, but a handful of twenties is always a good persuader. And dressed in a spare pair of bib overalls with a cap pulled low over my face, I drove the ancient decorators' Bedford Rascal to the rear door and loaded it up with the boxes we'd pulled out of the coffins.

I'll swear the van was only held together by the roof rack and some grubby looking twine, but the engine worked which was good enough for me. I squeezed back into the cab and made my way round to the main road, turning north. I took the long and scenic route back round to Lowestoft. By the time I got there, Fiquenet would be closing in on Ipswich with her police escort, unspecified tail, and load of hospital laundry.

21

(Tuesday)

DC Matthews woke me with a mug of coffee, a pile of toast, two aspirin, and a small zip-up case.

I looked at them sideways for a long moment before lifting my head from the keyboard. A pain shot through my neck and I winced as I made it into an upright position. My right hand ached and was still clutched round the mouse. I managed a bleary, "Thank you, Erika."

She smiled and left. I'm not sure she wasn't now laughing somewhere over photos of me on her phone. Whatever lights your bulb, I say.

Flexing my hand, I took a few moments to crawl fully into the land of the living, feeling the stubble on my chin, grateful I hadn't drooled on the keyboard, which had no doubt left a chequered pattern across one side of my face. The air in the room was stale and the lamp burned hot from having been on all night. Somewhere at the far end of the office, a vacuum cleaner started up.

The coffee was hot and the toast was filling, which is all it needed to be, I suppose. The aspirin would need a bit of time. The case went in my pocket for now. I took the last of the coffee down to the car park and got some fresh air. It was meant to wake me up, but all it managed was to make me realise I needed more sleep. And a shower. And maybe a different job.

Hopper was at his desk when I returned, speaking to someone on his phone. He nodded and I waved. Back in the room they had given me, I turned the light on and got back to my task. When I gripped the mouse, all those familiar cramps from school-days returned, but I kept at it. There was still a bit left to do.

I had spent most of the night making high resolution scans of all the documents we had dug up using an A3 scanner that Erika had rustled up from somewhere. It was a tedious job, but Sally wanted it done. In case the CIA asked for their paperwork back. Assuming it was theirs. We'd had a good laugh about that.

Presumably they were busy in Langley discussing whether to claim it as I worked the scanner. Asking for it would put their brand all over it and that risked making us curious. Well. More curious. If they disclaimed it, there was every chance we would give it to a probationer or retired researcher and ask them to assess it. Of course, if it did belong to the Company, we would hand it over. But we still wanted to know what it was. I wanted to know what it was. Because this ancient pile of paper is what Charlie died for.

It was tempting to read them as I worked, but I would never have got anywhere like that. So I stuck with it, scanning, checking each picture for clarity, moving on to the next document, picking up what I could of the content as I went along. Fighting to stay awake.

As well as the dental records, which filled four of the cases, there were notes, memos, reports, petty cash sheets, all the detritus of any bureaucracy. As any agent will tell you, this is a large part of intelligence work. Not just the stuff you have to do as part of your everyday work, but the fact that it creates a paper trail, is part of a narrative. This one was far from complete. But at least it hinted at a story, something that had been lacking until now.

It was a troubling account. There was a lot I didn't like about it. Not least, of course, is that in 1948, the United States of America was a signatory to an agreement it has never officially rescinded. The UK-USA Security Agreement. You can look up the content of the main Agreement, but take it from me, there was a lot more to it than that. And if the story I was unfolding was anywhere near true, it had all been left in shreds decades ago. But that's the trouble with hints and incomplete stories. They can so easily be taken the wrong way.

Which is why, when I had finished making the scans, I fished out the zip up case and opened it up. Inside was a 2TB solid state external hard drive. I plugged it into the computer and made a copy of the documents for myself. I knew it was wrong. I'd been hauled over the coals before for helping myself to copies of information that wasn't rightfully mine. But, as Charlie died for this I wasn't going to let it be pushed sideways into the hands of an inquiry team or lost in the bowels of Thames House. You might just as well douse the stuff with petrol and throw on a match. Which, lets face it, was another likely option.

Mind you, if this is what they had come back for they were either stupid or there was something here that I was missing. If these documents exposed a US operation on UK soil, why not just leave them buried? It was only the subsequent fuss that had led to them. If it had been left alone, the police would have reburied the bodies, had another open file in their system, and it would all have been forgotten in a few days. Even J. J. Pennyweather's mother's concerns about her son, presumably prompted by an item about the skeletons, would not have led AFOSI to anything other than a grave and a suicide.

However, given that Cichy and Navarro had been jumpy enough to spook Charlie and dump his body to try to throw us off the trail; given that someone had subsequently shot Cichy and Navarro was now on the run; given that there had been Russians in town, not to mention the smart boys I'd spotted at the hospital, I would really have to go with the latter.

The trouble was, my feelings weren't enough. And I couldn't get beyond those because I still couldn't see what was worth protecting in this way. OK, the treaty had been breached, but that was ancient history. A strongly worded memo from the DG of the Security Service to the Chief of CIA London Station would have covered it, perhaps with a covering letter from the Home Secretary. But there was something in front of me that said that would not be enough.

I can only put it down to being tired and emotionally involved. That's why the names didn't really sink in to begin with. The dental records weren't collected by place but by patient's name. They had been gathered from a number of different centres and collated somewhere central. Best guess was the Midlands, as that's where Pennyweather thought the lorry had come from. And whoever had gathered them had put them into alphabetical order. That meant there had been no hurry back then. This wasn't something being shut down so much as it was something being wound up. There is a difference.

If they were winding something up, it was because it had come to a natural end and they were quietly dismantling it, putting things in order, shipping out. There was no rush to get on the last helicopter out of the compound; no need to shred stuff. They wanted the records because they wanted to monitor the progress of whatever they had set in motion. And presumably they wanted to keep tabs on these people.

These people. Far too many for a network. And the level of resources and back-up spoke of something else. But if not a network, then what? Why so many people? Why dentists?

You are probably familiar with those puzzles that on first appearance seem to be random splodges of black on white. Stare at them long enough and a picture leaps out at you. Usually when you give up. Your conscious mind stops trying to impose order and the unconscious mind sees the hidden shape. Because there is always a pattern to an operation, a structure that holds it together and makes it work, no matter how hard you try to hide it, no matter how unusual it is.

With me, it was the names. Something nagged. So I went back, not quite certain of what I had seen. That record, for example, was from Edinburgh and covered the first half of the 1970s. A good few records before and I found the one that had passed without properly registering. Oxford. Early years of the 1970s. Possibly coincidence. They were both common names. But what were the odds of so many of the names on the list being so familiar? It was suddenly very cold in that windowless room. Because that is the kind of list that people will kill to protect.

I had finished making my copy, put a password on the disc, tidied and repacked the files, and was sitting in the room lost in thought when DS Hopper knocked and leaned in.

"Email from Dr Khurana."

Stiff and tired, I stood. "That was quick."

"Tell me about it," replied Hopper. "We usually have to wait weeks on serious cases."

We crossed to his desk and I peered at his screen. I read and re-read, but it didn't help. Hopper tapped a number on his landline and then passed the handset to me.

"Dr Khurana?" I asked when someone responded.

"Mr Grant?"

"It is."

"You got my email?"

"I'm staring at it now with a blank expression on my face. Could you manage an explanation using words of maybe just four syllables so we mere mortals can understand?"

I heard a laugh. "You have to remember this stuff has been in the ground a long time. I can tell you what we've found, but I'm not prepared to draw any conclusions from it."

"That's fine by me. This isn't likely to become a police matter."

I saw Hopper stop typing for a moment before he resumed the report he was working on. "Very well," said Dr Khurana in my ear, her voice faint for a moment.

"Safrole oil. Possibly. Or a similar methylenedioxy compound."

"Which means?"

"It is a precursor for MDMA. Ecstasy."

"Forty years ago?"

"There are a host of other drugs that use it. And Safrole oil has been used medicinally for centuries."

"What kind of drugs?"

"Not sure I can manage it in four syllables. There's the substituted methylenedioxy-phenethylamines. Psychoactive drugs that act as entactogens, psychedelics, entheogens, and stimulants."

"Entactogens? What are they?"

"They're also known as empathogens. Things like Ecstacy. Studies have shown that they induce the release of oxytocin, a hormone and neurotransmitter closely connected with social bonding. People who take these drugs say they increase their feelings of empathy and emotional closeness with those around them."

"Is this connected with LSD?"

Hopper had stopped any pretence of typing and was watching me closely.

"They're... cousins, if you like. Some chemical similarities, but a different set of responses. Psychedelics, because they work on perception, have a tendency to make a person focus inward on specifics. Entactogens promote connection."

"Food for thought."

"Possibly."

"OK. Something that might be on the menu. Thank you. Anything else?"

"That was about all we found in the samples we tested. We'll keep going if you want. I'll write up the report and e-mail it to Detective Sergeant Hopper."

"That's great. Thanks."

"And..."

"Yes?"

"We had someone poking around the Path lab last night, just like you said."

"Did you—"

"Yes. I had removed everything from our system. Had someone from IT rig the thing to make it look as if we are scheduled to look at the exhumations tomorrow. Nailed the boxes up nice and tight."

"Were they touched?"

"Not as far as I can tell."

"OK. Thank you, again."

"You're welcome," she said almost as if she meant it and then hung up.

I dropped the handset back into the cradle and stood staring into space. Sometimes I'm not as stupid as I look. Or feel.

"You all right?"

I looked down at Hopper. "Hmm? Oh. Yes. Just thinking. Did it look that painful?"

He grinned. "Have you slept much lately?"

"No. Sounds like a plan to me, though. There'll be a follow-up e-mail from Dr Khurana at some stage. Read it if you want. And can you copy that to..." I patted my pockets, but didn't find any cards. Instead I scrawled an e-mail address on a post-it note.

"Will do."

"And that stuff in there," I pointed to the room where I had been working. "Any chance it can go in the evidence locker until I take it to London?"

He looked at me for a moment. "We'll squeeze it in."

"Thanks."

I made my way down to the car park, turned my collar up against the warm, misty drizzle and made for my car.

22

(Tuesday evening)

Intelligence is a long, slow game. Mostly. It is about observing what everyone else does, especially the stuff they don't want you to watch. It is about looking for patterns and associations, trying to make predictions. Any intelligence officer will tell you it is a thankless task because most of the time you are looking at stuff that is irrelevant, and often you miss the stuff that is important. And the only time the outside world notices you is when you get things spectacularly wrong.

That's because everyone else is doing the same thing. Not only do they run general interference that is meant to misdirect and confuse, when they set up specific operations, they try to devise things that have no pattern or discernible associations. They want you to see disparate black splodges on a white background and miss the hidden picture.

Into this mix you throw the sort of operation I was on. Full of wild cards. There is little or no time to observe and make measured responses. Instead, you put in an experienced field operative who has a good instinct. Which means he is still alive and uncompromised. Then you let him play his instincts and react according to the best training you can give him.

Of course, this does not take into account random acts of madness or the idiocies of any of the parties involved. I had assumed that Navarro would have made his way to a fall back, maybe even fished out a false passport and been on a plane back to Virginia with a legend already prepared in case his bosses got curious. Of course, I was forgetting he had come in on his real passport. Or his work name passport. That's how we picked up his entry to start with.

Perhaps he'd assumed that openness was the best cover. It can work. But he and Cichy hadn't bargained with us, our long memories, and our suspicious natures. Or the inept bastard at Thames House who had sent a bright, young intelligence analyst out to his death in the field. Or that bright, young analyst's very angry friend.

And there were other players in the mix as well. Because Cichy and Navarro had upset their bosses. Big time. But hindsight is always a great way in which to view things. I should have kept all this in mind along with the consequences of what Navarro and Cichy had done both forty years ago and in the last few weeks. But I didn't. Not properly.

Alarm bells did begin to ring when I was woken by my phone. Hopper told me that one of their local patrol cars had been called to an incident and picked up a dishevelled man who had been trying to steal food and found himself facing the wrong end of a farmer's shotgun. By the time I had established it was the thief who had found himself at the wrong end of the gun and not the police, I was heading for the bathroom.

The alarm bells weren't loud then. Perhaps I mistook them for that touch of tinnitus I have had since a Russian gun went off next to my ear in Palmer's Green. Perhaps I just wanted to talk with Navarro to see if I could confirm any of my suspicions. Perhaps I just wanted to look in the face of one of the men who had dumped Charlie in the river.

I hadn't completely lost it, though, and before I set out, I made some arrangements of my own with Hopper and with Thames House. I sincerely hoped they wouldn't be needed, hoped they would be ready in time if they were. Because one thing was certain. If Navarro had been mentioned in any way over a police radio, the ghost unit whose shadows we had barely seen except when they wanted us to, would know all about it.

It wasn't far. I cut past Rendlesham Forest and then headed for the coast. On the way I took a call from Sally which we pretended hadn't taken place. Once in Orford I parked outside *The King's Head*. Hopper was already there. He got out of his car as I drew up then led the way. We crossed the quiet street and went past the board that proclaimed St Bartholomew's and the tourist signpost that pointed back toward the castle and off to the right toward the harbour.

It was a beautiful village. Comfortable. Warm red brick and roof tiles settled between the trees. I had been here once before. With Lesley. A day out from Aldeburgh just up the coast. We had been on a literary pilgrimage. Visited the post-apocalyptic landscape of Orford Ness just across the river. Climbed Orford Castle. And then spent the following week in Essex down at Tolleshunt D'Arcy. But that was a long time ago.

As we headed up the High Street, I could hear someone walking quickly behind us, familiar foot-steps trying to catch up.

"I think you've been followed," said Hopper quietly.

"I think I have," I replied.

How she had found me, I don't know. I thought I'd lost her. It had been annoying seeing her outside the cottage, sitting in that bloody great Cadillac, advertising to all and sundry where we both were. That's why I had ignored her and sped off, leaving her with a three point turn in a narrow lane. Oh well.

The old police station was a solid redbrick affair, a comfortable looking building that probably hadn't seen anything exciting since 1945 and was now closed, up for sale. The windows were boarded up, weeds grew in the front garden, and the whole place looked forlorn. The front door was unlocked from inside as we approached. A uniformed Sergeant looked up from his East Anglian Daily Times and smiled as the constable closed the door behind us.

"Afternoon, sir," he said to Hopper. "Not been in here for a while."

He flicked a glance back to the door as it opened again.

"She's with us," I said without turning round. I'd swear I could feel her sour smile hit me between the shoulder blades.

"Best lock up," I said to the bemused looking constable when Fiquenet was in.

He turned the key and slid the bolts across.

Hopper knew his way around and led us through the deserted building. I'd wanted Navarro kept well away from the system for now and under wraps as much as possible. The sergeant who had greeted us was the arresting officer and seemed at ease playing along with the shenanigans of the spooks. It got him back into his old station. He was happy.

There wasn't a lot to the building. The public section looked for all the world like an old-fashioned bank. A counter with a grille separated the reception area from the office. The sergeant buzzed us through a hefty door and made sure it was closed behind us. Hopper helped himself to a set of keys from the desk.

"Do you have a safe, Sergeant?"

He looked at me and nodded. I drew my gun, ejected the magazine, emptied the chamber and fed the round back in with the others. The Sergeant looked at Hopper who shrugged and said, "It's all above board."

We watched as the Beretta was locked away, then edged round a desk to an open door that gave on to a short corridor. On the left were stairs to the station sergeant's flat above, an open cupboard that housed a few spiders, and a nearly closed door behind which a cistern could be heard gurgling. There was a tiny kitchen as well, big enough to make tea and re-heat takeaways. There was still a kettle in there.

Opposite these there was just the one door. That was open as well. An all-in-one table with benches was bolted to the floor. On the table, against the wall, was the mains wiring for a DVD/tape recording unit. It didn't take much guessing to work out that it had been the interview room.

Our feet clacked on the worn lino and the air was heavy with the stale scent of cheap polish and cheaper disinfectant. The corridor turned to the right and we were faced with a closed door of vertical bars. Hopper unlocked this and we went through. He closed the door and locked it behind us.

There were four cells, two on either side. Three of the doors stood open. The fourth, the furthest on our right, contained Navarro.

I dropped the letterbox peephole cover and stared in. The CIA agent lay on the bed, asleep. A tray was on the floor by the bed. Empty fish and chip wrappings added their own bouquet to the unforgettable and unlovely aroma of the place.

He jerked upright at the sound of the key turning and was swinging his legs round as we entered the small room. He tried to look unimpressed, but he was tired and a wash of the face hadn't done much but highlight how dirty the rest of him was. It was a long time since he'd had to slum it in the field, albeit that field was in Vietnam.

"You," I said, "are in a deep pile of shit."

"Says who."

"For starters, the police," I said and saw Hopper grin in an altogether feral fashion I hadn't suspected him capable of. "Then British Intelligence. That would be me. And then there are your people back home."

"She's not CIA."

"Not any more," said Fiquenet. "I'm with the Air Force these days."

Navarro's sneer seemed to have got stuck on the front of his face. Perhaps he was calculating odds.

"So who do I get to dance with first?"

"That," I said, "would be me."

I looked at Hopper who held my gaze for a while before heading out of the cell. "I'll see about brewing some tea."

"How about you give him a hand?" I asked Fiquenet.

Like the gentleman I am, I waited until she was through the door and out of sight. Then, with a smile, I let my anger give me strength. Stepping forward I grabbed clothing in each hand, hauled Navarro off the bed, and threw him against the end wall.

He looked surprised more than anything else, gazing up at me from where he had slumped to the floor. Not as surprised as me. He was a big man and it had been a noisy fall.

"Everything all right in there?" It was Hopper, calling from the kitchen. His voice was casual, but I doubt he was happy.

"Just making room to sit down," I called back. "It's going to be a long session," I added for Navarro's sake. "And that, in case you were wondering, was for slamming the caravan door into my face." I smiled a thin smile. "Just wait until we get onto the really personal stuff."

He didn't look convinced, but he didn't do more than sit up with his back against the wall. I wasn't out to hurt him. Much. Just shake him out of his arrogance and get his attention.

We sat like that until Hopper re-appeared in the doorway. "Interview room?" he asked.

"OK. On your feet, Navarro."

"Am I under arrest?" he asked as he struggled up.

"It can be arranged," said Hopper. "What would you like? Malicious damage. Leaving the scene of a crime. Not reporting a murder. Attempted murder. Suspicion of murder."

Navarro shrugged, but he followed Hopper through to the interview room. There was nowhere else to go.

A couple of extra chairs had been put in the room and there was a tray on the table with plastic mugs of tea. Steam rose in pale, lazy columns. Navarro squeezed himself onto the fixed bench opposite Hopper. Fiquenet grabbed a chair and sat down behind Navarro. I stood by the door. When everyone was settled, I closed the door.

"I want—"

"What? A lawyer?" I asked. Navarro didn't say anything. "Someone from the Embassy, then?" Still he didn't talk. "Oh. I know. Chief of London Station. I know him well. Meet him once a week after the JIC meeting."

"You're on your own, pal," said Fiquenet quietly.

He looked at me and then at Hopper. Hopper smiled. I think Navarro was finally beginning to get the idea.

"So how about you answer a few questions, fill in a few details? Who knows? If you give me enough, I might just see what I can do to tuck you away somewhere safe."

There was a very long pause after that. It never does to get your hopes up in a situation like this, as interrogators will lie their balls off to get you to talk. But this was different. He knew he was comparatively safe here. And I might just be telling the truth. It had been known.

He studied his hands for a while and then looked up at me, waiting. I grabbed the other chair and settled myself at the end of the table between him and the door.

"What happened after Vietnam?"

"Huh?"

"Where were you posted?"

"Langley."

"Not for long," I said.

"Not for long," he agreed.

"I bet you loved Suffolk after all that."

"Listen, kid—"

"Don't try the hard guy stuff with me," I said calmly. "I spent years in East Germany and Czechoslovakia when there was still a fence, minefields, and killing fields to cross. And then I spent many more years in a nasty little civil war that you people could have cut the funding to overnight. So don't give me any of that shit."

Fiquenet had stood silently as I talked and stepped up behind him. "Play nice," she whispered in his ear. Navarro jumped and tried to twist in his seat. He couldn't manage it in the narrow space. Fiquenet sat down again.

"Suffolk," I said. "Tell me about Woodbridge AFB."

"What's to tell?"

"The CIA compound. What was its function?"

"I can't tell you stuff like that." He actually sounded outraged.

"OK," I said. "I'll tell you. Centre for CIA operations in Eastern Europe and Russia. Centre of operations and quartermaster stores for European stay-behind and roll-over networks in case of a Soviet invasion. One of the bases for U2 flights. Not used that often as the plane would hit Soviet radar before it got to operating height, but a useful fallback landing field. Also a home for one or two of the less savoury projects that met with Congressional disapproval. MK Ultra, for example."

"Ultra?" He looked puzzled. So did Fiquenet. "Ultra was closed down."

I shook my head. "No. Paperclip. Chatter. Bluebird. Artichoke. Delta. Ultra. Search. These things just evolve. One project gets closed down and reopens somewhere else with a different name, remit, and all the original research and most of the same personnel. Ultra paperwork was supposed to have been destroyed. Except it wasn't. Was it?"

"I don't know."

"Really? So you weren't a very high ranking officer then. You just followed orders. What do you know?"

Fiquenet was leaning forward in her chair by this time. Whether it was to catch an answer from Navarro or because of what I had said, I didn't know. Hopper just looked on with an impassive expression that he'd lowered into place when we came into the room.

"Tell me about the Forest."

"We came back for old time's sake." I wanted to know about forty years ago, but at least he was talking. Even if it was garbage.

"You and Cichy?"

"Yeah. We thought we'd have a look round the old joint. Have some warm beers. Talk over old times."

"In the Forest at midnight."

There was just the tiniest intake of breath there, but it was enough for me to know that I was finding a way in. It let him know that I knew. And every time I scored one of those, he would be left wondering just how much he could bend the truth and get away with it.

Hopper put his head on one side. It wasn't a big movement, but gave the effect of him looking at something through glass in the zoo, waiting to see how it would react to being poked with a stick.

"I suppose you mean the bodies they found."

"Something like that."

"We got curious. Saw it in the paper. Went to have a look."

"Saw it in the paper."

"Yes."

"Where? Which paper? McLean Connection? USA Today? Did it get into the Washington Post?"

"The Evening Star."

"Oh? But surely the story was run before you got here. Pick up an old copy at the local chippy?"

"Stefan. It was Stefan. He always kept an eye on the local press here."

"And it was the story of the bodies in Rendlesham Forest that brought you to the UK?"

Navarro shrugged. "If you say so."

"I do."

"So you go into the Forest. Late at night. Why? Why stumble about in the dark?"

His eyes flicked back and forth from me to Hopper. He eased himself in his seat, but he didn't look any more comfortable than before.

"I'll tell you, shall I?" I asked. "It's very simple. You didn't want to be seen. You didn't want to risk there being someone at the site. And to be doubly sure, you walked up through the Forest from the Capel Road. How am I doing so far?"

He wasn't moving any more; wasn't trying to look at anyone.

"When did you realise you had a tail? Was it then, or was it up in the Forest when you were looking at the site where the skeletons had been found?"

I gave him the chance to answer. I gave myself the chance to adjust the pressure valve.

"There's been so much going on, perhaps you're a little confused about events. Maybe you thought it was a deer. Who knows? It could just have been kids from the nearby camp site," I yelled, slamming a fist on the table. The cups jumped a fraction.

"It was Stefan."

"It was Stefan," I mimicked, a whine in my voice. "We'll ask him, shall we? Oh. We can't."

"He was always trigger happy. Guess that's why we got the pencil." He paused a moment. "We heard something when we were standing by those trees that were down."

"So you chased?"

"Stefan loosed off a couple of rounds high in that direction and we heard someone running."

"Did you hear him die? In the woods. Afraid. A long way from his wife and kid."

"You're breaking my heart."

Hopper sucked air over his teeth and narrowed his eyes. "Wrong answer," he said and stood. He picked up the tray of untouched drinks. The door to the interview room closed quietly behind him as he left.

"Deep shit," I said, barely controlling the urge to rip his throat out. "And I'm still your best hope."

"We didn't mean for anyone to get hurt."

"No? You just heard about some bodies in the woods and flew all the way from America to have a look. And then some poor fool stumbles across you in the woods."

"It's not very convincing is it," said Fiquenet from her corner.

"Of course, you could have reported it to the police. 'Oh dear, officer, we were taking a moonlit walk in the woods for old times sake and stumbled across a corpse.' But you didn't, did you? You bundled the poor sod up and drove to the nearest river where you threw him in. Did you bother to check whether he was still alive?"

"Seems to me you had something to hide."

Navarro made no attempt to turn to see Fiquenet. He was getting used to the technique.

"The question is, what? Going for a walk in the woods isn't going to raise eyebrows anywhere these days, especially if it was just to gawk at a crime scene. So tell me about forty years ago. Did you see the flying saucer?"

"What?"

"You were in the woods, several nights running. Just after Christmas 1980."

That got his interest, although he tried hard to conceal it. "What makes you say that?"

"Witnesses. Locals."

A flicker of the eyes. An attempt to clear his throat without anyone hearing.

"Three," I added. "In different parts of the Forest. They didn't know what they had seen, but they sure as hell knew they had seen it. And then there was all that flummery about the UFO. Your idea, was it? No matter. They kept quiet, those witnesses. Wise people. It was only when what they had seen was put together in the right order. It was only when someone else came along, investigating the death of a British Intelligence Officer—"

That was when Hopper came back in. I was all ready to curse him, but maybe he'd been listening.

"Sorry to interrupt," he said. I watched Navarro, saw the tension ebb a fraction. "Just been checking out reports of some shady looking types checking over cars in the town."

Navarro didn't like that. I can't say I was that happy, but he lost a good deal of colour from his face. I stood and turned to Hopper, putting a question into my face. He gave a faint nod.

"Won't be a moment," I said and left the room.

In the office, the uniformed Sergeant looked up from his paper.

"The DS says there have been some gentlemen casing motors."

"Ah. That they have."

"OK. Can I have my gun from the safe, please?" An eyebrow rose over his left eye. It looked comical, which I'm sure is a mistake a lot of local yobs had made in the past. "In case we decide to leave in a hurry," I added.

"I sincerely hope there isn't going to be any trouble."

"So do I, Sergeant. So do I."

He took some keys from a drawer and slid them along the desk to me.

I was pushing the magazine home as I came through the doorway of the interview room. Hopper got out of my chair and slid into the bench opposite Navarro as I closed the door. The slide moved easily as I fed a round into the chamber and smiled at Navarro who looked truly nervous for the first time. I dropped the hammer, put on the safety, and slid the gun into its holster in the small of my back.

"Friends of yours?" I asked, still smiling.

"What?"

"In the town."

He shook his head.

"I hate interruptions, don't you? You have to go all the way back to the—"

"You said there were witnesses."

"Oh yes. Natives. You'll know all about that, having served in Vietnam. Stories of how the VC would sit down at a table next to soldiers and share their food before heading back into the jungle. Stories of how they could blend into the foreground, how patrols could walk within six feet of them and never see them. Until it was too late."

"Ghost stories," he said. "Made up by frightened kids."

"Oh, but there's always a kernel of truth. Someone watched you in the Forest all through the winter of 1980. You and Cichy. And you didn't see them once, did you. They put it all in a detailed diary. Of course, they didn't know who or what they were seeing and everyone else thought they were a bit touched. They were afterwards. Right out of their head for months. Never the same after that."

"Oh? And what was the 'that'?" asked Fiquenet, for all the world like I was telling a story at a camp fire.

"Well, you see, this is where it gets a bit hazy. One of the witnesses. The witness to that bit. The crucial bit. Do you know? He got his brains blown out. With an Air Force issue Colt .45."

"Funny," said Fiquenet. "I could have sworn you told me they got the wrong guy." She was good at this.

"Oh yes. That's right. Slipped my mind. So tell me, Mr Navarro, just to clear up a few details you understand, what happened to the lorry? What happened to the crew? Just what was it that caused all that fuss in the Forest?"

He made a real effort this time and turned to look at Fiquenet. "No good looking at me," she said. "There's a rock and there's a hard place. Oliver Navarro somewhere between. The Brit really is your softest option right now."

The Brit smiled. He wasn't especially happy, but he smiled.

"Off the record?" Navarro asked after a while.

"It will all be hearsay," I said.

You can never tell how someone's mind works in these situations. Tough ones crack easily. Timid folk can become blindly stubborn. People who have been straight and honest all their lives start lying like there's no tomorrow, even when the truth would be the better option. All sorts of factors get to work. All you can do is try to find their weak points and exploit them.

I am not a trained interrogator. I could have had Navarro shipped to one of our places for a polite and prolonged chat, but I didn't think we had time for all that. Besides, the Americans would be all over us with extradition documents. It was more likely they already planned to go for the black van option – the quaintly termed extraordinary rendition.

So all we could do is wait while he made his mind up. Hopper escorted him to the bathroom and I began to worry he was stalling. I took some comfort from the fact Fiquenet didn't look too worried. She did more of this sort of thing than me. But then she usually had time on her side. And she might be playing her own game.

While Navarro was away from us working out the odds, figuring the angles, looking for a way out, and admiring the British plumbing, the rest of us made arrangements of our own.

With Navarro safely back in his seat, Hopper got the Sergeant to sort out some food supplies in case it turned into an all night session. It turned up shortly afterwards, discreetly, in the shopping bags of three local women. Pies and chips for our tea. There was extra milk as well. More tea bags.

While Hopper and Navarro ate in the interview room, I gave the nod to Fiquenet and we went to the kitchen to make a brew.

"Your assignment has been compromised," I said quietly as the kettle boiled.

She looked puzzled. "Someone looking at the vehicle—"

"It's not just your car. My people have had a request from the CIA for the documents. They didn't learn about them from me or Hopper."

"The hospital."

I shook my head. "I made sure of that."

"Shit."

"I'm assuming the team out there are the same ones who shot Cichy."

"I want to get Navarro and the papers to Providence Court."

I shrugged. "It's a long way to London. Let's just get him to talk first. Take it from there."

We settled back into the interview room where the odour of chips, vinegar, and sweat added a piquant layer to the background of pine disinfectant. Hopper switched the lights on. They flickered, dimmed and then flooded the room with a hard, greenish light.

"Your call," I said.

"I want protection. If I give what I know."

"Give what you know and I'll tell you what it's worth."

"He's still your best bet," said Fiquenet quietly, settling down to listen.

"It's worth protection."

I watched Navarro. He was still struggling. A lifetime of working with secrets, a lifetime of guarding your own back and hoarding what you have in order to give you an edge. Perhaps I was like that. Not that I knew much that was worth being chased round the country and getting shot at. Not any more.

Rubbing my right shoulder blade against the chair back to ease the itching of the scar, I waited. I had been out there in the cold, where he was. But I felt no sympathy. I didn't even know whether that should worry me.

"Our pension. It was meant to be our pension."

"Drugs?"

"Money."

"How so?"

"Cash."

"You're going to have to fill in the details."

"You're right about Ultra. We didn't know at the time. If we had, we'd have stayed well clear."

"So what was your job at Rendlesham?"

"Stefan, me, and a clerk, we ran the materials co-ordination office. For the CIA in the UK."

"I thought that was done out of London Station."

He swallowed. "The legal stuff, yeah."

I saw Fiquenet tense. It's a fine distinction between legal and illegal. A legal is an intelligence agent who has an official position as their cover. They usually work out of an embassy as an attaché, clerk, even a driver. Then there are units like the ones based at Rendlesham. Out stations, numbers stations, listening posts, operational centres for handling agents in and out of hostile territory. Illegals are all the rest. Some intelligence services pay lip service to these distinctions, and often the legals are there to run interference so that the illegals can get on with their work quietly.

It only becomes a problem when two countries have a pact. Like the US and the UK. There shouldn't be illegals working in the UK. They do of course, and always have done. Just as we have illegals in the States.

As long as the CIA restricted their target list to transitory non-nationals, we usually let them get on with it. It saves on our resources. Navarro's hesitance seemed to suggest these weren't those kind of illegals.

"You're racking up points," I said. "Go on."

"You don't get all the details, but you can work things out. Especially if you've been in the field yourself."

"Like you and Cichy."

"Sure. If a group needs certain items, it's fairly obvious from their list of requirements what they are involved with. We saw all sorts of stuff go through that office over a period of years."

"Good at it?"

"I guess. They kept us there a long time. And you start to see patterns, work things out."

"Such as?"

"An operation can take a long time to put in place, so you don't always notice. Money here. Equipment there. Stuff comes in. Stuff goes out. It gets moved around as well and you don't know about some of that."

"Drugs?"

"Like I say. Some stuff you don't know about."

"Money."

He nodded.

"Your pension."

"That was the idea."

"Must have been one hell of a pile."

"Four point two million."

Hopper whistled very softly.

"Dollars or pounds?"

"Pounds."

"And you're still working?" Navarro shrugged by way of an answer. "It's a serious amount of jam, even now. Back then. Enough to seed a..."

He looked at me and I looked back. It seems he wasn't prepared to say. Feed me information. Let me draw my own conclusions. Let me confirm my suspicions. I could live with that.

"What?" asked Hopper.

"How's your recent history?" I asked him.

"Never was my strong point."

"I've been reading some interesting analysis over the last few weeks. There was a point when it seemed we might get a majority Labour government that would push through nuclear disarmament and push for the removal of US nuclear weapons from UK soil. It didn't last long, because there was a downturn in the economy and a great deal of civil unrest."

"Power cuts. Miner's strike. All that."

"That's right. But it was much more than that," I said, looking at Navarro. "There was a suspicion at the time that it was co-ordinated..." I tailed off, literally light-headed at the implication of what I was thinking. Not just for the past, but for the now. The right now. "We were so obsessed with the Soviets we looked in the wrong direction and we didn't find anything of note. Pocket money into a few Trade Union accounts, cut price printing, cheap office space. Peanuts." I thought about it a bit more. "Even if anyone had thought to look in the right direction, it would have done no good. The people who cooked this up were far too practised."

"Are you serious?" asked Hopper. "All that stuff was..."

"Orchestrated. That's the word you're looking for. All the players were there and willing to act. It just needed someone to make sure it had the maximum required effect."

"Which was?"

"The election of the Conservative government in May 1979. Headed by a right-wing ideologue."

"Are you seriously suggesting that Maggie Thatcher was elected because of American interference?"

"Not directly. All they wanted was a right leaning government. Didn't matter who was in charge."

Hopper shook his head slowly. "I don't buy it. You can't keep that sort of thing secret."

"You don't have to because it was never the stated objective of a formal operation. And regime change is an old game as far as the CIA is concerned."

"But here?"

"Why not?" I let that sink in. "I suspect there were two strands to this. The first part contributed to the unrest that saw the Labour government thrown out on its ear. That would have been a very subtle matter of co-ordinating a nudge here, a whisper there, a discreet conversation with a newspaper owner somewhere else. That's all that was needed. But it was never a forgone conclusion. Had a Labour government been re-elected, there would have been real fun and games, especially if they had tried to push through disarmament."

Hopper was frowning, staring down at some point far past his shoes. He was probably trying to imagine civil unrest on that order and not liking what he saw. As a copper he would have been in the front line of a very dirty little war. It would have made the miner's strike look like a junior school playground squabble.

"But we got a Conservative government. One that famously loved all things American. So, when things had settled down, the CIA decided to dismantle the structure of the other strand of the operation. Stand down its agents, recall the materiel. How am I doing, Navarro?"

"Don't much see why you need me here. I might as well just..." He looked at the door.

I managed half a smile. "Nice try."

"So where's this going?" asked Fiquenet.

"The trucks. It wasn't just that one, was it?" Navarro shook his head. "How many?"

"They were coming in all year. We worked out a system that would avoid it looking like a regular pick up run."

"Is that why you brought stuff in by the Night Road to the back gate?"

"Sure. Sometimes. There was officer accommodation by the main gate so a forest road had already been designated as the Night Road to avoid disturbing base personnel. The East Gate was always manned. But like I said, it was also to avoid too much stuff coming through the main gate."

"Which the Russians watched."

"I guess."

"And where, more to the point, the RAF liaison office was."

He shrugged.

"And you knew what was on the trucks?"

"Mostly. We had to work out what would fit. Documents were done by the case load, but we never knew the contents. Same with cash. We knew which shipment, although we were never told the amounts. But it didn't take much to work out what a full case would carry."

"So how did you do it? That night."

"An old trick. There's a spot on the Night Road where you can't be seen from either end. We undermined the road. It was concrete laid onto the soil.

So we dug a channel and made it look like water had done the job. Not that anyone investigated. We kept it propped up with sawn logs. Plenty of those about. Took them out that evening and stacked them, like you see in other parts of the Forest."

"But you didn't wait in the Forest."

The laziness went out of his eyes. I cursed myself silently. It never does to reveal too much of what you know.

"No. The trucks had radios. If there was a problem they called it in. We fixed the frequency on the truck so it called us rather than the base. Went down to where it had tipped over." He faltered, spent a long moment thinking, perhaps wondering just how much we already knew. "That's when it began to go wrong."

"How do you mean?"

He sighed. "The truck was only meant to have paperwork in its load. Mostly cash. But there was all sorts of other stuff. It was a real mess in the back."

Fiquenet raised an eyebrow at me. I shook my head a fraction. She could have her turn later. If he wanted to leave the issue of four dead bodies out of it for now, I was willing to go along. Because that's the only way the ambush would have worked.

"What kind of stuff?"

"God knows. Bottles and vials. All smashed. Dripping liquid everywhere. It lit up with a bang, though. We got the stuff out we wanted. All the document cases. Swapped them, like for like."

"Like for like?"

"We adjusted the manifests. It was Christmas. There wasn't a CIA flight due back Stateside for a couple of weeks. We took document cases stuffed with old paperwork; put it in the back of the lorry."

"And kept all the ones with cash in."

"That was the plan."

"You think someone was on to you?"

"Would I be sitting here now?"

"So you emptied what you wanted from the lorry. Then what?"

"Kerosene. Flare. Woomph."

His eyes went out of focus for a moment. He came back to us quickly, but it looked like it had been a very long time to him. I hoped it was a particularly vicious nightmare he had been watching somewhere on the inside of his head.

"Stuff in there burned fierce," he said. "Real fierce. Must have been a whole pile of stuff in there."

"Entactogens and hallucinogens."

"Yeah. I only caught a whiff but, Jeez, I was high. Stefan didn't catch as much, but his feet were off the ground as well. I really don't remember much after that. Not what you'd call proper remembering. We pieced it together afterwards."

"Where did you take all the stuff you'd unloaded?"

"We had a station wagon on a fire road just uphill from the crash site. Everything got loaded into that. Just as well we did it before we torched the truck. We drove off to a cottage we had. I guess some other part of the brain takes over. I don't know how we made it there."

"You nearly didn't, according to one witness. He saw you come out of the Forest driving like a maniac. Phoned the police. They couldn't trace you."

"Lucky, I guess."

Four dead, a hijacked lorry ablaze in the Forest spewing out hallucinogenic and entactogenic fumes, and all he could think about was how lucky they were to get home. A real piece of work.

"How long before you discovered you didn't get what you thought you were going to get?"

"Next day. We slept a few hours. Woke up in some way out wonderland. Opened the cases. Fucking dental records."

"Anything else?"

"About twenty thousand in cash, if that's what you mean."

"And? Come on. Dental records. They made you panic?"

He got shifty, fidgety. "Dental records. That was enough."

"Yeah. That and the drugs. You knew what that meant, didn't you. Did you look at the names on the records?"

"Are you crazy? We might have been high, still, but we weren't stupid."

"So you went into the back garden of your cottage and burned them."

"You know what we did with them."

"Why?"

"We panicked. We were full of acid and that other stuff. What we did... It seemed like a good plan at the time."

"And in the meantime, the Air Force came to see what the glow was in the woods."

"Jeez. They must all have got a face full. Do you know the Forest? I do. Fucking years we spent there. Smoke and mist hangs in the trees. It doesn't blow away. The only thing that got blown away was those kids' minds."

"Is that why the UFO story was put out?"

"Yeah. That was the Research division. It was their stuff in the lorry. They pulled all those kids in and got to work on them. Found out what they thought they might have seen in the woods and played on that."

"High risk, wasn't it?"

"Who was gonna believe it? Except people no one else would take seriously."

"So you got ten thou apiece."

"Yeah. Some retirement fund. I really need the can again."

Hopper went with Navarro. I sat back in my chair, stretched my shoulders, and stared at the ceiling.

"You finished?" asked Fiquenet.

"If you mean have I had as much as I can take then, yes. Just about." I checked my phone for texts and nodded to myself. "We can get him up to London now if you like."

"I like. There's a lot of detail I want filled in. Specially those kids in the lorry."

"Oh, that's bound to be down to Stefan Cichy."

"No shit."

When they returned, I tipped the wink to Hopper who wandered off muttering something about a man and a dog. Navarro slid himself into the bench. Perhaps we should paint his name on the back.

"One thing puzzles me," I said.

"Just the one?"

He must have caught the look on my face as he put his hands up in a gesture of surrender.

"How did you know about Pennyweather so soon?"

He grimaced. "The kid made it easy, asking around the base after the..."

I let him falter. He'd have to face up to all that sooner or later. Probably a lot sooner than he wanted. I was happy to let him think otherwise. But a little turn of the screw wouldn't hurt just now.

"Not back then. Now. A few days ago. In the graveyard. You must have known who he was or you wouldn't have tried to silence him. Again."

I'd have given him an Oscar for it if I'd thought it was acting. After he had stared at me for long enough to know he wasn't going to get any more, he strained round in his seat and looked at Fiquenet.

"What's he talking about?"

"You tell me," she said. "I was there. Someone shot at Pennyweather."

He gave her about the same amount of incomprehension before turning back to me. Pennies began to drop for Navarro.

"Jeez."

"A warning?" asked Fiquenet.

"Since when did they give a warning? The boys and girls at Langley haven't been sitting on their backsides all this time. Someone there figured out what was going on and saw Pennyweather as a threat."

"A threat? He didn't know anything."

"He knew a British subject had been murdered by the CIA," I said. "That would be enough, don't you think?"

Hopper had appeared in the doorway. "All ready," he said.

"Thanks." I turned to Navarro. "We're moving."

"I like it here."

"Shame. Say goodbye. Hands on the table."

Navarro frowned. Hopper produced a pair of cuffs.

"Hey. What is this?"

"We're driving up to London. I don't want you changing your mind and thinking you can jump out at a set of lights."

He sneered. "Think these would stop me?"

I drew my Beretta. "They'd slow you down long enough for me to stop you with this. And given that the young man you dumped in the river was a close personal friend of mine, I wouldn't be aiming at your legs."

He stopped sneering.

23

(Wednesday, early morning)

I stood at the back door of the old police station, sniffing the salty night air in the hope of clearing the odour of disinfectant and sanctimonious shit that clung in my nostrils. Navarro was the sort of person whose very presence made me feel like I needed a shower. He soiled the very atmosphere just by moving through it. Fiquenet was welcome to him.

Hopper returned from a casual stroll round the block and crossed the small, weed-grown car park. "What was all that business about drugs and dental records?" he asked quietly as he stepped up beside me.

"If I told you, I'd—"

"You'd have to shoot me. I know."

"—have to get you to sign the Act."

"OK."

"You must be mad," I said. "Don't get mixed up with spooks."

I heard him snort. "Says the man who tried to recruit me. Anyway, some of them..."

"Not Fiquenet?"

"Get lost. Just tell me."

"If I'm right, there was a whole other strand to what the Americans were doing through the 70s. You have to remember that our Intelligence Services had been gutted by the Soviets. They had people on the inside and close to the top floor of both the Security Service and the Secret Intelligence Service. A sieve was watertight by comparison. And where we weren't leaking, the very thought we might be was enough to paralyse us. As you can imagine, the Americans weren't happy about that."

"Didn't they have similar problems?"

"Not if you listen to them, no. And truth be told, we were in a lot worse state."

"So?"

"So it sounds like the Americans decided that if it worked for the Soviets, they could do it as well. But on a larger scale."

"Yes, but what?"

"The Russians had agents of influence all over the place, especially in the UK. The problem they almost all of them had was that at some time, early in their lives and careers, they'd had contact with Soviet agents. Russians, East Germans, it doesn't matter. The fact is there was a link and that made them vulnerable. But what if you could create an agent of influence without the contact, without them even knowing they were one."

"Is that possible? Surely people have to be… recruited, trained, that sort of thing."

"Entactogens engender empathy. If you get dosed up in the right mixture, a skilful person can enhance your natural sympathies and reinforce tendencies to the point that certain behaviours and decisions will almost inevitably follow a certain path."

There was a moment's silence, and then a cool breeze soughed through the leaves of a large tree in a nearby garden.

"Take someone impressionable who has expressed a love of things American," I said. "Dose them with entactogens. Subject them to pro American imagery and sentiments. Do it on a regular basis for three or four years."

"So what?"

"Do that to high flying students at Cambridge and Oxford. Other top universities."

He thought about it. "Shit."

"Exactly. A whole generation of local and national politicians, civil servants, company CEOs and other high fliers, not to mention journalists, all emotionally disposed to side with the US. Agents of influence who don't even know what they are. They don't need networks or handlers. Technically they are not spies so it doesn't breach the letter of the US-UK Accord. And if you have enough of them, it doesn't matter if one or two change their minds about their careers or break out of the patterns they've had reinforced. The net effect will be pro-American."

"But how…" I let him think about that as well. "Dentists."

"Exactly. Perfect place."

"Bloody hell."

"Neat isn't it."

"But…"

I held up my hand to stop him. "I have no idea. It could all be in my sordid imagination. On the other hand…"

"Have you two finished?"

We turned. Fiquenet was standing behind us in the darkened passage. I watched her for a moment, but if she'd heard any of what I'd said, she didn't look like she wanted to discuss it.

"I'm ready," I said.

Hopper took out a phone and tapped one of his pre-sets. It was answered straight away. "Go."

I did pretty much the same with my own phone. "Go."

We went back inside and got Navarro out of the cell. Hopper handed me the torch I had asked for and we went back to the rear door. We didn't have to wait long. Hopper's phone rang. He listened and nodded.

"Good luck," he said quietly and headed back to the police station.

I went first, followed by Navarro and then Fiquenet. We crossed the small car park to the road where a

Land Rover was just pulling into the kerb. The driver, from Thames House, got out, keys in the ignition and the engine running. Without a word or a look he walked on along the back road and disappeared into shadow.

The Land Rover was an old Defender 110 Station Wagon, looking like it was held together by mud and dung. There were straw bales in the back concealing the boxes of documents that Hopper had arranged to have loaded.

Fiquenet and Navarro climbed in the back, Fiquenet behind me. I wedged the torch where I could reach it easily, belted up, and took a couple of seconds refreshing my memory about the layout. Keeping the lights off, I pulled away.

"Where are we going?" asked Navarro.

"I told you," said Fiquenet. "London. And don't you dare start asking if we're there yet."

"But where in London?"

"Hey," I said, "It's a secret. Now try to look like a local and shut up. I'm trying to concentrate here."

I am not a fan of night driving. Especially with someone in the back who is a target.

For all it looked like something a farmer would want to trade in before it fell apart, the Defender ran sweet and quiet. It handled well and the brakes were good and tight. Towards the edge of the town I took a sudden left where Hopper had shown me on the map and passed in front of the Primary School and then along behind a fire station. Conveniently open gates let us onto a track between fields.

I switched on the lights and pushed down on the accelerator. We sped into the tunnel of light, shadows and hedgerow shapes whipping past on either side. It wasn't the smoothest ride, but it wasn't a road, either. Which might give us the head start I was looking for.

For a moment there was open space and a house on our left as we flashed across a road and then the tunnel returned, with the barely seen forms of trees rearing on both sides.

"Jeez. Are trying to get us killed?"

"Quite the opposite, Ollie."

The track emerged onto the edge of a large wheat field and I switched off the main beams. A long line of mature trees continued on our left, flickering in the dark as we passed. Ruts and bumps made us sway and I could see dust rising red in the rear lights. I would have preferred something with infra-red beams, but you work with what you can get in the timescale available.

After the field and more trees, the surroundings opened out again with rough grass either side of the track, a hint of trees in the dark distance. I eased my foot off the accelerator a touch and we began to slow. There were turnings ahead I didn't want to miss. The track curved round to the left and the lights of a large house appeared between the trees in the distance. Somewhere nearby would be a turning to the left that led to the buildings.

As I reached that turning, I glanced to the right. There was a long, straight road carved into darkness by the lights of an approaching vehicle. It might be nothing. People going home after a drink in town. A farmer working late. Kids out for a late night cruise. The vehicle was a long way off, but you get a feeling for these things.

I cut my lights altogether and dropped speed, peering into the dark, wrenching the wheel when I saw the road on the right. Hitting the pedal again, I put the main beam back on as soon as we were in amongst the trees. In the mirror, watching for lights, I saw Fiquenet turn and peer over the top of the straw and through the rear window.

That first stretch of road was straight. At about five hundreds yards it turned gently to the right. As we went into the curve, headlights flashed in the rear view mirror. I swore softly.

A denser patch of woodland swallowed us and the track began to twist. I killed the speed a little. Somewhere up ahead we would come to proper roads.

"Did it turn off?" Fiquenet asked more out of hope than anything else.

"Nowhere to go."

"Any sharp bends coming up?"

"Probably. What have you got in mind?"

"Laser."

"Risky. I'll let you know when."

There was a click as Fiquenet undid her seat belt so she could get herself into a good position.

Lights of a house appeared. "Hold tight." I hit the brakes and we slid to a stop at a junction. I gave it a few seconds, giving the other vehicle a chance to close the gap. Happy the road was clear, I hit the accelerator and we crossed into Tunstall Forest. Another vehicle followed close behind.

"Better make it soon," said Fiquenet.

I worked through the gears and put on speed as fast as I could, switching on the main beams. After a few seconds a sharp bend loomed. I killed the lights and yelled, "Now."

It was a powerful laser. I was aware of it waving around in the back for a moment while she targeted the eyes of the following driver. A small red spot danced in the rear view mirror and, as we wove round the bend on the wrong side of the road, I caught a glimpse of a dark shape shoot across the road. There was a loud bang and the vehicle disappeared in a cloud of dust and foliage as it failed to leap a deep ditch.

I took my eye off the mirror and got the Defender straightened up, piling on the speed again. The road was straight and clear after that. Which is why we were doing about eighty when we hit the stinger.

Contrary to movie mythology, vehicles do not leap into the air, perform corkscrew manoeuvres, and roll for four hundred yards before bursting into flames when they hit a nail in the road. Vehicles are designed to be stable, proper off-road vehicles more so. It takes a stunt driver, ramps, compressed air rams and all other manner of special effects tricks to get a car to fly, even temporarily.

I was aware, far too late, of something lying across the road, heard the tyres go, and felt the steering shudder. A lot goes through your mind at a time like that quite aside from assessing the immediate situation, controlling the vehicle, and swearing at your own stupidity.

Mind you it was a hell of a time to remember not everyone is as short-staffed as we are. They were clearly working at least two teams. One to tail and push. The others based at points I had to head for. Once the tail had a route, the others would work back and set an ambush. And they'd had all afternoon to study maps, satellite imagery, and drive the terrain.

All that training I'd done in the past in Herefordshire and in and around Painscastle, the experiences I'd had in Ireland, kicked in straight away. I shut off the headlights to give my night vision a chance of establishing and concentrated on bringing the Defender to a stop in a position I wanted. My passengers knew the score so I didn't waste time worrying about them.

Somewhere far behind us would be whoever managed to climb out of the tail vehicle and closer would be the person who had laid the spike stick across the road. In front...

A dark shape pulled across the road, emerging from a forest road to the right as I slewed the Defender in that direction and let it stop at an angle. There was a moment's silence and stillness. I hit my seatbelt release and popped the door. It was a very good place for an ambush. After midnight. Lonely road in the heart of a forest. A good place to escape if you got away from the crossfire.

Three shadowy figures detached from the darkness of the van that had blocked the road and spread out, moving swiftly toward us. There was a movement from behind me and I saw a small dot of red light dance on the front passenger door window.

They probably mistook it for a laser gun sight. Windows blurred and collapsed in a shower of fragments. There was that tinny pinking sound as bullets hit the body work, almost lost in the rapid three shot of automatic weapons.

God alone knows where she'd been hiding it, but Fiquenet produced a gun and popped off several rounds.

Half deafened from the pistol going off at very close quarters I was still able to hear them open up again in return, heard a grunt from Navarro and an obscenity from Fiquenet.

By this stage I was bent double and leaning out of my side of the vehicle. There was a lull, but I knew it wouldn't last. I twisted, and saw Navarro was slumped forward, saw Fiquenet's face was a world of pain.

"Give me your gun," I said as loudly as I dared.

She didn't move.

"Your gun."

With an effort, she reached forward over the back of my seat and dropped it into my hand. It was slick with blood.

Slithering out head first, I ended up on the tarmac in an ungainly heap. Once I managed to get my feet under myself, I called into the silent night air. "I'm coming out. We're hit bad."

Taking further silence as assent and not wanting to give anyone any more time to get behind me, I stood leaning on the wing with the engine between me and our assailants.

A voice off to the left called out. "Move round to this side of the vehicle. Hands high."

"I'm hurt," I replied, edging round the front of the Land Rover. It was dark between the trees, but there was light enough to see where they stood. Well spread, leaning into their guns, wearing vests. And when someone is wearing a vest you have to get really ugly. Unless you are assured of a headshot, which means dangerously close range, you have to disable them first to get close enough to finish them. That means the groin.

Now these customers were no doubt tough. Veterans of conflict. But they were cocky, thought they were above the law, thought they were invulnerable. They hadn't even bothered with suppressors. And with superior fire power they no doubt assumed they had the upper hand. But I still slipped off regularly to Hereford where I am put through the grinder so I wasn't going to be left on the tarmac without first taking down as many of the bastards as I could.

My right hand was held high, showing Fiquenet's pistol. It was small. A Glock 26, commonly used as a back-up pistol. I kept my left arm twisted close to my body, my head on one side as if curled round a pain. There was a slight sway in there as well for good effect. I'd learned to do it for real.

You look for a mistake. Adrenalin floods the system and gives you extra speed, sharper vision, and quicker reflexes. You hope the mistake comes before the fear kicks in and the tremors start.

The one on the left moved forward to cover Navarro and Fiquenet. It was the big one with the neat beard we'd seen in the hospital. It put him very close.

"Put your weapon on the ground," he said.

I went very slowly down on one knee, keeping Fiquenet's gun in sight to give him something to watch. When my knee touched the ground and I was in a stable position, I lifted my left hand and put three bullets into his head with my Beretta, firing in the general direction of the other two with the Glock. As he hit the road, I turned the Beretta and downed another as he returned fire. The third was running for the cover of their van.

I emptied both guns in his direction, saw a window go milky and collapse, saw the van lurch slightly as a tyre went. The Glock was no further use so I let it drop, ejected the magazine of the Beretta and slid in one of my spares as I crabbed across to the nearest body. Several shots hit the front of the Land Rover and the door beside me.

The downed man's weapon was a Heckler & Koch MP5K machine pistol. There were spare magazines in his belt. I holstered my Beretta and made for the trees, emptying the H&K at the van and reloading as I jumped a narrow ditch.

That left me with the Land Rover to defend and no idea how many reinforcements might be on the way. Adjusting the machine pistol to triple shot, I moved as quietly as I could in the direction of the tail vehicle and the stinger. Anyone from that direction would approach with caution, but they wouldn't yet know the odds had been shortened in my favour.

I didn't go far and I didn't have to wait. Someone was moving fast toward the scene of the shooting at a crouch. I could barely see him, but I could see the gun.

"Drop your wea—"

He didn't wait. I shot him as he swung in my direction.

The engine of the van that had pulled out in front of us turned over and I ran back in that direction, leaned against the back of the Land Rover to steady myself, flicked the safety down to automatic, and emptied the rest of the magazine into the van's cab. The engine kept running. The van didn't move.

Out of habit, I replaced the magazine and then moved forward across the open space. He'd been hit in the neck and had bled out all over the place. It was a mess, but gun battles aren't slick or clean. There's a lot of noise, confusion, running, gasping for breath. And with the odds against you, you have to shoot to kill.

Once I'd secured all the loose weaponry, I hobbled back to the Land Rover and settled myself down in a defensive position, fumbling in my pocket for my phone. In the relative silence, somewhere beyond the ringing in my ears, I thought I could hear sirens. That's when I realized some of the blood was my own. That's when the shivering started.

24

(An afternoon)

Warm, afternoon sunshine filled the quiet room, a slight breeze carrying in the distant sounds of the city. Delicate plasterwork coving had taken on a deformed blobbiness under years of repainting with white emulsion. The walls were a sun bleached aquamarine. It was like being at the bottom of an empty swimming pool.

In other rooms, people talked in hushed tones, phones warbled politely. There were footsteps that came and went, the clatter of trolleys. It was a whole other world out there. A world of antiseptic smells and briskness, of weak tea with one biscuit. It was a world I was not especially fond of, but you have to make the best of it.

It was a sign of the times that this had once been a fully functioning if very small hospital. They had patched me up a few years ago. Now the operating theatre and the surgeons had gone. All that was left was a glorified nursing home to which I had been sent after the surgical work at the RCDM in Selly Oak.

A morning session of physiotherapy had left me tired and a less than flavoursome lunch had left me longing for one of Harry Yao's specials. I tried to take my mind off those and a hundred more pressing concerns with a book, but somehow the pillows were pushed into a more comfortable position, and the struggle to keep my eyes open was just too much.

"Come on, come on, we can't have you lying there all day."

The voice jerked me awake. I hauled myself with care into a sitting position and looked across at Sally. She stood in the doorway with a large, full shopping bag slung from one shoulder.

"You sound just like the physiotherapist."

"And how is the leg?"

"Bloody sore."

We watched each other across the sunny silence. I don't know what she saw in my face, but there was a definite shadow beneath her smile.

"Are you going to keep those?" She pointed to the little jar that contained the fragments of bullet they'd taken from my leg. It stood next to the toy car Georgie had left for me to play with if I got bored.

"They're a reminder."

And perhaps a cryptic sign: Danger! Minefield.

I patted the bed. "We must stop meeting like this," I said, unnerved by the intensity of Sally's expression. "Has no one written a report for me to sign?"

She put on her office face and crossed the room, putting her bag on the floor and sitting in the chair beside the bed. "You'll have to do your own work this time."

"I never was very good at fiction." The shadow began to look thundery so I put my hands up in surrender. "I give in. I give in. I had enough of a bollocking from young George. Then Rose did it all over again with all the swear words added."

Sally managed a pale smile. "That one would be for Charlie."

I nodded, silent for a moment. "So. What brings you here on a sunny afternoon?"

"I thought you might be bored." She reached down and produced a backgammon board from her bag. It was the one from my flat. The one she had taught me on all those years ago, the first time I had been in hospital.

As she opened it up I reached out and put my hand on top of hers. She squeezed my fingers. Her hand was trembling. Not much. It could have been anything. Perhaps even just my imagination.

"What are the stakes?"

"High."

She reached down again and produced a tin of Dark Chocolate Gingers. A whole tin. High stakes, indeed.

"And information?"

She sighed and her shoulders sagged a fraction. "Still looking for a neat ending?"

"No. But when the Americans start using gung-ho mercenaries against British nationals on British soil, I'm inclined to want to know a bit more. Especially when that British national is me."

Sally didn't answer straight away. It was difficult to know what she might be thinking. After all, I'd killed four of them. But they were my nightmares and I wasn't sharing. Not with Sally. Whatever was going through her mind, she decided to keep to herself. "The US Ambassador was invited to make a visit to the Cockpit. CIA Chief of Station came with him. Guess what…"

"The CIA formally denies any knowledge of what happened, but they would like their paper work back please, because they just hate to litter up other people's countries."

"Do I detect a hint of bitterness?"

"So who was it?" I asked. "Xe Services Ltd?"

"Too high profile these days, but it might have been an affiliate. We haven't been able to identify the… corpses. The survivors have already been 'extradited' to the States and we'll no doubt never see or hear of them again. The vehicles are clones and we haven't been able to trace where they came from. Yet. The Suffolk Police put out a statement about rival drug gangs fighting over a shipment."

"I bet the press are having a field day with that. What about the Russians?"

"They buggered off as soon as the shooting started. Happy to see us and the Americans at each others' throats."

"Oh – and who did they leave behind we weren't supposed to notice?"

"Never you mind. You don't work at Thames House any more, remember? But while we're on the subject of the Russians, Rose received a bouquet of twenty flowers. George a model car, a ZIL. Both signed 'Flagtail'."

We both gave that some thought. It was a nice gesture. Perhaps the cheeky sod wanted to defect, after all.

I shrugged. "Pennyweather?"

"Who? Oh. The poor boy who died decades ago."

I decided to take the hint. "OK." Squeezing a stone. "Let's try Fiquenet and Navarro."

"Special Agent Fiquenet was discharged as fit enough to travel and returned to the States yesterday on a US Air Force hospital plane. Badly grazed. No serious damage."

"Alone?"

"Only if you count a couple of corpses in the hold as company."

I don't know why she was being so cagey. "What about the stuff I scanned?"

That didn't even get an answer. Which told me why Sally was being so circumspect. She glanced at the open door of my room. The clinic belonged to Thames House, but that was no reason not to be careful. Indeed, quite the opposite. "Frankly," she said very quietly, arranging the pieces on the board, "nobody knows what to do with it. There's no proof there was ever such an operation. That this isn't some Russian stunt to try to implicate the Americans."

I nearly laughed. "There's some pretty damning circumstantial evidence."

"That's not enough to act on—"

"It was for the Americans," I pointed out.

"—and even if it is true, it hasn't exactly compromised the integrity of the realm."

"Other than dragging us into a number of dubious armed conflicts round the globe and increasing the likelihood of terrorist acts against British targets, you mean. That and leaving the EU, which really does suit the Russians, not to mention the possible break up of the UK."

"All of which can be attributed to other causes. And, anyway, who do we take it to?"

"So I don't have much of a report to write. Unless you want it all buried in a new set of Worthington files."

"Damn." Her phone was ringing. She held it up to her ear, her face blank. I pretended I wasn't trying to listen. Which wasn't difficult as I couldn't hear a thing.

"I have to go," she said when she'd put her phone away. "Consolation prize," she added pushing the tin of biscuits toward me. "Save me some."

"Don't be too long, then."

Her eyes flicked back and forth across my face. "We'll be seeing more of each other." I tried to absorb that. Promise. Threat. Prophecy. Who cared? I liked it.

"And no more work in the field," she added as she crossed to the door.

"Like I get a say, but I'll have a talk with my boss about that."

"You already have."

I blame it on the bullet wound, and the after effects of anaesthetic, weeks of boredom in a hospital bed dulling my mind, but it took me a moment to work out. By that time, my new boss had gone.